Sabrina Jeffries is the N... 38 novels and 9 works of ... pseudonyms Deborah M... ever time not spent writing in a coffee-fueled haze of dreams and madness is spent traveling with her husband and adult autistic son or indulging in one of her passions – jigsaw puzzles, chocolate, and music... over 7 million books in print in 18 different languages, ... Carolina author never regrets tossing aside a budding career in academics for the sheer joy of writing fun fiction, and hopes that one day a book of hers will end up saving the world. She always dreams big.

For more information, visit her at www.sabrinajeffries.com, on Facebook at www.facebook.com/SabrinaJeffriesAuthor or on Twitter @SabrinaJeffries.

Praise for Sabrina Jeffries, queen of the sexy regency romance:

'Anyone who loves romance must read Sabrina Jeffries!' Lisa Kleypas, *New York Times* bestselling author

'Irresistible . . . Larger-than-life characters, sprightly dialogue, and a steamy romance will draw you into this delicious captive/captor tale' *Romantic Times* (top pick)

'Another excellent series of books which will alternatively have you laughing, crying and running the gamut of emotions . . . I guarantee you will have a tear in your eye' *Romance Reviews Today*

'The sexual tension crackles across the pages of this witty, deliciously sensual, secret-laden story' *Library Journal*

'Exceptionally entertaining and splendidly sexy' *Booklist*

'An enchanting story brimming with sincere emotions and compelling scenarios . . . an outstanding love story of emotional discoveries and soaring passions, with a delightful touch of humor plus suspense' *Single Titles*

'Scorching . . . From cover to c...

'Full of all the intriguing char... dialogue that Jeffries's readers ... *Weekly* (starred review)

SABRINA
JEFFRIES
THE STUDY OF SEDUCTION

headline
ETERNAL

The right of Sabrina Jeffries to be identified as the Author of
the Work has been asserted by her in accordance with the
Copyright, Designs and Patents Act 1988.

Published by arrangement with Pocket Books,
a division of Simon & Schuster, Inc.

First published in Great Britain in 2016
by HEADLINE ETERNAL
An imprint of HEADLINE PUBLISHING GROUP

1

Cataloguing in Publication Data is available from the British Library

ISBN 978 1 4722 3216 8

Typeset in 11.8/14 pt Berling LT Std by Jouve (UK)

Printed and bound in Great Britain by CPI Group (UK) Ltd,
Croydon, CR0 4YY

Headline's policy is to use papers that are natural, renewable and recyclable
products and made from wood grown in well-managed forests and other
controlled sources. The logging and manufacturing processes are expected
to conform to the environmental regulations of the country of origin.

HEADLINE PUBLISHING GROUP
An Hachette UK Company
Carmelite House
50 Victoria Embankment
London EC4Y 0DZ

www.headlineeternal.com
www.headline.co.uk
www.hachette.co.uk

*For my husband, Rene, who's about as close
to being Edwin as a man can get, but without the
math/engineering skills.*

*And for Becky Timblin and Kim Ham, whose
support despite their many challenges this year meant
worlds to me. Y'all are the best!*

Acknowledgments

A big thank-you to sex educator Dr. Emily Nagoski, whose input on my characters and information on the subject of female sexuality was invaluable. Any mistakes in the book are my own.

One

London
April 1830

"You have lost your bloody mind."

When every member in the reading room of St. George's Club turned to look at Edwin Barlow, Earl of Blakeborough, he realized how loudly he'd spoken.

The place was more crowded than usual, now that everyone was back in London and night was falling. Gentlemen wanted a few drinks before they plunged into the maelstrom that was the Season.

With a quelling glance that sent the curious onlookers scrambling to mind their own business, Edwin returned his attention to Warren Corry, the Marquess of Knightford. "This plan of yours can't possibly work."

"Of course it can."

Warren was Edwin's closest friend. Really, his only friend, aside from his sister's new husband, Jeremy Keane. Edwin didn't make friends easily, probably because he didn't suffer fools easily. And society was full of fools.

That was precisely why Edwin, Keane, and Warren had started this club—so they could separate the fools from the fine men. So they could protect the women in their lives from fortune hunters, gamblers, rakehells, and every other variety of scoundrel in London.

In a matter of months, the club had swollen from three to thirty members, all good men eager to share information about which of their peers couldn't be trusted with women. Until now, Edwin hadn't realized that so many gentlemen's female relations needed protecting from sly and not-so-sly attempts on their virtue . . . and fortunes.

Warren was clearly taking that mission very seriously. Perhaps too seriously.

"Clarissa will never agree," Edwin said.

"She has no choice."

Edwin narrowed his gaze on Warren. "You actually believe you can convince your sharp-tongued cousin to let me squire her about town during the Season?"

"Only until I return. And why not?" Warren said, though he took a long swig of brandy as if to fortify himself for the fight. "It isn't as if she hates you."

"No, indeed," Edwin said sarcastically. "She only challenges my every remark, ignores my advice, and tweaks my nose incessantly. The last time I saw her, she called me the Blakeborough Bear and said I belonged in the Tower of London menagerie, where ordinary people could be spared my growls."

Warren burst into laughter. When Edwin lifted an eyebrow at him, Warren's laugh petered out into a cough. "Sorry, old boy. But you have to admit that's amusing."

"Not nearly as amusing as it will be to watch you try to talk her into this," Edwin drawled as he settled back in his chair.

Rather than giving Warren pause, that made the blasted idiot ask, "Does that mean you'll do it?"

"The point is moot. She's not going to agree."

"Don't be too sure. You mustn't take her pokes at you as anything more than her usual mischief-making. You let her exaggerations get under your skin, which only tempts her to plague you more. You should just ignore her when she starts her nonsense."

Ignore Clarissa? Impossible. He'd spent the past few years trying unsuccessfully to unwrap the mystery that was Lady Clarissa Lindsey. Her barbed wit fired his temper, her provocative smile inflamed him, and her shadowed eyes haunted his sleep. He could no more ignore her than he could ignore a rainbowed sunset . . . or a savage storm.

For three months now, she'd been isolated at Warren's hunting lodge, Hatton Hall, and Edwin had felt every second of her absence. That was why the idea of spending time with her sent his blood pumping.

Not with anticipation. Certainly not. Couldn't be.

"What do you say, old boy?" Warren held Edwin's gaze. "I need you. *She* needs you."

Edwin ignored the leap in his pulse. Clarissa didn't need *anyone*, least of all him. Thanks to the fortune left to her by her late father, the Earl of Margrave, she didn't have to marry for love or anything else. Apparently, the woman had some fool notion she was better off without a husband, given that she'd reportedly refused dozens of marriage proposals since her debut years ago.

But it wasn't her fortune that had men falling all over themselves trying to catch her eye. It was her quick wit and effervescent personality, her ability to draw a man in and put him off at the same time. It was her astonishing beauty. She was the fair-haired, green-eyed, porcelain-skinned darling of society, and she almost certainly knew it.

Which was why he rather enjoyed the prospect of watching Warren attempt to convince her she should go about town with a gruff curmudgeon like himself. "Assuming that she and I both agree to this insanity—how long would I have her on my hands?"

"It shouldn't be more than a month. However long it takes me to deal with her brother in Portugal. I can't leave Niall stranded on the Continent with all the unrest there right now."

"I suppose she's already heard why you're going."

"Actually, no. She doesn't even know about his letter yet, which was waiting for me when we arrived from Shropshire for the Season. I wanted to be sure you would agree to keep an eye on her before I told her. But once she learns that this involves Niall, she'll want me to take this trip, and she'll realize I won't do that unless I'm sure she's safe."

"From this Durand fellow." After all, there was a reason for this charade Warren was proposing.

Warren's jaw hardened. "Count Geraud Durand, yes."

Settling back into his chair, Edwin drummed his fingers on his thigh. "If I'm to do this, you'd better tell me everything you know about this Frenchman."

"Haven't you met him?"

Edwin lifted an eyebrow.

"Oh, right. Not your circle of influence. But surely you've heard of him."

"He's the French ambassador's lackey."

"If he were a lackey, he wouldn't be a problem. He's the man's first secretary. And because the ambassador had to return to France right after Christmas, Durand is now running the embassy as the charge d'affaires. The position gives him a great deal of power."

"Then what the devil does he want with Clarissa?"

"A wife. He asked her to marry him in Bath some months ago."

That stunned Edwin. Warren had initially described Durand as an admirer who'd been plaguing her.

Not that Edwin was surprised at anyone's desiring Clarissa to distraction. Most men did. But men in the field of diplomacy generally preferred wives who were . . . well . . . not inclined to speak their minds and flirt outrageously.

"She turned him down," Warren went on. "That's why we had to return to London. Unfortunately, he followed us here. He seemed to have made it his mission to gain her, no matter what. He was at every public event we attended. Twice, he tried to accost her on the street."

"*Accost* her? Were those your words or Clarissa's? Because even you said she's prone to exaggeration."

"This was no exaggeration." His lips thinned into a grim line. "The bastard frightened her enough that she started avoiding going out in public, and you know that's not like her. So after we spent Christmas at your brother-in-law's, I whisked her and her mother off to Shropshire where I knew he dared not follow, since by then he had to serve as charge d'affaires here. I'd hoped our absence would give his ardor time to cool."

"And has it?"

"I don't know. We've only just returned, so it's not as if I've had time to assess the situation. But I'm not taking any chances. She has to be protected while I'm trying to sort out her brother's troubles."

Edwin cast him a measuring glance. "You don't mean to bring Niall back to England, do you? They'll arrest him for murder as soon as he sets foot on English soil."

"I know. Damned fool, fighting a duel over some woman. He ought to have known better." Frustration furrowed Warren's brow. "To be honest, I have no idea *what* to do with him. But I must work out something. He can't continue abroad like this indefinitely. And I can't continue to manage my properties *and* his, even with Clarissa's help."

Edwin snorted. "Clarissa helps?"

"There's more to her than you realize."

Ah, but Edwin did realize it. Granted, he wouldn't have expected her to have any skill at estate management, but despite her outrageous manner, he sometimes glimpsed a seriousness in her that reminded him of his own.

Or perhaps she merely had periodic bouts of dyspepsia. Hard to know with Clarissa. She was entirely unpredictable. Which was why she always threw him out of sorts.

Warren waved over a servant and ordered another brandy. "Honestly, accompanying her won't be as trying as you think. Don't you need to go out into society this Season anyway? Aren't you bent on marrying?"

"Yes." He was bent on siring an heir, anyway, which required wedding *someone*. Though God only knew who that might be.

"You see? It's perfect. You have to go on the marriage mart. Clarissa wants to enjoy the Season, and I want her to find a husband. It's an ideal situation."

"If you say so." How he could successfully court anyone with Clarissa hanging about was anyone's guess, but he supposed it might improve his stern reputation if he had a lighthearted woman on his arm at the usual balls. Assuming she would even agree to take his arm. That was by no means certain with Clarissa.

"You were still recovering from the loss of Jane last Season, so this will be your first real attempt to secure a wife since Jane jilted you. Do you have any particular lady in mind?"

"No. I know what I want. But God only knows if I can find a *who* to go with it. I haven't made a serious search, because I had my hands full with Samuel and Yvette. And then there was the false start with Jane." Edwin sighed. "But I suppose I must begin looking."

"And what are your requirements for a wife? Other than that she be of breeding age, I suppose."

Chafing at Knightford's astute perception that this endeavor was about finding a woman to bear him an heir, Edwin glanced out the window that overlooked Pall Mall. "I would prefer a woman who's responsible and uncomplicated."

"Like your mother, you mean."

He didn't answer, preferring not to lie. His mother

hadn't been remotely uncomplicated, but no one knew that except Edwin and his brother Samuel. Not even their sister Yvette was aware of how complicated their mother had been . . . and what had made her so. Edwin had worked hard to spare Yvette that awful knowledge.

"I want a woman who's quiet and sensible," Edwin went on.

"In other words, someone you can keep under your thumb. The way your father kept your mother under his thumb."

A swell of painful memories made acid burn his throat. "Father didn't keep her under his thumb; he ignored her." For reasons that Edwin unfortunately knew and had difficulty accepting. "I will never do that to my wife."

"You will if she's as dull as what you describe." Warren leaned back in his chair. "When I get around to choosing a wife, I want a lively wench who will keep me well entertained." He winked. "If you know what I mean."

Edwin rolled his eyes. "Remind me again why we asked you to join St. George's? You're as bad as the men we're guarding our women against."

"Ah, but I don't prey on innocents. Any woman who lands in my bed jumped there of her own accord. And I daresay that's true of any number of fellows here."

It probably was. Even Edwin had taken a mistress in his twenties when the turmoil within his family had kept him too busy to look for a wife and his loneliness had grown too acute to endure. That hadn't, however, been very satisfying. Knowing that a woman was with you only for your rank and money was somehow more lonely than not having a woman at all.

Although with Yvette married and out of the house, he'd started to feel the disadvantages of a solitary life. So once more he'd be looking for a wife, always an awkward experience. Women expected a man to gush about being in love, and he simply couldn't. Love was a fictional construct dreamed up by novelists. His parents' marriage had proved that.

But it wasn't wise to tell a woman his philosophy. Unfortunately, neither could he lie about it. He wasn't like his scoundrel brother, who was presently serving a sentence of transportation for kidnapping. Edwin couldn't spin a clever yarn or hide an opinion beneath a facile compliment.

Sadly, most women seemed to prefer facile compliments to blunt truths any day. For that matter, some *men* were like that.

Hence, his dearth of friends and his difficulty finding a suitable wife. "When will you broach this with Clarissa?"

Warren looked at his pocket watch. "At dinner, which should be in . . . oh . . . half an hour. I was hoping you'd come."

"*Now?*"

"Why not? Might as well get it over with, eh? And I *am* leaving for Portugal in the morning."

Devil take it. Edwin would have liked more time to prepare. He wasn't the spontaneous sort. "Planning to have us join forces against her, are you?"

"That wasn't my intention initially, no." Warren gulped some brandy. "When we left Hatton Hall for

London, I'd hoped that by now Yvette and Keane would have returned from America, and they could simply take her under their wing. Yvette can talk Clarissa into just about anything."

Edwin smiled. His sister could talk *anyone* into anything, even him.

"But I gather they're still abroad," Warren said.

"It may be a few more weeks before they return. Sorry."

"Well, it can't be helped. At least my aunt will be there to help persuade her."

Edwin suppressed a snort. Lady Margrave, Clarissa's mother, was a flighty female who rarely offered sound advice, so Clarissa rarely heeded her. He doubted that this time would be any different.

Warren surveyed the reading room. "You know, this place turned out quite cozy. It's not as sophisticated a setting as some clubs, but it's comfortable. You and Keane ought to be pleased with yourselves. Between Keane's artistic eye and your mechanical ingenuity, the place doesn't even look like a tavern anymore."

"We had plenty of help with the practical aspects of décor from Yvette and her mother-in-law."

"That explains the female touches," Warren said, "which are refreshing. I mean, the dark woods and leather give it a nice masculine feel, but there's something to be said for decent draperies, too. The ones at White's are funereal."

"I'm glad you approve."

Warren's gaze snapped back to him. "I'm sorry I couldn't be around to help. And that I have to run off again." He rose. "So, are you coming or not?"

The casual words were belied by Warren's tight expression.

They both knew that Edwin hadn't yet agreed to the plan. And why hadn't he? Because the thought of spending weeks in Clarissa's company put him on edge as nothing else could.

But it didn't matter. Warren was his friend and wouldn't hesitate to help if the shoe was on the other foot. So neither would Edwin.

He stood. "I'm coming."

~~~

As soon as the door to Clarissa's bedchamber closed behind the servant who'd left a message for her mother, the aging widow turned to her daughter in a panic. "I cannot believe your cousin did this!" She leaned heavily on her cane. "Warren knows better than to invite an eligible bachelor for dinner with no warning. What was he thinking?"

Clarissa raised an eyebrow at her mother's reflection in the looking glass. "He was thinking that it's just Edwin, whom we've known for ages. And who has come to dine before."

"I don't know if pigeon pie is quite suitable enough for guests," Mama said, as if Clarissa hadn't spoken. "Oh, dear, and we are fresh out of Madeira! Edwin loves his Madeira, you know."

"Mama—"

"And the pickled onions were entirely too sour the last time we ate them. I was hoping to use them up tonight, but if Edwin is coming—"

"Mama, calm down! It's not as if we're expecting the Tsar of Russia." She smiled into the mirror. "Although Edwin *would* make a fine tsar. All he'd have to do is be his usual autocratic and dictatorial self."

Thankfully, that observation broke her mother out of her fretting. "And he would look quite the part, too, wouldn't he? All that black hair and that chiseled jaw."

And broad shoulders and regal bearing and slate-gray eyes as coldly beautiful as a Russian night spangled with stars.

Clarissa scowled at herself. She must be addled to be thinking of Edwin so poetically. Though he *was* sinfully handsome. In a sort of standoffish way. And she hadn't seen him in ages. Absence makes the heart grow fonder, and all that.

"Why, I can almost imagine him in an ermine cape and one of those tall, furry hats," Mama said.

Clarissa laughed. "Edwin would only wear such a pretentious thing to a coronation, and then only because he had to."

His manner of dress was always correct, but terribly sober.

Unlike hers. She examined her gown in the mirror and smiled. Edwin would probably look sternly upon this confection of lace and lavender bows. Secretly it wasn't her favorite, either—a bit too fussy for her taste—but she'd expected to be dining only with Warren and Mama, and had just thrown on the first thing she'd found in her closet.

Oh, well. No time to change, and besides, she would never change her gown for *him*. Let Edwin give her one of his ruthlessly critical glances; she would not be cowed.

Indeed, it was merely force of habit that had her pinching her cheeks until they glowed nicely pink. It was not because she wanted to look pretty for Edwin. No, indeed.

"You know, my girl," Mama said, "if you were a bit nicer to that man, you could probably have him wrapped about your finger in a matter of weeks."

"Oh, I doubt that. Edwin is far too inflexible to be wrapped about anything. More's the pity." Clarissa would dearly love to see the woman who could manage *that*.

But it wouldn't be her. Edwin, of all people, would never accept her as she was, especially once he knew the full extent of her youthful mistakes. And her narrow escape from the obsessive attentions of Count Durand a few months ago had only made her more determined to avoid bending to any man's demands of what a wife should be.

You can never escape me, my dearest Clarissa.

A shudder swept her as she thrust the count's final words to the back of her mind. They were just the sort of dramatic nonsense men thought women wanted to hear. But to her knowledge, he hadn't hunted for her. He hadn't been loitering in the street outside Warren's town house once they arrived. No doubt he'd moved on to another pretty woman.

And if he hadn't?

Then she would be firmer in her refusal this time. Years ago she'd allowed a man to bully her, and it had shattered her life.

Never again.

Pasting a brilliant smile to her lips, she whirled to face her mother. "Shall we go down?"

"Not yet, my angel. The servant said the gentlemen are already here, so we should keep them waiting. You must never let a man be too sure of you."

"It's *Edwin*, Mama," she said tightly. "He's sure of everything and everyone, no matter what I do." With her usual coaxing smile, she offered her arm to her mother. Mama had broken her hip in her early forties and it hadn't knitted properly, so navigating stairs was difficult for her. "Come now, I know you're dying for a glass of wine. I certainly am."

"Oh, all right." Leaning on Clarissa's arm, Mama let herself be led to the door. "But you must promise to give him a compliment first thing. Men like that."

"Right," Clarissa said noncommittally.

"And don't contradict him all the time. Men despise fractious women."

"Uh-huh."

"And do *not* spout your witticisms incessantly. It's very mannish. Not to mention . . . ."

As they made their slow way down the stairs, Clarissa let her mother drone on, only half listening to the usual recitation of little tricks designed to hook a man and reel him in. Those might have enabled her Cit of a mother to snag an earl, but they smacked of deception to Clarissa.

If a man couldn't like her as she was, what was the point? Clarissa could barely hide her true opinions from Mama. How was she to do it with a husband?

Not that she ever intended to *have* a husband. Granted, she wouldn't mind having children, but that required taking a man into her bed—and the very thought made her hands grow clammy and her throat close up.

No. Marriage was not for her.

". . . and do be sure to save the biggest slice of cake for Edwin," Mama said as they reached the bottom of the stairs.

"Nonsense. I'm not saving *anything* for Edwin."

"That's only fair," drawled Edwin from somewhere in the shadows to the right of the staircase. "I'm not saving anything for you, either."

Striving to hide her surprise, she halted as he came into the light.

"Edwin!" Mama cried. "My dear boy!" She held out her hand.

Dutifully, he came forward to take it. "You're looking well, Lady Margrave." He bent to brush a kiss to Mama's cheek.

No kiss for Clarissa, of course. He was too much the gentleman for that.

"You're looking rather fine yourself," Mama chirped as she drew back to survey him.

And Lord, but he was, in his tailcoat of dark-blue wool and his waistcoat and trousers of plain white poplin. Even his cravat was simply tied, which only accentuated the masculine lines of his jaw and sharp planes of his features, so starkly handsome.

How had he managed to grow even more attractive in a mere three months? And why on earth was she gawking at him? This was *Edwin*, for pity's sake. It would swell his head even more if he knew what she was thinking.

Instead, she teased him. "Don't tell me—you were so impatient for us to come down that you've been pacing the foyer in anticipation."

The idea was ludicrous, of course. *Impatient* wasn't

even in Edwin's vocabulary. If ever a man believed that slow and steady won the race, it was he.

And he clearly recognized the irony, for he flashed her one of his rare smiles. "Actually, I was fetching this from the library. Warren told me he was done with it." His eyes gleamed in the lamplight as he held out a book. "Of course, if you wish to read it yourself . . ."

"Doubtful," she said. "Any book *you* loaned him has to be deadly dull."

"You mean, because it lacks gallant highwaymen rescuing virtuous ladies."

"Or virtuous ladies rescuing gallant highwaymen. Either would be preferable to one of your dry tomes on . . . what? Chess? Engineering? Philosophy of the most boring sort?"

"Clarissa," Mama chided.

But Edwin merely laughed, as she'd hoped he would. She took great pride in the fact that she could sometimes make him laugh. No other woman seemed able to. No other woman dared try.

"Mechanical engineering," he said. "However did you guess?"

"Because I know you all too well, sir."

He sobered, his gaze turning oddly intense even for him. "Do you? I'm not so sure."

The words hung in the air a moment in frozen silence before that was shattered by her cousin's approach.

"I found another book you might enjoy, old boy," Warren said as he bent to kiss first his aunt, then Clarissa. "It's about automatons."

She rolled her eyes as Warren handed it to Edwin. Of course, keen interest leapt in Edwin's face the moment he scanned the cover. The earl did love his automatons, to the point where he even made his own, though Clarissa had never been deemed worthy enough to actually see one.

"Looks intriguing, thanks. I'll get it back to you as soon as I'm done."

"No hurry." Warren shot her a veiled glance. "As you well know, I won't need it anytime soon."

Whatever was that about?

Before she could ponder it, Warren offered Mama his arm. "Come, Aunt, let's get you off your feet while we have our wine before dinner. Don't want to tax your hip overmuch."

"Thank you, my lad," she cooed, and let him lead her to the breakfast room. "That is ever so thoughtful of you! But then, you always were a dear. Why, I remember when . . ."

As Mama prattled on, Edwin was left to come behind with Clarissa. "So," he murmured, "exactly what were you refusing to save for me?"

It took her a moment to remember that he'd overheard her earlier. "The biggest slice of cake."

"I don't like cake."

"I know. That's why I'm not wasting it on you. You won't appreciate it, and you'd probably eat it just to be polite."

He slanted a serious glance at her. "Perhaps I'd give it to you, instead."

"I doubt that, but we'll never know, shall we?" she said lightly. "I'm saving it for myself, regardless."

"So I heard."

"Because you were eavesdropping." Mischief seized her. "How rude of you."

As they passed into the breakfast room, he shrugged. "If you don't want people hearing your pronouncements, you shouldn't talk at the volume of a dockworker."

Mama paused while settling onto the settee. "A dockworker! For shame, Edwin—what a thing to say to a lady! Have you no pretty compliments to offer?"

When he stood blatantly unrepentant, Clarissa said, "If Edwin knew how to compliment ladies, Mama, he would be too popular in society to settle for having dinner with the mere likes of *us*."

"There's no settling involved, I assure you," he said irritably.

She was congratulating herself on getting beneath his cool reserve again when Warren stepped in. "Play nice now, cousin. We need him."

"For what?" Clarissa asked.

Instead of answering, Warren gestured to the settee. "You'd better sit down. I've got something to tell you and your mother."

Two

A short while later, Edwin watched as Clarissa demanded answers of her cousin. "And this letter from Niall requesting your help was just sitting here waiting for you? How long?"

"Only a few days," Warren said.

"They should have sent it on!"

"We would have missed it, then. We were already on our way here."

"And why did he send it to you, not us?"

"Because he wanted to keep you and your mother out of it if he could."

Lady Margrave gave a bone-chilling cry. "Heaven help us all! My poor boy is in danger—I just know it! Or he's gambled away all his funds!"

"I'm sure it's nothing like that," Warren said through gritted teeth.

"And Niall would never be so foolish as to lose everything at the tables," Clarissa said grimly.

"He could have taken up with a bad crowd over in Portugal!" Lady Margrave protested. "I mean, if he was daft enough to get into a duel over some soiled dove all those years ago—"

"Mama!" Clarissa said, with a furtive glance at Edwin. "That's enough."

"It's not as if the whole world doesn't know how your brother ended up in exile," Edwin said. "Blasted young bucks and their dueling. It's been the bane of half the families in England."

A flush of embarrassment stained Clarissa's cheeks. At least, he assumed it was embarrassment. What else could it be?

Stiffening, she turned to Warren. "When are we leaving?"

"*We* are not leaving," Warren said with a scowl. "You and your mother are staying here while I go to Portugal."

"Mama can stay, but why can't *I* go with you? I can help."

Warren eyed her askance. "Do what? I don't even know what I'll be facing. Niall's message was cryptic, and his circumstances unclear. All I know is that he needs me to help him out of a spot. I'm not dragging you with me when I'm unsure what to expect."

"You cannot go, my dear," Lady Margrave cried. "You might be captured by pirates! They roam those seas, you know."

"Now, Mama, the likelihood of my being cap—"

"Oh, dear, dear, no. You mustn't go. Only think what might happen to you!" Clutching her chest, Lady Margrave fumbled in a jeweled box on a table next to the settee. "I need my salts. Where are my salts?"

Without a word, Clarissa rang for a servant, then walked over and pulled a vial out of the box. "There,

there, Mama." With astonishing patience, she knelt to wave the vial under her mother's nose, then urged her to lie down on the settee. "Just rest a moment while I have a word with Warren, all right?"

The lady's maid hurried in at that moment, and Clarissa said, "Mama is feeling faint. Please sit with her. His lordship and I will be right back."

She headed for the door that adjoined the library, and Warren followed. Edwin hesitated, but it seemed only right that he join them, given that he was supposed to be part of Warren's plan.

And she barely seemed to note Edwin's presence, too intent on berating Warren. "This is madness! I can't believe you mean to go without me! If Niall is in trouble—"

"There's naught you can do about it," Warren snapped. "You're staying here, and that's final."

Muttering curses, she roamed the library like a caged lioness. Tendrils of her hair were escaping their pins, her cheeks were flushed, and her strides were so quick, they gave him glimpses of ankle. God, but she was glorious in a temper.

Edwin had never seen her angry. Cross, yes. Sarcastic, oh yes.

But in a fury? Never. And now that he was witnessing it, he found it fascinating. Considering that he generally hated dealing with emotional women, that surprised him.

She rounded on Warren. "So you're going to leave us here to worry ourselves sick over you and Niall for the next month or so."

Edwin couldn't suppress his snort. Now she rounded on *him*. Damn.

"Do you have something to say, Lord Blakeborough?"

The formality of her words should have given him pause. It didn't. "Warren and Niall are grown men. They can take care of themselves, and will probably do it better without you tagging along."

Planting her hands on her hips, she narrowed her eyes at him. "Stay out of this. It does not concern you."

"Actually, it does," Warren broke in. "While I'm away, Edwin is going to accompany you and your mother to whatever social engagements you wish to attend."

The emotions that played over her face were intriguing. Surprise, then confusion . . . then more of that amazing anger that brought such fetching color into her cheeks. Edwin couldn't stop staring. Was the flush all-encompassing? Did it extend beneath her clothing?

God, he must stop thinking about what was beneath her clothing.

"Whyever would Edwin need to do that?" she bit out.

"To protect you from Durand," Edwin said bluntly.

For a second, she paled. Or perhaps he'd imagined it, for almost instantly she spat, "That is beyond ridiculous."

Warren's dark eyes glittered. "Is it?" He marched up to her. "Ever since you refused the man's proposal, he's dogged you at every turn. You were frightened enough of him after his last appearance to beg me to bring you and your mother to Hatton Hall for the rest of the winter."

If Edwin hadn't been watching her closely, he wouldn't have seen her convulsive swallow. And that one little motion made something knot in his gut. Because that was another thing he'd never seen—Clarissa afraid. It disturbed him more than he expected.

It also made him question his assumption that she might be exaggerating the situation.

She drew herself up. "That was months ago." Her voice tightened ever so slightly. "Surely Count Durand has gotten over this nonsense by now."

"Or your absence has made him even more obsessed," Warren said. "I can't take the chance that it's the latter. Unless you want to return to Shropshire—"

"Absolutely not!" Clarissa set her shoulders firmly. "I will not miss the Season because of that . . . that ridiculous man. He probably only wanted me for my fortune, anyway, like the rest of them."

"I don't think so," Warren said. "Durand comes from a long line of wealthy French aristocrats. His family fled the revolution for England early enough to retain most of their assets, and once they returned to France after the war, they were able to insinuate themselves into royal circles."

"So the Frenchman spent some time in England before he was actually posted here?" Edwin asked.

"He was born in Sussex," Clarissa said dully. "And raised there, too, until his family went back."

"He's that young?"

"About your age, yes."

Hmm. "So, not some aging roué looking for a young bride to bear him sons."

"Hardly," Warren said. "And he refused to take no for an answer."

"Why was that, if not for Clarissa's fortune?" Edwin asked.

She whirled on him, eyes blazing. "Oh, I don't know. Perhaps he was foolish enough to think me pretty. Or engaging. Or—"

"I'm sure Edwin didn't mean that the way it came out," Warren said soothingly.

She stared Edwin down. "Didn't you?"

God. He'd never been good at deciphering women. He weighed his words. "I meant that men who don't take no for an answer generally have a reason for their . . . obsession, if you will." He thought of his mother. No, that wasn't the same at all. "I'm merely trying to get at what the reason might be." When she continued to stare balefully at him, he thought to add, "Beyond your beauty and wit, that is."

She rolled her eyes. "You really cannot give a woman a compliment without being bullied into it, can you?"

That startled him. "I can. I just don't always think to do so. I'm not like my smooth-talking brother."

Something flitted over her features. Sympathy? No, it couldn't be. Not with Clarissa.

Yet when she spoke again, her voice was softer. "No one would ever mistake you for Samuel, Edwin. And that's something you should be proud of."

He was still reeling from those unexpectedly thoughtful words when she cleared her throat and added in a harder voice, "But that doesn't mean I want you scowling over me like a watchdog for the next few weeks."

That was more the Clarissa he knew.

"Now, cousin," Warren began, "Edwin was kind enough to agree to do this, and given that he doesn't much enjoy society—"

"Exactly!" she snapped. "He'll be worse than you—chiding me and curbing my enjoyments and glowering at anyone who dares to approach."

"That last strategy is why I never have to put up with idiots at social occasions," Edwin said dryly.

"It's also why you have no friends," Clarissa shot back.

"Clarissa, that's enough!" Warren barked. "You're being rude to a man who only wants to help."

Edwin tensed. He shouldn't care one way or the other if Clarissa balked. Indeed, it would be a boon—he wouldn't have to deal with her moods and her unpredictability. He could walk away, having done what Warren asked.

But for some absurd reason, that didn't sit well with him. "Why don't you give us a moment alone, all right?" Edwin asked his friend.

Warren glanced from Edwin to Clarissa. "Fine. Perhaps *you* can talk some sense into her." He headed for the door. "I'll go attend to my aunt."

As soon as Warren left, a hush settled upon the room. Edwin said nothing. He might not have experienced Clarissa in high dudgeon before, but he'd certainly dealt with Yvette enough to learn the effectiveness of quiet calm upon an enraged female.

Clarissa crossed her arms over her chest. "I suppose you're going to tell me that I'm being difficult."

"No."

As the minutes spun out between them, she

tipped up her chin. "Then you're going to try to tell me that I have no choice in the matter. But Warren is not really—"

"Your guardian. Yes, I know. You're too old for that. But your father did leave him in charge of your fortune and did ask him to look after you. So that's what Warren is trying to do. And you always have a choice. I'd never take that from you."

When he allowed the silence to build again, she regarded him with rank suspicion. "You're going to remind me of my duty to my family?"

That made him smile. "Hardly. Seems to me that you're already fulfilling your duty to your family admirably." Before she could retort, he added, "But if you don't agree to this, Warren will worry about you while he's off dealing with your brother, so his mind won't be on what he's doing. And that will hamper his ability to get Niall out of whatever mess he's in."

Gritting her teeth, she glanced away. "It's surprisingly devious of you to come up with that, Edwin."

"Not a bit. It's the truth."

"Then Warren should let me go with him. He can keep watch over me better that way."

"And you will slow him down. Is that what you want? For him to arrive too late to help your brother?"

Her gaze swung back to him, a roil of flashing green that took his breath away. "Why should I slow him down?"

He shrugged. "You'll need servants. You can't travel without a maid at the very least, so arrangements will have to be made, more luggage accounted for, more time spent in customs—"

"Enough." She fisted her hands at her sides. "I hate it when you're logical."

"I'm always logical. You hate it when I'm right."

To his surprise, her lips twitched as if fighting a smile. "That, too."

With his blood pounding, he searched her face. "Would it really be so terrible to spend time in my company?"

"No, of course not." Whirling away from him, she went to stare out the window at the back garden. "I just hate that the count has more power over my life at present than I do. And we don't even know if he's still interested!"

"True. But if he is and he continues to plague you, wouldn't you prefer to have someone in your corner?"

A sigh shuddered out of her. "*Are* you in my corner, Edwin?"

The question tightened an unfamiliar knot in his chest. "I am always in your corner." When she didn't respond, he added, "I should hope we are friends at the very least."

"Friends?" She turned to cast him an enigmatic look that threw him off-balance. "Is that what we are? I've never been quite sure."

Neither had he, but he wouldn't admit that to *her*. "We are for the next few weeks. I gave Warren my word that I would look after you."

For some reason, that seemed to provoke her. "I am *not* a child!" A hurt look crossed her face. "I'm a grown woman perfectly capable of handling some . . . unruly suitor."

That was when it dawned on him why she was so angry about this. She was a proud woman. And

being a proud man, he could understand not wanting to rely on anyone else for help.

"Of course you're capable. No one doubts that."
When she glared at him, he realized he needed to
change tacks. "Indeed, I envy you your ability to nav-
igate society when I am so very bad at it."

Her stance softened to skepticism. "You're not that
bad."

"You're not the first person to point out that I
don't compliment ladies sufficiently. So whatever
time we can spend together might help us both. I'll
keep Warren happy by accompanying you, and you
can give me some strategies for moving about society more effectively. It would be a fair exchange."

She eyed him warily. "You think so, do you?"

"I *am* looking for a wife, you know. And finding
one would be much easier if I didn't insult women
every time I opened my mouth."

Apparently that struck her as amusing, for she
flashed him a rueful smile. "True."

He could put up with her attempts to instruct
him if it meant keeping her out of the clutches of
Durand. He owed it to Warren. "You can even play
matchmaker, if you wish. Help me pick the perfect
wife. This can work to our mutual benefit."

"You're better at smooth talk than you think," she
said archly, but she was still smiling, which he took
as a good sign. "Oh, very well, when you put it that
way, how can I refuse? But you must promise not to
curtail my pleasures too much. You'll accompany me
to parties and such, but nothing more—no lectures
about how I must behave or whom I must avoid."

"Of course. You're not my sister. If you want to

dance the night away with some arse, it's not my concern." His voice hardened. "As long as the arse is not Durand."

"Trust me," she said acidly, "it will *never* be Durand."

"Then we're agreed." He held his breath. He didn't know why, but it mattered to him that she regard him as capable of protecting her. *Worthy* of it, even. Which was idiotic.

But Clarissa did tend to inspire the idiotic in him.

She finally nodded. "We're agreed."

Three

Clarissa did enjoy a lively ball. And it was probably good that this was her first engagement with Edwin since they'd come to an agreement two days ago. Nothing taxed the earl's patience like a crowded ballroom. So if he made it through this without growling at everyone—and her—then she could trust his word that he would allow her to enjoy the Season.

As she danced with a young major who happened to be a duke's son, she scanned the room for Count Durand. So far she hadn't seen the Frenchman, but that didn't exactly steady her nerves. He might be in the card room. Or watching her slyly from the gallery. That would be just his style.

"Wishing for a better partner, Lady Clarissa?" Major Wilkins asked peevishly.

Forcing her attention back to the fellow, she gave him her best flirtatious smile. "Certainly not. Hoping to avoid a bad one later."

He brightened, clearly sensing an opportunity to be of gentlemanly service to her. "Anyone in particular?"

As they briefly parted in the dance, she considered telling him the truth. It couldn't hurt to have a spy in society warning her of when the Frenchman was about. "Count Durand, actually. Have you seen him here this evening?"

"No. I don't believe he's in attendance. Demmed Frenchman knows better than to brave a ballroom full of English officers with long memories."

Since her companion couldn't have been a day over ten when the war ended, she had to stifle a laugh. "Oh, Major, I'm sure you're right. He wouldn't dare risk a confrontation with a fierce fellow like you."

The officer preened a bit as he bent closer than was proper. "If he did, I would defend your honor most vigorously."

She inched back. "How gallant of you!" But she didn't believe a word. For peacetime soldiers like Major Wilkins, a dagger was more a fashionable accessory than a weapon.

As they parted in the dance again, her eyes strayed to where Edwin stood across the room with her mother, his expression deceptively bland. Now *there* was a man who could use a dagger to good effect if necessary. Though she doubted he carried one. No doubt Edwin abhorred violence. Brawling in public wasn't correct, after all.

The officer followed the direction of her gaze. "Is that the Earl of Blakeborough?"

"In the flesh."

"I didn't think he liked to go into society. They say he's rather a dull sort."

Edwin was a lot of things, but "dull" wasn't one of them.

She and the major swung about the alternate couple, and when they were in line again, she said, "The earl is looking for a wife." She felt a perverse need to defend him. "Nothing unusual in that."

"Then he should dance. How better to get to know a woman?" Major Wilkins's gaze dropped to her bosom and stuck as he made his chassé to the right. "And women prefer a man who can show a good leg."

After their chassé to the left, Clarissa trod on the toes attached to his "good leg," jerking his attention back to her face.

She smiled thinly. "And here I thought that women prefer a man who can show good manners. Silly me."

The insult went right past him. "I should hope a gentleman can show both."

"Indeed. Let me know when you intend to start."

He blinked. "I beg your pardon?"

"Nothing." Thank *heaven* the dance was ending, and she could escape. Even Mama's nattering was preferable to this puffed-up partridge's lewd behavior.

They bowed to each other, and he led her toward her companions. As they approached, Edwin watched her with an enigmatic stare. He continued to do so as greetings were exchanged and she waited for the major to move on to the next pair of bosoms.

But the officer lingered to chat. Wonderful. Now she had to make polite conversation. And clearly Edwin, who now stoically drank his champagne, wouldn't be any help at all.

Fortunately, Mama was always willing to step in. "So, Major Wilkins, you're the Duke of Hastings's youngest, are you not?"

He nodded stiffly. Clearly he didn't like being reminded that he was at the bottom rung of his lofty lineage.

"And are you married?" her mother prodded.

He must not have minded that question so much, for he slid a sly glance at Clarissa. "Unfortunately, no, ma'am. Though I'm not averse to the idea."

"I should hope not," Mama said. "An officer of your consequence requires a wife, preferably a pretty one to move him forward in society."

"Yes," Edwin muttered, "a pretty one is always preferable to one with sense."

Clarissa couldn't resist poking the bear. "Don't you think it possible for a woman to have both?"

Edwin shrugged. "Possible? Yes. Usual in our circles? No."

"Then you must consider *me* a most unusual woman. Or else you think me either ugly or dim-witted."

"You know that I think you neither one." Edwin's gaze locked with hers. "And this is starting to feel distinctly like a trap."

"A trap of your own making," she quipped. "I wasn't the one to say that beauty in a woman is preferable to brains."

"I did not say—"

"Careful, now." The major nudged Edwin. "The lady will have you tied up in knots before you know it."

"And Clarissa is very good at tying knots," Mama said cheerily. "Why, she recently tatted the most splendid little coin purse you ever did see. It had a sweet button on the . . ."

For once, Clarissa appreciated Mama's nonsense. It

saved her from an escalating argument with Edwin, who never seemed to know when she was teasing him. Even now, he stood ramrod straight, his jaw carved from stone. However did he manage to shave that chin when it was always so rigid?

"I can well believe that your daughter excels in the feminine arts," Major Wilkins was saying in an attempt to ingratiate himself with her mother. "Clearly Lady Clarissa is possessed of every womanly virtue."

"Not to mention a sizable dowry," Edwin said, an edge to his voice.

The officer looked uncertain of how to respond to that in a gentlemanly manner. "While I'm sure that is true, I should think . . . That is . . ." It took him a moment to find his bearings. "A fortune is of no consequence in matters of the heart, after all."

Edwin lifted an eyebrow, and Clarissa choked back a laugh.

"Don't be silly," Mama said. "A fortune is always of consequence. Which is why my late husband made sure that our children were well provided for. *Very* well." She nudged Clarissa none too subtly. "Eh, my dear?"

Oh, Lord. Mama would probably give up her best fur to see Clarissa snag a duke's son, youngest of the bunch or no. Particularly since Clarissa kept refusing the suits of older sons.

Thankfully, Clarissa was saved from more matchmaking by the sound of waltz music.

"Forgive me, Major," Clarissa said hastily, "but I promised Lord Blakeborough the first waltz."

"Lucky fellow," the officer said with a frown.

"Lucky, indeed." Edwin knew perfectly well she

was lying, but fortunately he didn't let on. He simply offered her his arm and led her off.

As soon as they took the floor, she set out to appease him. "I'm sorry for the subterfuge, but—"

"It's fine." He led her through the steps with typical precision. "I suppose I'll have more luck finding a wife if I practice the usual ballroom sports."

"You don't require practice."

His gaze sharpened on her. "No need to flatter me. I know my limits."

Clearly he was still annoyed over their little exchange. "I mean it, Edwin. You're not the most poetic of dancers, but you keep time well, don't tread on my toes, and never miss a step. That's more than I can say for plenty of men."

"Take care," he drawled. "You might lead me to think you actually like me."

"I do like you. Sometimes." She thrust out her chin. "But I also can't resist provoking you. You get so deliciously annoyed. And you take my remarks far too seriously."

A grudging smile crossed his lips. "Warren told me much the same thing."

"Didn't you believe him?"

"I never know what to believe when it comes to you."

"Well, believe this at least: I think you're a perfectly accomplished dancer. I certainly prefer you over the major."

That brought his gruff manner back. "I don't know how you can endure that fool."

"Unfortunately, enduring fools is what a woman must do to have a little fun."

His hand tensed on her waist. "You have a peculiar notion of what's fun. Wouldn't you prefer a quiet conversation at dinner or a stroll about a museum to dancing with idiots?"

"I happen to enjoy dancing. And sadly, I require a partner for it. Thank goodness even idiots can be good dancers."

He glanced over to where Major Wilkins was still standing with her mother. "Are you sure that *he* knows you're merely amusing yourself with him?"

"Well, if Mama hadn't started blathering on about my dowry, he would have known it when I refused to dance with him again. She's bound and determined to get me married, and any fool will do, apparently."

"In this case, I hope you ignore her."

"Don't worry. I'm not about to marry a man who doesn't know when to stop ogling my bosom."

His mouth thinned into a hard line. "He was ogling your bosom?"

"Oh, don't turn into a watchdog again. Men ogle women's bosoms all the time. A female can wear the most innocuous gown ever, and some fellow will stare at her chest as if waiting for her clothes to rip open and reveal her nakedness. And when she's wearing a ball gown . . ."

She trailed off, remembering a night she'd rather forget.

His hand tightened on hers. "I don't do that, do I?"

Forcing her attention back to him, she smiled. "Of course not. You're a gentleman. Besides, you have no interest in my bosom."

"I wouldn't go *that* far. I'm not dead, you know."

As if to prove it, he let his gaze dip down for the merest of moments.

If she'd seen one ounce of leering in that quick look, anything to indicate that he thought of her disrespectfully, she would have been disappointed. But his look was more akin to hunger. No, not hunger—*yearning.* As if he saw what he wanted, yet knew he couldn't have it.

Good Lord, she was flying into pure fancy now. Edwin was only making a point, as usual. Whatever "yearning" she saw was all in her head. And she didn't want him to have any yearning anyway. Because that could easily lead in an entirely unpleasant direction, as she knew only too well.

"Come now," she said, "you must admit you never show me any attention of that kind. That's why I'm forced to accept offers from men like the major. You rarely attend balls and even if you do, you don't ask me to stand up with you." She smirked at him. "So you see, it's all your fault that I must entertain myself with fools."

His face darkened. "I *have* asked you to dance with me."

"Once. At my debut. But not since."

That seemed to startle him, for he glanced away. "Has it really been that long since we stood up together?"

"Seven years. The last time was at my very first ball. And even that was out of pity."

He scowled at her. "It was not."

"No? Yvette didn't put you up to it? Beg you not to leave me hanging out there, waiting for someone to ask me?"

"She didn't have to beg," he grumbled. "I agreed to it readily."

"I can't imagine why," she said lightly. "I'm sure you found a dance with a naïve young chit like me perfectly boring."

"Now *that* is patently untrue." Something indecipherable leapt into his eyes that made a delicious shiver skitter down her spine. "I may find you provoking and impetuous and reckless at times, but never once have I found you boring."

Suddenly she couldn't breathe, catapulted back to the memory of her come-out. Nervous and anxious after all the "advice" Mama had given her, she'd stood quaking at the edge of the floor, certain that no one would ask her to stand up with him. So when her best friend's brother had asked, she'd nearly kissed him right then and there. It had shown her a new side of Edwin—the one that was an eligible gentleman, and not just an irritating brotherly planet in the orbit of her friend.

Now, as they glided through the dance once more in perfect accord, it was as if they relived that night. The rhythm had beaten through both of them, matching her frenzied pulse at having her first dance with a real man. The scent of a hundred beeswax candles had swirled about the room, along with a glittering throng of young beauties and their beaus.

His eyes had shone more softly upon her in that moment than ever before. The way they shone now.

This time when his silvery gaze drifted down, it was to fix on her mouth. Her *mouth*. Oh, heavens. A sensation startled to life in her stomach that she had never thought to feel for Edwin. Unsettling. Provocative.

Absolutely unacceptable.

"So," she said, to break the spell, "have you determined which woman you might wish to court?"

His face closed up. "Not yet."

"You have *no one* in mind? Not a single person?"

"Well, when you put it that way . . . I suppose Lady Horatia Wise is a possibility."

"Admiral Nelson's goddaughter? She's a pillar of ice. You wouldn't want her, to be sure. She'd freeze you right out of your bed."

He arched an eyebrow. "Miss Trevor, then."

"A pillar of rock. Stubborn as a mule, or so I'm told. The two of you would butt heads until your heads fell off, and then where would you be? Besides, no one had ever heard of her until she came into society with her aunt, which I find highly suspicious."

The words earned her another rare smile. "So whom do *you* propose? Lady Anne? Lady Maribella?"

"Horrors! Lady Anne wears ridiculous hats. And Lady Maribella has the silliest laugh I've ever heard. It would drive you mad in under a month."

He cocked his head. "What happened to your playing matchmaker? You're doing rather the opposite of that."

"I suppose you're right." She could hardly admit that the idea of his actually marrying someone—anyone—seemed wrong somehow. He was meant to be always a bachelor. As she intended to be always a spinster.

The waltz ended and he led her from the floor, allowing her to survey the eligible women in the room.

"Let me see," she said. "What about Lady Jane Walker? She lost her mother recently and might be eager to get away from the memories her house probably provokes."

"I was engaged to a Jane. I hardly want another."

"Then Lady Beatrice. She's very pretty."

"And thus will expect plenty of pretty compliments. Which, as you know, I'm not good at."

"Miss Lamont?"

"Too French. I don't really understand Frenchwomen. Or Frenchmen, for that matter." Instead of taking her back to where her mother and the major stood, he made a sharp turn toward the refreshments room. "Speaking of Frenchmen, have you seen any sign of Durand?"

"No. And Major Wilkins said he wasn't in attendance."

"Thank God."

She eyed him closely. "Since that's the case, it's fine if you want to go home. I know how much you hate these things."

"I'm not leaving without you and your mother, and it's early yet for you." He met her gaze. "But if you don't mind, I may escape to the card room for a bit."

"Of course I don't mind." She glanced back over her shoulder to where the major was obviously anticipating her return to Mama's side. "And I will escape to the retiring room."

They parted ways then. Fortunately, by the time she emerged from powdering her nose and sweetening her breath, Major Wilkins was "showing a good leg" with someone else.

The next hour passed uneventfully. She danced a reel, two quadrilles, and another waltz, then paused to down some champagne. Not seeing her mother about, she decided to head toward the floor again and wait for someone to ask her for the next set. The champagne made her lightheaded, and she was enjoying just watching the dancers when a footman came to her side.

"Pardon me, milady," he said, "but I was asked to inform you that your mother has fallen ill and is lying down in the drawing room."

Oh, dear. Mama's spurious fits of illness generally only came on when she wanted to get out of doing something. So she might actually be sick this time.

Clarissa picked up her reticule from where she'd left it on a table and hurried to the drawing room, prepared to administer the requisite smelling salts. But when she burst through the door, she saw no one there.

Had Mama already recovered and returned to the ballroom? Or had she been so ill that their hostess had moved her to a more comfortable room?

Only after the door clicked shut behind her did the truth dawn on her.

"Good evening, Lady Clarissa."

A chill swept down her spine. She would recognize that faintly accented voice anywhere. God rot him and his sly ways.

Steeling herself, she turned to fix Count Geraud Durand with her iciest look. "Resorting to deceit now, sir? Surely that's beneath you."

His handsome features fell. "How else am I to see

you alone? My trick wouldn't have worked if your guards had learned I was in attendance."

"My *guards?*"

"Your friends and family watch you like a hawk." A fierce light shone in his blue eyes as he approached her. But something calculating glimmered in them, too, that had always given her pause. Always made her wary.

Though her stomach churned, she stood her ground. Showing weakness with men was invariably a mistake. If she had been stronger years ago, her brother would not be in exile.

So she must be firm. Put the count in his place once and for all. "My family wouldn't need to watch me if you would stop hounding me."

"Hounding you? I haven't seen you in three months!"

"I've been away." Straightening her evening gloves with feigned nonchalance, she gauged the distance to the door. "You could hardly expect me to remain in London when not a soul of consequence is here. I much prefer a steady diet of house parties and gaiety, as you well know."

"You might prefer it, but that's not where you've been." He speared his fingers through the blond mane that had made him the focus of many an English girl's fantasies. But not hers, not after she'd become better acquainted with him. "You've been in Shropshire."

Her heart began to pound. They'd chosen Shropshire because Warren's hunting lodge wasn't well known. Yet somehow he'd found out. "And you say you haven't been hounding me."

He gave a Gallic shrug. "I made a few discreet

inquiries, that's all. At first I thought perhaps you'd gone to join your brother abroad."

She stiffened. "Why would you think that?"

"You told me once that you wished you could visit him. I assumed you might have decided to do so."

"And lead the English authorities right to him, if anyone happened to be watching? I'm no fool."

"No, but you are being manipulated by the rest of your family. Imagine my shock when I learned that you were right here in England, being kept from me by your cousin." He stepped nearer still. "Knightford knew full well that I couldn't leave London with the ambassador away."

"Yes. He did." She stared him down, determined not to let him gain the upper hand. "So did I. He was only doing as I asked."

"I don't believe you." As she stifled a curse, he added, "I know that deep down, you sense our connection. You may claim otherwise, but you recognize that we're meant to be together."

Oh, Lord, what now? He truly believed what he was saying. She walked over to part the curtains, as if to look out at the night street. Hopefully he wouldn't be aware that the window was actually a set of French doors opening onto a balcony that connected with the card room next door.

"Admit it," he said from behind her, far closer than she liked. "You and I belong together."

"If I thought so, I would have accepted your proposal of marriage." Stealthily, she reached for the handle.

"You refused my proposal because your cousin commanded it."

She tried the handle. It was locked.

Panic built in her chest. She was trapped. And the last time she'd been trapped alone with a man . . .

No, she wouldn't give in to hysterics. She mustn't! Count Durand mustn't see her quake before him. Fear was the enemy.

Forcing a smile, she faced him, alarmed to find him only a few feet away. "I refused your proposal because I'm in love with someone else." The minute she blurted out the lie, she regretted it. Count Durand might be the sort of fellow for whom such a declaration would make matters worse.

But he merely laughed. "That's absurd. My spies have seen no evidence of that."

Anger spiraled inside her, and she clung desperately to it, hoping to banish her fear. "Spies? You've been *spying* on me?"

"I told you. I shall never let you escape me."

Her blood faltered. *Be strong,* she told herself. *You can bluff your way through this.*

She donned her haughtiest manner. "If you're trying to convince me of your love, that isn't the way to go about it." With a sniff, she rushed past him.

But she wasn't quick enough. Catching her by the arm, he jerked her back around and pushed her against the wall.

"Then I shall have to convince you some other way," he growled, before taking her mouth with his.

A tiny part of her screamed, *Fight!* But the rest of her froze. Dark memories from years ago swamped her. A night in an orangery. Soft kisses twisting into hard ones. A man's rough hands groping, ripping . . .

Her ears began to ring. Her vision was tunneling

now, and her head spinning . . . Oh, Lord, no, no, no. She couldn't faint. Not now. Not with him!

Then the door slammed open beyond them, and through a dim fog, she heard Edwin say, "Let go of her, you bastard, or I'll beat you within an inch of your life!"

Four

It took all of Edwin's strength not to hurtle across the room and plant a facer on Durand. But laying out the charge d'affaires of the French embassy would set tongues to wagging, and the last thing they needed was rumors swirling about Clarissa and Durand. The man would use them to force her into marriage.

The very idea made Edwin's blood run cold. Especially when she stood stock-still, trembling, her face white. Seeing her so shaken cut through him like a knife of ice. If the man hadn't stopped trying to kiss her at that moment, Edwin might have pummeled the bastard anyway.

"Step away from her." Edwin held his hands curled into fists before him in a pugilist's stance. "Now!"

Durand frowned. "Stay out of this, Blakeborough. It's none of your concern."

"The devil it isn't." Edwin said the first thing that came into his head. "She's my fiancée."

Bloody hell. Had he actually said that? He'd never been good at lies, and that was a colossal one.

But he wouldn't back out of it now. Too much was at stake. "So I'll thank you to keep your hands off her unless you want to end up laid out on the floor."

Looking panicked, Clarissa rushed over to put herself between them. "That's enough, both of you!" She grabbed Edwin's rigid arm and dragged on it until he reluctantly lowered his fist. "There will be no brawling. There *must* be no brawling." Her imploring gaze said, *This must remain private.*

Damn it. She was right.

"You heard the lady," Durand said with a smug tone. "There's no need for brawling. Especially since we both know you're lying about being her fiancé."

She whirled on the man with a fierce look. "He is not." Then she grabbed Edwin's hand. "I just told you I'm in love with someone else. You simply refused to listen."

Even knowing she was bluffing about being in love didn't diminish the power of those words. Or the strange sensation of her fingers clinging to his hand so intimately. As if she needed him.

God help him, he would be here for her, no matter how many lies he had to spout. She was still shaken. He could tell.

It brought anger roaring up inside him once more. "I suggest you leave, Durand, or I won't be accountable for my actions." *That* was certainly not a lie.

The Frenchman laughed dismissively. "And what do you think you could do?"

Edwin's free hand was still clenched in a fist at his side. "Not for nothing did my brother spend all his time with pugilists. They taught him how to fight, and he taught me. I'm happy to demonstrate what I learned."

Rabidly eager, in fact. He couldn't explain the violence of his anger, but it was a palpable, twisting creature inside him. If Durand made one move toward Clarissa, Edwin would gleefully punch the arse in the jaw.

Eyes narrowing, Durand glanced from him to Clarissa. "Your fiancé, eh? If that's true, then why is this the first I'm hearing of it?"

"We're keeping it secret until my cousin returns." Clarissa sounded far calmer than Edwin felt, though the surprising strength with which she gripped his hand belied her tone. "Edwin hasn't had the chance to ask Lord Knightford for my hand formally."

"Why not?" Durand crossed his arms over his chest. "Knightford brought you to town only a couple of days ago, didn't he?"

Edwin's gut twisted into a knot. The man knew her comings and goings that well? "Not that it's any of your concern, but he had to leave right away again on business." Edwin stared down into Clarissa's face with what he hoped was a convincing lover-like expression as he prepared to lie his arse off. "Besides, I wanted to speak to her before I approached him. So I did. Yesterday. Unfortunately, by then he was already gone."

The Frenchman scowled. "I don't believe either of you. Here's what I think happened." Ignoring Edwin entirely, Durand sidled nearer, and Clarissa pressed herself against Edwin's side so instinctively that it worried him. "Knightford had to leave on business, and he was afraid that if he left her ladyship alone, I might persuade her to give me a chance. So he asked his good friend to stand in for him as her protector."

"And why would I agree to that?" Edwin asked.

"Yes," she said swiftly. "Why would he agree—or then make up a story about an engagement? And why would I support it, instead of just telling Edwin to leave you and me alone?"

Durand fixed his gaze on her. "Because they've poisoned you against me. But don't worry. I shan't relinquish my pursuit just because this arse is trying to keep you from me."

Edwin pushed between her and Durand. "Come near her again, and I will make you regret it."

Durand chuckled. "She *let* me kiss her, you fool."

"I did not!" Clarissa cried.

"And the minute your back is turned," Durand went on, ignoring her, "she won't be able to resist finding me. You'll see. All that this ploy of yours does is delay the inevitable."

A cold chill ran down Edwin's spine. The man was mad. And madmen were always dangerous. "Get. Out." Edwin stared him down. "Before I decide to give you that demonstration in pugilism after all."

The arse held up his hands. "Whatever you wish, my lord. I shall look forward to proving you wrong about Lady Clarissa and me." After casting a lingering look at Clarissa, he left.

She collapsed onto the settee like an automaton falling to bits. It alarmed Edwin. He didn't like her color. Or the fear in her eyes. He should have taken Warren's concerns more seriously. But what the devil was wrong with Durand? Why would he want a woman who so obviously didn't want him?

After walking to the door to make sure the Frenchman was truly gone, he filled a glass of brandy from a nearby decanter and returned to her side. "Drink this."

"Isn't it a bit soon in our engagement to be plying me with spirits?" she quipped, but she took the glass from him with shaky hands. She sipped some and grimaced. "Good Lord. Gentlemen drink this swill routinely?"

He knew a desperate attempt to hide distress when he saw one. With some difficulty, he tried to match her light tone, hoping to encourage her to talk about what had just happened. "We have it for breakfast. And I'm sure our host would be appalled to hear you calling his fine French brandy swill."

She gulped some, obviously having discovered its power to help one forget, and he took the glass from her. "Not too much; you'll make yourself sick. And I don't want to have to carry you out in my arms and cause a scandal."

"No, though that would probably convince Durand of our engagement." She stared off across the room, her eyes distant.

"Better now?" he asked, fighting the urge to seize her and hold her. She would *not* appreciate that.

"I'm fine." She forced a tremulous smile. "Really. He merely . . . took me off guard is all."

Edwin might not be good at reading people, but he knew one thing. She was *not* fine. "Perhaps I should call in your mother."

"Don't you dare!" A bitter laugh escaped her. "Mama wouldn't be any help. And anyway, she's the reason I ended up in here in the first place. A servant told me that she was ill and needed me in the drawing room, so I came."

"He lured you here, in other words."

Rubbing her arms as if to bring warmth to her chilled blood, she nodded. "I can't believe I fell for it." She was silent for a long moment. Then she started, and her gaze shot to him. "Edwin, I didn't let him kiss me, you know."

"I didn't think you had."

As if she hadn't heard him, she went on hastily, "When I wouldn't fall into his arms, he . . . he . . ."

"Pushed a kiss upon you," Edwin said tightly, wishing he'd torn the man off her by force.

A haunted look crept into her eyes. "I should have . . . slapped him or scratched him or something, but I . . . froze. I couldn't fight, I couldn't do anything. I—"

"You were afraid. He had you trapped."

"Yes!" The gratitude in her eyes fairly slayed him. She rose to face him. "He mistook my rigidity for acquiescence. But it wasn't. And I didn't encourage the kiss. I truly didn't!"

"I believe you. I can tell when a woman is avoiding a man." He approached her. "And this incident proves that he's still obsessed with you. Disturbingly so."

She began to pace in short, quick steps that matched her short, quick breaths. "I had hoped the blackguard would have forgotten about me by now."

How could anyone forget about Clarissa? She was vibrant, alive. Everything most men wanted in a woman.

Most men. Not him.

Liar. "Clearly he has not." He gazed steadily at her. "Was he always like this?"

She shook her head. "Not at first. He simply courted me like any other gentleman. I—I suppose he took my flirtatiousness for encouragement."

"No," he said firmly. The words reminded him too much of his mother's for comfort. "A gentleman always proceeds with caution until he's sure of his reception."

"He's French. Perhaps he doesn't know how to behave."

Edwin snorted. "He was born and raised here, was he not? He knows the rules. He simply chooses to ignore them. You cannot possibly think that bribing a footman to lie about your mother being ill and then accosting you alone, with no chaperone, is considered acceptable behavior anywhere, here *or* in France."

"No, I suppose not. Though when he proposed and I refused him, he accused me of leading him on." She lifted her gaze to Edwin. "I swear I did not."

"Of course not." He hesitated before raising a delicate subject. "Why *did* you refuse him, anyway, if he'd behaved honorably up until that point?"

She worried her lower lip with her teeth. "He kept trying to get me alone, and he sent me private notes. I don't like that sort of . . . behavior. He always had something, well, *off* about him. Not quite normal, you know?"

"I do know." Edwin had known another man like that. The one who had ruined his mother's life. "Which is why it's imperative that you not go off alone again for any reason. Take me with you if you must venture out. It's best to err on the side of caution, since the man is obviously behaving irrationally."

An anxious frown crossed her brow as she whirled on him. "True, but you shouldn't have told him we were engaged. I have no intention of marrying you."

He stiffened. "Of course not."

As if she realized what she'd said, she winced. "I'm sorry. I didn't mean that the way it—"

"It's fine. I know how you feel about me." He was grumpy Edwin, the fellow whose company no woman could abide for long. The man who knew love was a lie.

He would resent the reputation, except that it was all true.

"It-it's not you," she said hastily. "I have no intention of marrying *anyone*. That's the other reason I didn't consider accepting Durand's proposal."

"Right."

She was merely trying to soothe his pride. The damned woman was too softhearted for her own good.

"I'm being honest," she persisted. "It has nothing to do with you or—"

"I was only trying to get him away from you, devil take it! I didn't mean anything by it." He rubbed the back of his neck. "I don't know why you're making such a fuss."

She swallowed hard. "Because Durand will run off and tell everyone, and then the two of us will be placed in a difficult—"

"He wouldn't do that. It wouldn't suit his plan."

Clarissa gaped at him. "What plan?"

"To win you. If he tells the world that we're engaged, he lessens his own chances at getting you back."

"He has *no* chance of getting me back."

"I know, but *he* clearly doesn't know that. Or acknowledge it. And he has to realize that ending an engagement publicly would be messy for us; he'll assume that we'd rather marry than cause a scandal. So it's better for him to keep it secret, too, in hopes that he can end it privately by winning you. That's the better strategy."

"Do you always think in terms of strategies?"

Edwin shrugged. "I'm a chess player. And in life, as in chess, strategy is everything. Durand knows that. So, as long as we give him enough evidence to believe that we're telling the truth, while at the same time not alerting the rest of the world to it, we'll be fine."

"You're suggesting that we—"

"Pretend to be 'secretly' engaged for Durand's benefit. Yes."

She blanched. "That won't work."

"Why not?" He lifted an eyebrow. "Surely you can be nice to me long enough to convince him. And no one expects *me* to be nice. All I have to do is be attentive."

"Oh, Lord, that alone will start people speculating about our new intimacy. And since telling Mama any kind of secret is just asking for trouble, she'll spin a future for us out of what she witnesses, and will start insinuating that we have an understanding, and next thing I know I'll be trapped into—"

"For God's sake," he bit out, growing annoyed by

her obvious loathing for the idea of ever wedding him. "If anyone will lose anything by having our supposed 'engagement' found out, it will be *me*. You said you'd never marry me. So you'd have to jilt me to get out of it."

She blinked. "Well . . . yes. Exactly."

"And since I've been jilted once already," he went on irritably, "being jilted again would make it even more difficult for me to find a wife. So if *I'm* not worried about the consequences if our 'engagement' is revealed, I damned well don't know why *you* should be."

"I just don't . . . see how it would work."

"Do you have a better suggestion? I'd call the arse out, but that would almost certainly lead people to assume there's something serious between you and me."

To his surprise, horror suffused her features. "You are *not* dueling with that scoundrel. Don't even think it!"

"I do know how to handle a pistol." Blast it, did she consider him incapable of winning a duel?

"That's not the point."

"Fine. What's *your* plan?"

She let out a long sigh. "All right. Let's say we pretend to be 'secretly' engaged around Durand. How are we supposed to convince him that it's real if we can't actually behave like an engaged couple?"

"I have no idea. *You're* the expert on flitting about society. Perhaps we should make sure he sees us holding hands in private, or even kissing or—"

"You're such a *man*," she cut in. "All of you go right to the physical."

He eyed her askance. "Shall we have him read our minds instead?"

"Very amusing." She pursed her lips. "But we can be more subtle. Give the illusion of your being on the verge of making an offer to me. We can flirt, tease, dance—" When he groaned, she added, with an arch glance, "Yes, we must dance as often as is proper without declaring ourselves. That's a given."

"Bloody hell," he muttered.

"Stop cursing. Besides, you're a better dancer than you let on. You'll be fine." Her expression softened. "Who knows? You might even learn how to put some poetry into your poussette."

"Since I don't know or care what a poussette is, I'm not sure how I could put poetry into it. And I really don't see how my circling woodenly about a ballroom with you proves anything to anyone."

"It proves you're willing to endure a pastime you're not fond of, just for the chance of touching me and holding me. Besides . . ."

As she went on describing the advantages of gamboling together in public, he slid behind a chair to hide the effect her words had provoked. He was stuck on the "touching me and holding me" part. Because he wanted to touch and hold her.

Years ago, Samuel, his practiced seducer of a brother, had told him that women responded very well to the usual kisses in the usual spots, but also to ones placed on strategic points all over the body. His brother had even claimed that some women could find their release merely from such caresses.

Though Edwin was skeptical about that last, he'd always wanted to try rousing a woman the way Samuel described. And the idea of doing it with Clarissa now filled his head. He imagined kissing Clarissa's inner arm, dragging his tongue along the soft skin of her throat, brushing his hand over the tiny dip in her—

"Edwin?" she prodded. "Do you agree?"

"Er . . . yes, of course." God only knew what he was agreeing to. That's what he got for woolgathering—that, and an arousal growing more prominent by the moment.

What the devil? This hadn't happened to him since he was a green lad lusting after tavern wenches. "But you'll have to help me with the flirting. It's not my strong suit."

"Don't worry. Just follow my lead, and listen to your instincts. I'm sure you have them. You just ignore them."

Or suppress them whenever it came to her, which he must continue to do. Because his instincts said to pull her close and kiss her the way Durand *should* have—like a lover, not a bully. His instincts said she might welcome such a kiss.

His instincts were doubtless quite wrong.

As if she could read his mind, she sharpened her gaze on him. "Are you sure you want to do this? It hardly seems fair to you." She approached him slowly. "I mean, how long are we talking about continuing this sham?"

He fought to clear his head of erotic images. "However long it takes for Durand to get the message."

"But that might be ages. What if you have to spend the entire Season pretending to court me for Count Durand's benefit? How does that help you find a wife?"

"You let me worry about that."

"You're not getting any younger, you know."

God, what did she think—he was doddering on the edge of the grave? "Thanks for reminding me."

"Seriously, Edwin—"

"I doubt our sham will go on too long. Consider it this way: If you help me with my flirting and court-ing and such nonsense, then by the time we're finally rid of that fool, I'll be so far advanced in my strategies to secure a wife that it will take me no effort at all."

She gazed heavenward. "Oh, Lord. I'm really going to have my work cut out for me, aren't I?"

"I beg your pardon?"

Coming up next to him, she slid her hand into the crook of his arm. "Well, first of all, stop refer-ring to flirting and courting as 'nonsense' in front of any woman you're actually interested in. And sec-ond, you have got to stop thinking in terms of strat-egies and 'securing a wife.' The important thing to remember is . . ."

His mind wandered again as she led him from the room, instructing him the whole way. But this time his thoughts weren't on undressing her. This time all he could think was that he'd gained himself yet another fiancée who was never going to marry him.

Bad enough that Jane had thrown him over. Though they'd never been more than friends and the only thing Jane had hurt was his pride, watching her fall for another man's claptrap about "true love" had still stung. It had been unexpected, too, since she was a sensible woman otherwise.

But Clarissa wasn't Jane. She took nothing—other than Durand's obsession, apparently—very seriously.

And even if she *wanted* to marry Edwin, he would never consider marrying her. If he ever got close to the bright flame that was Lady Clarissa Lindsey, she would singe him but good. He'd rather be alone than to wed her and find that her infatuation was temporary.

He refused to have his heart pummeled when she lost interest in her husband and moved on to her next conquest. He refused to wake up one day, like his mother, to discover that his marriage was all a lie. That his spouse had never been in his corner. That Clarissa's love or infatuation or whatever one called it could not withstand the rough times of a marriage.

Edwin had watched his mother die with his father's name on her lips and her heart breaking, and all because Father had been off at a private opium club in London, indulging in his favorite vice to erase his memories of the past. Even "love" had not prevented his father from sinking into that abyss.

Before Edwin would risk having that happen to *him*, he would settle for a perfectly conventional, boring union with some responsible chit who was happy to live the usual life of a well-bred lady— bearing him children and managing his household and not making him think or feel.

Because quiet comfort with any ordinary female was surely preferable to a possibility of untold pain with a certain frivolous beauty.

Five

Meeks's Mechanical Museum had probably never seen such an influx of people. But having been appropriated by Lady Maribella's parents for her eighteenth birthday, it was overrun with the beau monde in full flower, oohing and ahhing over such creations as a tiny clockwork coach drawn by two horses, and a mechanical flute player, which, once wound up, entertained an entire room.

Clarissa turned her attention to Edwin, who was frowning as he observed a mechanical spider in its advance forward. "You don't look very pleased," she said. "I'd think you'd be delirious at being able to attend a social occasion you can actually enjoy for once."

"I would be happier if Meeks had added anything new since the last time I was here."

"When was that?"

"Two months ago. I brought the lads."

Ah yes, from Preston Charity School for Boys, which Edwin supported. Thanks to Yvette, Clarissa and her

mother had given to the cause more than once themselves. "I'm sure they enjoyed it immensely."

"They seemed to. They usually do."

"Usually? How often do you come here, for pity's
sake?"

He shrugged. "A few times a year. More, if I hear
that there's something new. It provides an excellent counterpoint to the lads' lessons in physics and
mathematics."

"And I suppose you also get ideas for your own
creations," she teased.

A faint smile crossed his lips. "That, too."

"One day I hope to see these automatons of
yours."

"So you can mock my endeavors the way Yvette
does? No, thank you."

She patted his arm. "I wouldn't do that."

"You've spent the past three days critiquing my
manner of speech, my behavior toward ladies, and
my opinions. I can hardly see why you would stop at
mocking my favorite pastime."

"If you would actually pay attention to my criti-
cisms," she said with a sniff, "I'd have no need to continue them."

He lifted an eyebrow. "I doubt that. I suspect that
you enjoy giving directions."

"Only when they're heeded."

"I heed them when I can. But I doubt I will ever
succeed in making my manner of speech 'amiable'
enough to satisfy your stringent requirements." His
voice hardened. "And I am *not* going to alter my
opinions about life and the world simply to acquire
a wife."

"I don't want you to alter them. Just don't voice them to ladies."

"So I can surprise my wife on our wedding night when she finds out what I really think? That hardly seems a good plan."

She huffed out a frustrated breath. "*You're* the one who asked me to help you. I assumed that it meant you would accept my help."

He cursed under his breath. "I'm trying." With a glance about the room, he changed the subject. "At least there's no sign of Durand. For a while there, he seemed to be at every event we attended."

And Edwin had bared his teeth every time the man had ventured near her. Indeed, the earl's fierce protectiveness toward her had come as a shock. He'd never before seemed to care so deeply about what happened to her.

"Perhaps your plan is working," she said.

"Or he's plotting a more indirect way to get to you."

A shiver swept over her before she could suppress it. It infuriated her. She'd worked for years to put her fear behind her, to fight off the bad dreams and the nervousness. Now, that dratted Durand threatened to overset all her hard-won control.

She refused to let him. "Lord, I hope he's abandoned his interest. If he hasn't, it will send Mama into even more of a 'spell' than she's in at present."

Her mother had begged to be excused from this party because she was having one of her "spells." Privately, Clarissa had suspected that Mama was simply trying to allow her and Edwin a chance to be alone, but Clarissa had said nothing to him about it and merely asked that they take his open phaeton for propriety's sake.

Miss Trevor and Lady Maribella hurried up to them. "Have you seen the boy draughtsman who draws sketches, Lady Clarissa?" Miss Trevor asked. "You must come look at it! It's in the next room."

The women tried to pull Clarissa away from Edwin, but she grabbed his arm. "His lordship and I will both come. He's very knowledgeable about automatons. Perhaps he can give us some idea of how they work."

"That would be wonderful," Miss Trevor said without enthusiasm as she led the way into the other room. Clearly, the woman knew his reputation for being blunt and reticent.

But Lady Maribella must not have, for she gushed, "There's a writer and a piano player, too. All three are positively amazing!"

"As opposed to negatively amazing, I suppose," Edwin muttered under his breath as they followed at a more leisurely pace.

"Hush," Clarissa chided, though she stifled a laugh. "She's young."

"*You're* young. But you still know how to use the English language."

"Why, Lord Blakeborough," Clarissa said sweetly, "I do believe you're giving me a compliment. You see? It's not that difficult."

"I never have trouble giving compliments to women I admire."

Her pulse quickened. He admired her? Truly?

Miss Trevor had halted in front of them quickly enough to hear his last two words, which she pounced on. "What is it that you admire, Lord Blakeborough? Do tell."

When Edwin frowned, Clarissa said hastily, "He was just saying how much he liked your gown, Miss Trevor. It's a work of art."

The young lady glanced to him as if for affirmation.

Edwin smiled blandly. "A work of art. Truly."

"Why, thank you, my lord." She cast him an assessing look, then hurried off to whisper in Lady Maribella's ear.

"A work of the worst art I've ever seen," Edwin muttered.

"Edwin!" Clarissa hissed.

"Don't tell me you like that riot of stripes and plaids and atrocious ribbons."

She paused, torn between confessing the truth and discouraging his bluntness. But she didn't want him to think her utterly brainless. "I'll admit that her gown is . . . rather unfortunate."

"'Rather unfortunate' is kinder than it deserves."

"True." She nudged him. "And yet, the two ladies are now regarding you with more fondness, are they not?"

Indeed, Miss Trevor and Lady Maribella were having quite the whispered conversation across the room, punctuated by furtive looks of interest at Edwin.

He rolled his eyes. "That's only because you lied to Miss Trevor, which I will never do."

"You don't have to. Just look for the good things in her, in all of them, and focus on those. Surely you can find one good thing to compliment in every woman you meet."

"I doubt it."

"Try."

Lady Anne and Lady Jane were joining Miss Trevor and Lady Maribella now, and the four approached Clarissa and Edwin with coy smiles. "So, what do you think of the automatons, Lady Clarissa?" Lady Anne asked.

"I don't know," Clarissa said. "I must see them up close."

She and Edwin approached the trio of mechanisms roped off from the room: a young lady who played what was actually an organ, judging from the bellows attached; a boy who drafted images; and another boy who wrote on real paper using real ink and quill. Each was only slightly smaller than a real child, and all were perfectly proportioned. The placard for them read, THE MUSICIAN, THE DRAUGHTSMAN, AND THE WRITER, BY MONSIEUR JAQUET-DROZ.

Edwin nodded to a fellow behind the velvet rope, and the man obligingly wound up the clockwork writer, who began to pen what appeared to be a letter.

"Isn't it amazing?" Lady Maribella gushed as she followed the automaton's quill with her gaze.

Edwin murmured in Clarissa's ear, "It would be far more amazing if he wrote something worth reading."

Clarissa whispered, "Say that again, only loud enough for them to hear."

He frowned at her, but said in a voice that carried, "It would be far more impressive if he wrote a treatise on physics."

The ladies tittered.

"*Now* you have their attention," Clarissa said under

her breath. When he arched an eyebrow, she raised her voice and asked, "What is your opinion of that figure?" She pointed to the draughtsman, who was drawing an intricate image.

"Have you noticed what he's sketching?" Edwin asked.

That prompted the rest of them to go and watch until the automaton completed its work.

"It's a carriage being driven by Cupid and pulled by a butterfly," Edwin supplied as the ladies were still trying to make it out. "A nonsensical drawing, to be sure. Why would Cupid use a carriage instead of just flying off himself to do whatever he wishes?"

"Perhaps he's tired," Lady Maribella said.

"Or simply not very bright," Edwin said.

Miss Trevor's eyes gleamed. "Exactly, my lord. And how does one harness a butterfly, anyway? Only think how tiny and gossamer the reins would have to be."

"And then they wouldn't be strong enough to haul a carriage," Edwin pointed out.

Lady Maribella tipped up her chin. "You two have no imagination. I think it's a very pretty sketch."

"As do I," Clarissa said soothingly to the young woman. "Very whimsical."

Edwin eyed her askance.

Miss Trevor caught that and grinned. "What do you think of the musician, my lord?"

"The clockwork is ingenious. I believe that Jaquet-Droz used a series of cams with . . ." When Clarissa frowned at him, Edwin released an exasperated breath, then finished sulkily, "It's very intricate."

"Look there!" Lady Anne said, pointing at the rise

and fall of the mechanism's chest. "She even breathes, as if she's alive."

"Lots of things breathe," Edwin snapped. "An altar may breathe 'ambrosial odors,' but that doesn't mean it will walk out of the temple."

The ladies started, then giggled.

"Why, Lord Blakeborough," Miss Trevor said, taking his other arm with a melting smile, "you are surprisingly droll."

Edwin appeared nonplussed. Clarissa was certain no one had ever called him droll, and his comical expression made her bite back a smile.

"Tell me, sir," Clarissa said, "isn't that line about the 'ambrosial odors' from *Paradise Lost*?"

His gaze swung back to her. "I thought you only read gothic novels."

"I do." She slid him a teasing look. "Fortunately, Milton's poem was quoted in one."

"That's cheating. It's like using a tune from an opera for a nursery rhyme."

The ladies laughed outright, and he actually smiled. Perhaps that was the key—to draw his fire so he might sharpen his wit on *her*. "And what, pray tell, is your problem with gothic novels, anyway?"

"That they exist," he said bluntly.

Miss Trevor went into gales of laughter. Clarissa didn't find it so amusing, especially since the other women undoubtedly read them, too. "That is *not* an answer."

"You expect a serious answer to a frivolous question?" he said.

"Why is it any more frivolous to enjoy a good tale

of adventure in a book than to watch a similar tale on the stage?" Clarissa asked.

"The last time I checked, there were no governesses wandering around castles in plays."

"No, but there are ghosts in *Macbeth*. And *Hamlet*."

"She's got you there, Lord Blakeborough," Miss Trevor put in.

He ignored her. "It's Shakespeare," he told Clarissa. "Surely you aren't going to compare the likes of *The Monk* to Shakespeare."

Since she hated *The Monk*, that wasn't possible. Feeling cornered, she crossed her arms over her chest. "When was the last time you even went to a play?" Take *that*, Mr. Oh-So-Sure-of-Your-Opinions.

"I go occasionally," he said, a tad defensively.

"*I* go regularly, so I should hope that my opinion on the subject has more weight."

"It certainly has more weight with *you*," he said. "Though I'm not sure how much weight it has with anyone else."

The ladies tittered again and formed themselves into a group about him, as if to protect him from her. The irony of it didn't escape her. Good Lord, she'd created a monster.

She was about to give him quite the set-down when Lady Maribella's mother stepped into the room to announce that tea and cakes were being served in the garden.

At once the ladies headed that way, but when Miss Trevor tried to tug Edwin with her, he murmured some excuse and hung back to accompany Clarissa. With a glare, she hurried past him.

That didn't work. Curse his long strides. He kept

pace with her easily. "I swear I have no idea what just happened," he murmured.

"I do," she said crossly. "You gathered a group of sycophants to applaud your every word."

"I was only doing what you advised."

A pox on him. "I know."

"But I didn't expect it to actually work."

She sighed. "People enjoy criticism of anything or anyone but themselves. As long as you aim your barbs away from your subject, you'll impress the ladies."

"But not you."

"You aimed your barbs at *me*, so, no. But it doesn't matter. You're not trying to impress me."

They were the last to leave the building, so he stopped her before she could go out into the garden. "And if I were? What must a man do to impress you?"

The direct question made her suspicious. It wasn't like him to speak of her as if she might be a woman who interested him romantically. "Rather like you and your automatons, I'm not about to tell you and risk your mockery."

A sudden remorse flickered in his eyes. "I shouldn't have mocked your reading tastes in front of the other women."

The unexpected apology did something funny to her insides. "Why not?" she said, hating the hint of breathlessness in her voice. "You mock my reading tastes all the time."

"As you do mine. But when it's done before an audience, it takes on a different tone. It's less like a 'merry war,' to use Shakespeare's term, than a personal attack. While it may have entertained them, it's something a boorish clod would do—and I'm trying to learn not to behave like one."

That showed more insight into personal relations than Clarissa expected. "You're being too hard on yourself." When his gaze warmed, she felt a strange panic. Edwin was proving far more appealing than she'd realized. Hastily, she added, "Besides, I'm used to your boorish ways."

"Ah." But he smiled. He wasn't taken in. "Used to them or not, you know I must learn to alter them for the nonce. So let me make sure I understand the strategy: I can say cutting things as long as they're directed at other than the ladies I wish to impress."

"Exactly."

"I shall never understand women." Though they could see everyone milling about the garden, eating and drinking a few yards from them, inside the museum it was deserted. Somehow being on this side of the threshold gave the illusion that they were private, although all it would take was for someone to veer close to the doorway to hear them.

As if he realized that, he lowered his voice. "At least I don't have to blather a lot of ridiculous compliments."

"Of course you do. You need both—wit to demonstrate your intelligence, and compliments to demonstrate your amiability."

"Oh, for God's sake, that makes no sense."

"Why?"

He shrugged. "I have no interest in courting those silly chits. Well, perhaps Miss Trevor would suit, if she didn't have such poor taste in clothes. But as for

the rest, I'd rather die a bachelor than marry one of
them. So why bother complimenting them?"

"It's precisely *because* you have no interest in
them that they're perfect for you to practice upon.
You have nothing to lose."

"And nothing to gain, either."

"I tell you what. If you can offer one genuine
compliment to each of our four companions before
we leave, I shall give you a reward."

Interest sparked in his eyes. "What sort of reward?
And please tell me it won't be a dance."

She laughed. "I shall let you choose. Whatever
you wish."

"All right." Did she imagine it or had his breath
suddenly quickened? He jerked his gaze from her.
"So, a reward." He imbued the last word with such
meaning that it sent a quiver of anticipation through
her.

Good Lord. Perhaps she shouldn't have given him
carte blanche so recklessly.

No, Edwin would never abuse the privilege by
asking for something . . . rakish. He wouldn't.

But you wish he would.

Her cheeks heated. Certainly not. That was ridiculous.

"You're blushing, minx," he said under his breath.

Now it wasn't just her cheeks heating but other
parts of her. It had been years since that happened.
Yet in the past four days, she'd felt that cursed melting warmth in her belly more and more frequently.
If the man weren't so infuriating, she might actually
think she was coming to like him.

It simply wouldn't do. "You're stalling. You still

have to give four compliments, you know. Or lose your reward."

He eyed her steadily. "Very well. Let's get this over with."

Before she could protest that he was missing the point, he stalked out into the garden and up to Lady Anne. "That is the most interesting hat I have ever seen," he said bluntly.

Clarissa choked back a frustrated laugh. Edwin could be so direct.

Fortunately, Lady Anne took "interesting" as a compliment. "Do you think so? It's my favorite." Beaming at him, the young lady affectionately patted the bonnet that resembled a platter of moldy fruit and began to wax eloquent about hats.

He endured her soliloquy for several moments before saying, "Excuse me, I forgot I needed to speak to Lady Maribella about a matter of some importance." After bowing to Lady Anne, he shot Clarissa a cheeky grin as he strolled over to Lady Maribella and Lady Jane, who stood next to the refreshments table.

Clarissa glared at him, which didn't seem to faze him one bit. Determined to hear what he said, she sidled over to pick up a glass of negus, as if that had been her sole purpose in approaching the table. Did Edwin really mean to fire his compliments at his targets in rapid succession just to obtain a reward?

Ooh, that was so like him. He disliked small talk.

"Lord Blakeborough!" Lady Maribella exclaimed before he could say a word. "Isn't this just the prettiest little garden you ever saw?"

Clarissa snorted. The woman clearly had a fondness for hyperbole and inane observations. She would sorely tax Edwin's patience.

"It is quite a little garden, yes," he said. "It suits you."

Hmm. Should Clarissa count that? The trace of irony in his voice said it wasn't *entirely* a compliment.

But Lady Maribella took it as one, for she giggled and blushed and said, "Oh, you are such a charmer, sir."

When the ridiculous claim made Clarissa choke on her negus, Edwin's gleaming gaze shot to her over the heads of his companions. "It's easy to be a charmer with such fine inspiration standing before me."

Clarissa froze. He clearly did *not* mean Lady Maribella and Lady Jane, so the compliment shouldn't count one whit. Yet the rough thrum with which he said it, and the heat in his expression before he returned his gaze to the other two ladies, made her weak in the knees. If that didn't suffice to prove him *capable* of flattering a woman, she didn't know what would.

Then Lady Jane said, "Which flowers do you like best, sir? I like the jonquils because they remind me of Mama. She used to love them so."

A lump caught in Clarissa's throat. Much as her own mother taxed her patience, she couldn't imagine losing her at as young an age as Lady Jane had lost hers.

Edwin smiled softly at the girl. "I'm sure she didn't love them half as much as that smile of yours. It would brighten any sickroom."

He clearly meant it, and that only thickened the lump in Clarissa's throat. Whenever Edwin showed the kindly side he generally kept deeply buried, it made her question her assumptions about him.

Until he spoke again. "Ah, I see Miss Trevor over there. Forgive me, but I must speak to her." Then he was off again, striding across the garden.

What was this, a race? As usual, the devious fellow was accomplishing his task with the least amount of time and bother, which was *not* what she meant for him to do at all. She followed at a distance, rather eager to see what he would come up with as a compliment for the intrepid young woman.

Without even a preamble, he said, "Miss Trevor, I couldn't help noticing that you have an excellent sense of humor."

"Why, thank you, my lord. So do you." Miss Trevor cast a speculative glance past him to Clarissa, who smiled and then turned and pretended to be admiring a plant. A rather ugly one. With spikes. Which she wished she could use on Miss Trevor.

Heavens, where had *that* come from?

Well, perhaps Miss Trevor would suit.

Oh, yes, that must be where. But only because Clarissa hated to see Edwin marry someone so obviously wrong for him. Not because she was jealous of any woman who actually garnered Edwin's interest. Not. One. Bit.

"As soon as we can be alone, I mean to claim my reward."

She jumped, then scowled at Edwin. "Good Lord, don't surprise me like that. I thought you were still talking to Miss Trevor."

"No need. I complimented her already."

Clarissa looked over to see Miss Trevor now wandering over to Lady Anne, probably to discuss the very abrupt Lord Blakeborough. She lowered her voice. "That was *not* the point of the exercise. You were supposed to engage in polite chitchat and bury the compliment in it."

There was a decided glint of humor in his eyes. "You didn't say that. You said to offer four genuine compliments. So I did."

"But—"

"Are you reneging on your offer of a reward?" he asked with a lift of his eyebrow.

He *would* see it that way. "Of course not," she mumbled.

"Good. Because I've decided what I want. Later, when we get a chance to be alone, I want to kiss the inside of your bare arm."

Her stomach flipped over. "That's a very odd request."

"You said 'anything.'"

"But . . . but why *that*?"

"You didn't say I had to explain. You didn't put any parameters on the reward. If you wanted a different outcome, you should have been more specific. You only demanded that I give—"

"Fine," she said, to forestall his litany of logic. "If that is what you wish, you may kiss the inside of my arm. Once."

His gaze burned into hers. "Your *bare* arm," he corrected her.

She gave an exasperated breath. "Yes, of course. My *bare* arm."

"Excellent."

As he marched back into the museum, she told herself that a kiss on her arm was nothing. It wasn't like a kiss on the mouth. It was hardly even intimate.

So why was her pulse leaping like a flying fish in anticipation?

Six

Edwin couldn't help noticing Clarissa's uncharacteristic silence on their way home. Generally, she chattered to her mother about each event they attended, describing who was wearing what, the drollest comments she'd heard, the latest gossip she'd gleaned in the retiring room. And he let her and her mother natter on, content just to slip into his own thoughts.

But her mother wasn't with them, so the ride felt more intimate than usual, even with his tiger on the perch behind them. Night was falling, and her body slid against him every time they made a turn.

Sometimes he made the turn purposely sharp for that very reason. Not for nothing did he have an extensive knowledge of physics and how bodies behaved in motion.

After one such turn, Clarissa muttered an oath under her breath. "I'm astonished that you own a phaeton. And that you drive it so fast. I would have expected you to be more . . . well . . ."

"Boring?" he said tightly.

"Cautious. As a general rule, you aren't reckless."

"As long as one first assesses a rig to determine its limits, it is not reckless to drive it to the full extent of its capabilities."

"Clearly when you did your assessing," she grumbled, "you did not take your passenger into account. But then, that is typical of you."

Of course he'd taken his passenger into account. That was why he was making all these sharp turns, though he could hardly tell her that.

He glanced over to see her clutching her large silk bonnet with one hand and the side of the phaeton with the other. She looked quite fetching doing it, too, with her plaid gown of soft blues and reds ruffling in the wind. "You seem to have a great many ideas about me that bear no resemblance to my true character."

"I could say the same for you. Though it's not *my* fault we don't know each other better. You tend to run off whenever I'm around."

"Because you and Yvette chatter incessantly. There's only so much a man can endure."

"Well, if you think *we're* chatterboxes, you should see Miss Trevor." Clarissa slanted a glance at him. "Indeed, I feel I should warn you about her. She's clever, I'll grant you, but I don't think the two of you would suit."

He bit back a smile. "In other words, *you* don't want to marry me, but you don't want anyone else to marry me, either."

Judging from the way she jerked her gaze back to the road, he'd hit the mark. "It's not that I don't want to marry you in particular," she said. "I told you, I have no intention of marrying anyone."

"And why is that?"

Her face grew shuttered. "I'm not the romantic sort, that's all."

"You don't have to be the romantic sort to marry."

"No, but you have to be affectionate, at least." She stared blindly ahead at the road. "And I am also not the affectionate sort."

"I see." But he didn't see at all. He couldn't imagine her as a cold, unfeeling woman, no matter what she seemed to think.

She babbled on. "Men want affectionate wives. They deserve them, just as women deserve affectionate husbands. Since I can't provide that, I wouldn't think it fair to marry a man under false pretenses."

"If you say so. But that's all the more reason you shouldn't try to dictate whom *I* should marry."

Not that it would ever be Miss Trevor. He couldn't endure a wife who dressed so outrageously. But he wasn't going to tell Clarissa that. He was having too much fun watching her attempt to manage his future.

"I'm not trying to dictate it. I just think that you . . . and Miss Trevor . . ." She glanced over to see him smirking at her, and muttered, "Oh, forget it."

"No, do go on. You've told me she's stubborn as a mule and that you find her sudden appearance in society suspicious, but beyond that, you haven't said exactly *why* we won't suit. Unless the reason is simply that you don't like her."

"I like her perfectly well. Just not for you."

"Because?"

Clasping her hands primly in her lap, she murmured, "It wouldn't be polite to say."

"Which means you have no reason."

"I should think I know what type of woman you're looking for."

"Oh, you do, do you?" he said with a laugh. "And what type is that?"

"The type who won't make a fuss. Who's a pillar of society and follows every propriety. Who will cater to your every whim."

Just like that, his amusement vanished. Grimly he steered the phaeton around a hole. "I don't have 'whims.'"

"You know what I mean," she said, clearly exasperated. "You're looking for a woman who will march to the beat of your drum."

Blast it, he was tired of people accusing him of such a thing. First Warren, now Clarissa. Her image of him as a morally superior arse had begun to grate.

It was precisely why he'd asked for his reward—to show her that he, too, could rouse desire in a woman. In *her*. That he was capable of pleasing a woman, and not just running roughshod over her. It was a matter of pride.

A matter of lust, you mean, his conscience said.

That, too. Even though he knew it couldn't go anywhere. *Mustn't* go anywhere.

Still, he had to set her straight on one thing. "I am not a bully, whatever you may think of me."

"I wasn't saying—"

"I want a companion in life, someone with her own ideas and opinions. But yes, I do want a woman who is quiet and responsible. If you must see that as a wife who 'won't make a fuss,' go ahead. I see it as calming."

Calming might be, as Warren said, a tad dull, but it was far better than the seething tempest that had been his parents' marriage.

"Well, that would never be Miss Trevor," she said triumphantly. "You wouldn't have a moment's calm with her."

She was probably right. "Fine," he clipped out. "You've made your point." It was absurd to argue about a woman he never meant to pursue anyway.

They rode a while in silence.

"So," she said at last, "what are you planning to do this evening?"

Claim my reward. No, that was what she wanted him to say, so she could demand to be told the when and where of it. He was not playing that game. If she wanted to know, she could ask him outright. Indeed, he was rather surprised she hadn't already. Clarissa didn't usually mince words.

"I'll probably go to the club, have a drink, read a book. I don't know. I haven't thought that far ahead. Why?"

"I just . . . I wondered if you were staying for dinner."

He cast her a sidelong look. Her cheeks were as flushed as he'd ever seen them. She was clearly dancing around the issue of the reward, and he was tempted to prolong the dance, to see how far she'd go.

"With your mother ill," he said, "I hardly think that's wise."

She snorted. "Mama isn't ill. She's very blatantly trying to throw us together for her own purposes."

"Ah. Does she know of your refusal to marry?"

"She does not. And I'd prefer to keep it that way."

"Yet another reason I shouldn't stay for dinner," he said dryly. "*I'd* prefer not to lie."

"You don't have to lie. Just don't volunteer the information." She steadied her shoulders. "And of course you should stay for dinner. Mama will be disappointed if you don't."

He *wanted* to stay. Because the idea of kissing her arm and seeing her reaction had consumed him half the day.

They drew up in front, and his tiger hopped down to take the reins from him. "I'll be remaining for dinner," Edwin told the lad. "So you might as well have your supper with the stable boys."

"Thank you, milord." The groom jumped into the front of the curricle and sent the horses trotting round to the mews.

As soon as they entered the house, they were met by a footman, who informed them that her ladyship had retired.

"Oh!" Clarissa said, clearly startled. "So early? And without eating?"

"She asked for a tray in her room, my lady," the servant said as he took Clarissa's bonnet and pelisse.

Edwin was rather gratified by the disappointment that flashed over Clarissa's face, especially since it mirrored his own. She bit her lower lip. "Well then . . . oh, dear . . ."

"I should go," he said. A tête-à-tête dinner with Clarissa might scandalize the servants, no matter what her mother was aiming for.

"I suppose you should." Suddenly she brightened. "But while we're waiting for your phaeton to be brought back round, I've something to show you in the library."

It was all he could do not to laugh. She could be so transparent. And he wasn't giving her an inch. "Oh? And what might that be?"

Looking as if she wished to thump him on the head, she said, "It's a book, of course. A very *rewarding* one."

"Ah." As hints went, that was a straightforward one. "Of course."

"It won't take long," she said brightly.

He sincerely hoped it took longer than she expected. Because he'd been waiting hours for this moment. And he meant to enjoy it at his leisure.

"Very well." He gestured toward the hallway. "Lead on, my lady."

The moment they entered the library, Clarissa's stomach knotted up. It was odd, really, that she should be so edgy around Edwin. Though it had taken her a long while after her disastrous debut to stop panicking every time a man touched her, since then she'd shared a few kisses with the occasional suitor, partly just to prove to herself that she could endure them.

But none of the kisses had been more than exercises. None of the men had been anyone she cared about. This was Edwin. He was different. So it was probably a good thing he only meant to kiss her arm.

Still, to be on the safe side, she led him to a corner of the library that couldn't be seen from the door.

The last thing she needed was a servant happening upon them and misinterpreting what he saw.

Summoning an expression of quiet calm, she turned and threw Edwin's own words back at him. "Let's get this over with, shall we?"

Edwin cast her an enigmatic look. "What, exactly?"

"The *reward*, for pity's sake!" She glared at him. "You know what I mean."

To her mortification, he chuckled. "I do, but it is much more fun watching you beat around the bush."

With a roll of her eyes, she thrust her arm out. "You, sir, can be quite a tease. I wouldn't have thought it."

"As I said, you don't know me as well as you think." Turning her hand over so the pearl buttons of her cuffs were at his disposal, he began to unfasten them with slow, intent interest.

Very slow. Very intent. It was different from anything she'd experienced. There were only three buttons, yet he took his time, until she was ready to scream at him to be done with it. Because the attention he gave to unveiling her wrist, inch by inch, was doing funny things to her insides. Unfamiliar things.

Years ago, the man she called the Vile Seducer, now long dead, had roughly extinguished her smoldering interest in men. Yet Edwin, with his capable fingers that made her shiver with every touch, was sparking something deep in her belly.

Something she'd never thought to feel again.

When he finished her buttons, he paused, his hand lightly encircling her wrist. As if he could detect the wild thrum of her blood through her veins, he murmured, "For a woman who claims not to be affectionate or romantic, you're oddly nervous." He met her gaze. "I won't bite, you know."

"Of course not," she snapped.

His eyes narrowed, shining like sleet on slate in the candlelit room. "No need to get testy. You agreed to this, remember?"

She forced herself to breathe, to smile. "Of course."

But she hadn't expected it to be such an overwhelming feast of sensation. As he bent over her arm, the scent of his hair—tinged with musk and cloves—wafted to her, faint but distinctly Edwin. He pushed her sleeve up, baring the tender skin inside the bend of her elbow, and the merest brush of his thumb sent her blood racing.

Then his lips were on her arm. Her naked arm. She could feel the rough scrape of his whiskers, hear the clock ticking seconds that seemed to slow as his mouth pressed into the pulse beating frantically just *there*.

The kiss was tender but firm and more intimate than she could possibly have imagined. Her knees went weak, especially when he lingered there to draw in a long breath as if to inhale her fragrance.

Still holding her wrist, he lifted his head to stare at her with eyes more fathomless than they'd seemed scant seconds ago. She couldn't look away.

So, to break the spell, she asked, "Why kiss me there?"

A faint smile touched his lips. "Call it one of those whims you seem to think I have." He straightened, then tugged her closer. "And here's another."

Then he kissed her lips.

Oh *yes*. Until he'd done it, she hadn't realized it was what she'd been waiting for. Edwin to kiss her mouth. So she could see, could know, if he truly was as different from her interpretation of him as he claimed.

In this, at least, he was. He didn't demand; he offered. His mouth toyed with hers, as slowly and intently as his fingers unbuttoning her sleeve. It made her insane. She was used to men pushing, forcing, taking. She wasn't used to patience or silken temptation, breaths mingling and lips caressing in equal measure.

And when he slid his tongue inside her mouth, it didn't so much startle as intrigue her. She'd been kissed like that before, but not so eloquently. It made her restless for more.

Hardly even aware she did it, she wrapped her arms about his neck. Then everything got more interesting. The *kiss* got more interesting. He sucked on her tongue and she slipped it into his mouth, something she'd never done. Their tongues engaged in a "merry war" that made her dizzy with the sweet ache of it.

His kiss grew bolder, but she didn't mind. She wanted it bolder still. She slid her hand inside his coat, shocked to find his heart beating as rapidly as hers. The kiss went on and on, battering her defenses, tempting her to let go . . . until he pulled her flush up against him.

She froze. She could feel the thickness inside his trousers, and she knew what it meant. Pain, humiliation. *Danger*.

Jerking away, she whispered, "No. Enough." She

waited fearfully for his protest, waited for him to fight her, to try to subdue her.

Instead, he ran his fingers through his hair and said raggedly, "Enough. Right."

She fought to get her breathing under control. "Edwin, I'm sorry I—"

"You have nothing to be sorry about." He was already slipping into his formal manner. "I overstepped my bounds. You're always well within your rights to remind me where they are."

No man had ever said that to her. It sounded too good to be true. But then, she and Edwin had done little more than kiss. Perhaps if matters had progressed further . . .

She tamped down a stab of fear. This was Edwin, after all. "Thank you. I can always count on you to be a gentleman."

He eyed her steadily, as if sensing that her words were as much a plea as anything. "And I can always count on you to be a lady."

He spoke the words with perfect sincerity, yet her throat felt suddenly tight and raw. How little he knew.

"Tomorrow, then," he said. "I shall fetch you and your mother at nine to take you to services."

All she could manage was a nod.

He looked as if he were about to remark on her uncharacteristic silence, then sighed. "I'll show myself out."

The moment he cleared the door, she collapsed into the nearest chair. Heavens. Edwin could kiss. He could feel.

He could be aroused. By her. By *kissing* her.

She didn't know what to think about that.

But one thing was certain. The next time she thought about offering him a reward, she would put the idea right out of her head.

Before it got her into trouble.

Seven

Still shaken by his reaction to the kiss with Clarissa, Edwin paused at the door of Warren's town house to speak to the head footman. "Have you seen Count Durand hereabouts?"

"No, milord. I've been watching the street as you requested, but haven't seen the Frenchman."

Relieved that the arse wasn't hanging about the house at least, Edwin rode from Mayfair to Pall Mall as if the hounds of hell were at his back. His "reward" had gone better than he expected. If he didn't watch it, he might yet find himself leg-shackled to Clarissa. And that would be disastrous.

He felt again the rapid beat of her blood against his lips as he kissed her inner arm. He saw again her expression as he straightened—a heightened look of awareness and arousal that had prompted him to kiss her lovely mouth. To plunder and taste and wish he could continue drinking from her lips for days.

A curse erupted from him. *Drinking from her lips*, indeed. He didn't want to do any such ridiculous thing. What he wanted was to have her in his bed. Which couldn't happen unless they married.

Remembering her reaction to him at the end, he gritted his teeth. When a woman recoiled from a man's embrace with alarm in her eyes, it didn't bode well for her wanting to marry the fellow.

Until that moment, she'd seemed to like him well enough. Of course, Clarissa was a known flirt, so sometimes it was hard to tell the difference between flirtation and genuine liking. Perhaps she'd merely been toying with him before.

But then, why not finish their kiss with a laugh and a teasing remark? Or a coy refusal, as some other woman might have done?

He shook his head. He would never understand her, and there was no reason even to make the attempt. This would end as soon as Warren returned. If Edwin had his druthers, it would end even sooner.

It could end tomorrow if Durand was disposed of.

The thought leapt into his head with startling clarity. Yes, perhaps he should attack things from that front. Surely the Frenchman had some weakness, some secret in his past that could be held over his head to make him stop his pursuit of Clarissa. And Edwin knew just the person to ask about it.

He went straight to the club, hoping that the Baron Fulkham, undersecretary of state for war and the colonies, would show up tonight. The baron had recently joined because his late brother's widow was being vigorously courted, and he needed to make sure she didn't end up in bad hands. While he was rarely present during the day, he did come in the evenings to enjoy a cigar and play cards with friends.

Fortunately, the card room was right where Edwin found him. Unfortunately, Fulkham was playing cards with Lord Rathmoor, the man who'd married Edwin's former fiancée.

Fulkham looked up before Edwin could retreat. "Evening, Blakeborough," the baron said, with a furtive glance at Rathmoor. "Someone said you were at Lady Maribella's party. We didn't expect to see you so soon."

That was probably why the man had felt comfortable inviting Rathmoor to the club as a guest. Meanwhile, Rathmoor looked anything but comfortable. Damn. This would be harder than Edwin thought.

"I was at the party but didn't stay to the end," he answered.

"Come play with us," Fulkham said. "Rathmoor is slaughtering me at vingt-un and needs some competition."

Edwin hesitated. He'd have to be cautious in questioning the baron as it was, since he barely knew the man. With Rathmoor there, it would be even more difficult.

Still, much as Rathmoor probably resented Edwin for attempting to marry Jane, Edwin knew the viscount was discreet.

That was why Edwin preferred dealing with men. A man asked direct questions, got direct answers, and nobody pressed him for more. There was none of this nonsense about compliments and such.

Besides, as a former Bow Street runner, Rathmoor might be able to shed some light on Durand. As long as Edwin didn't let on that this had anything to do with Clarissa, there'd be no chance of either man's leaking information that could harm her reputation.

A card game might be the perfect venue for asking questions that seemed casual. Especially a French card game. It was an obvious opening.

"I believe I *will* join you." Edwin took a seat between the two men. "What are the stakes?"

"Five pounds to start." Fulkham lifted an eyebrow. "Unless that's too rich for your blood."

"It's fine." Edwin enjoyed cards most of the time, especially since he rarely lost, but tonight he would be hard-pressed to keep his mind on the game.

They determined that Rathmoor would be dealer. With a grim expression, he shuffled the cards, his movements rigid. Perhaps Edwin should directly address the difficult issue between them before going on to more productive subjects.

"How is Jane?" Edwin hadn't seen her since her wedding to Rathmoor several months ago, so it should be a perfectly acceptable question.

Given the way Rathmoor stiffened, perhaps not. "She's well," he clipped out and dealt each of them two cards.

Edwin examined his cards and did some quick mental calculations, then indicated he wanted another card. "I understand you're renovating Rathmoor Park."

Rathmoor's gaze shot to him, still wary. "We are."

The other two men both took another card as well.

Edwin chose to stand at nineteen. "I'm sure Jane will be a great asset in that endeavor. She has a keen sense of how to decorate effectively."

Rathmoor softened a fraction. "She does indeed. How did you know?"

"After my father died and I wanted to redo the

town house, she made several helpful suggestions. Yvette was very grateful for the advice, since I had put her in charge of the furnishings."

"Jane has a knack for such things." Rathmoor examined his cards and chose to stand at seventeen. "She's good at managing people."

Fulkham asked for another card, and then chose to stand, too.

"She certainly is." As they each turned their one facedown card over, it occurred to Edwin that Jane had tried to manage him from time to time, and he'd chafed at it. She'd gone about it so single-mindedly, much as his sister had always done.

But Clarissa teased and challenged him, which he found vastly more enjoyable. Living with Jane would probably have been more trying than he'd realized at the time. Rathmoor seemed happy enough with her, but that was because the man fancied himself "in love."

At least Yvette was no longer trying to manage Edwin's life. Though sometimes he missed that.

"Congratulations, Blakeborough," Rathmoor said, "you win this one."

"Hmm?" Edwin looked down to see he had turned up a two to go with his nineteen. Twenty-one.

Rathmoor had twenty, and Fulkham had gone bust.

But the baron didn't seem perturbed by that, for he laughed. "Your mind is a million miles away, isn't it?"

"Sorry." Edwin swept the sovereigns to his side of the table. "I was woolgathering about my sister."

"Surely you needn't worry about her now that

she's married." Rathmoor sounded less uncomfortable than before as he picked up the cards and shuffled.

"No," Edwin answered. "Keane is a good man. He's proved to be far more reliable than rumor had led me to believe. And until he came along, she had to fight off scoundrels." He slanted a glance at Fulkham. "Speaking of scoundrels, someone asked me about the Count Durand's character." That was almost true.

"The charge d'affaires?"

"Yes." Edwin cut the cards for Rathmoor, who began to deal. "Have you heard anything about him? He seems quite the smooth-talking fellow."

"That's necessary for a man in the diplomatic profession," Fulkham said.

"If he's the charge d'affaires, shouldn't he be intent on doing his duty by the ambassador and not running around courting women?" Edwin tapped for another card. "The person who wanted information about him was upset by his pursuit of a certain female relation."

"Durand is a typical Frenchman, that's all," Rathmoor said dismissively. "Eloquent with the ladies. Rather like my half brother, who has just enough French in him to be dangerous."

Edwin didn't want to let the conversation wander into some tangent about Rathmoor's relations. "But Durand hasn't a reputation for, say, seducing gentlewomen, does he?" He figured both men would take the question in stride, since that *was* the purpose of the club, after all—to separate the wheat from the chaff regarding suitors.

"Not to my knowledge." Fulkham tapped to demand

another card. "The man *is* unmarried, after all. He's probably looking for a wife."

"So he has no skeletons in his past," Edwin persisted.

Rathmoor dealt another card to the baron. "It wouldn't matter if he did. I suppose if he'd committed some indiscretion you could shame him in society with it, but that's about all you could do."

"And even that would be inadvisable," Fulkham added. "Matters are rather strained right now between France and England. The last thing we need is some brouhaha over the charge d'affaires' skeletons, whatever they may be. Besides, unless it was the worst sort of criminal act, he would be immune to prosecution as a diplomat."

That hadn't occurred to Edwin. And so far the man hadn't committed any criminal act that Edwin knew of. Which meant it would be very difficult to banish Durand from London.

Fulkham cast him a warning glance. "I would advise your curious friend not to take on a man like the count. Durand is connected to several powerful gentlemen in France, and has a few important connections in England as well."

Do they know he's half-mad? Edwin nearly asked. But he couldn't say that. He'd have to explain, and that would mean risking Clarissa's reputation.

"Well, then, I suppose that is that," Edwin said smoothly. "Thank you for the information. My friend will be relieved."

Edwin would simply have to hope that Durand's absence at the party earlier today meant that the man had finally gotten the message and was staying away. Because going on the offensive with the charge d'affaires didn't appear a viable option. Which meant Edwin would of necessity be spending more time with Clarissa.

When his pulse quickened at the thought, he cursed himself for a fool. Pray God Durand was out of their hair soon. Otherwise, Edwin was in for a long and difficult Season.

"You had best go dress for dinner, my dear," Clarissa's mother said. "His lordship will be here in an hour."

"There's plenty of time," Clarissa muttered.

The drawing room was cozy at this time of day, with the late-afternoon sun streaming in, and she was in no hurry. Indeed, she dreaded the evening ahead. She almost wished Edwin wasn't coming to dine on this rare night when she and Mama had no engagements.

Yesterday, when he'd accompanied them to services, he'd been as stiff as a poker and had barely spoken two words. No doubt her final reaction to his kiss on Saturday night had insulted him. Lord only knew how surly he'd be at dinner.

But before she could think about going to dress, the butler appeared in the drawing room doorway to announce Edwin's arrival.

She jumped to her feet, patting her hair feverishly. Good Lord, he was early! And when he entered, she noticed he was rather formally attired for dinner. He even wore a many-caped dress cloak that he'd apparently not allowed the footman to remove.

"We weren't expecting you yet, sir." She tried to catch a glimpse of herself in the mirror across the room. No doubt she looked a fright.

If she did, he didn't seem to notice. "I fear there's been a change of plans, ladies," Edwin said distractedly.

Mama bolted upright. "Nothing has happened to Warren or Niall, has it?"

Edwin looked startled. "No, no, nothing like that."

"Warren has scarcely been gone a week, Mama," Clarissa said. "He's probably still on the ship to Portugal. He certainly couldn't have met with Niall yet." Though she dreaded what he might learn when he did—that *she* was the cause of Niall's exile. It was a constant source of shame and guilt for her.

But Niall would never reveal it. He'd kept her secret from Mama and her cousin all these years; why should he betray it now?

"Oh. Yes, you're right." Mama sank back in her seat. "So what is this 'change of plans,' Edwin?"

"I entirely forgot that I'm obligated to attend the opening of a new enterprise tonight. I won't be able to stay for dinner. You're welcome to go with me, but if you prefer not to, I'll understand. It's rather sudden, I know."

He said it almost as if he hoped they wouldn't go. No doubt he was tiring of fulfilling his promise to Warren now that Count Durand's interest in her seemed to have waned.

Fine. She hadn't wanted to dine with him, anyway. She was looking forward to a lovely evening alone with Mama. Truly, she was.

"What is the opening for?" Mama asked.

"I'm sure it's nothing that would interest us, Mama." Clarissa glided over to the window with studied nonchalance. "It's probably a lecture hall or an exhibit of machines or something equally dull."

"Actually, my Lady Spitfire," he drawled, "it's the reopening of the Olympic Theatre."

She froze, then whirled on him. "Madame Vestris's Olympic Theatre?"

"You know about it?"

"Are you mad? *Everyone* knows about it! If not for the fact that Mama and I were sequestered in the country for months, I would have bought tickets to *Olympic Revels* as soon as they went on sale." She narrowed her gaze on him. "There've been none to be had for love or money these past few weeks. So how did you get them?"

He shrugged. "I'm an investor. I have three tickets, actually, but with Keane and Yvette in America—"

"You're an investor." She couldn't keep the incredulity from her voice. "In the Olympic Theatre."

"You needn't look so shocked. When Madame Vestris approached me, I agreed to put some money on her venture if she'd agree to hire a couple of the more promising lads from Preston Charity School for posts in her business office."

"You know Madame Vestris?" she breathed. "The most celebrated opera singer, dancer, and actress in London?"

With a sudden gleam in his eyes, he waved three tickets in the air. "I could introduce you."

She gaped at them, then snapped her mouth shut. "Give me twenty minutes to get ready." Picking up her skirts, she hurried for the door. "We're most certainly going with you."

"Twenty minutes?" Edwin snorted. "I ought to make a wager on that. I'd win handily."

She paused to stick her tongue out at him, then rushed into the hall.

"But Clarissa," Mama called from behind her, "what about dinner?"

"Tonight we shall live on music!" Clarissa cried with a dramatic wave of her arm.

"Music isn't very filling, my dear!" Mama cried.

But Clarissa was already rushing up the stairs, calling for her maid. Madame Vestris! The town had been buzzing for the past month about the actress's venture—how she'd renovated the theater in its entirety, how she meant to provide spectacular entertainments. The famous contralto and another actress were partners in it, and no one could wait to see what they had in store.

Clarissa had nearly cried when she'd realized she couldn't get tickets. And Edwin had meant to go *without* them? She would punish him for that, just see if she didn't. She had the perfect gown for it, too. If he *did* notice her bosoms, as he'd said at the ball, then she would certainly make him notice them tonight. And choke on his disapproval of her attire, as well.

When, an hour and a half later, she and Mama descended the stairs in full regalia, complete with satin opera cloaks, she caught Edwin glancing at his pocket watch.

"Don't blame *me* if we're late," she told him with

a side glance at her mother. "I wasn't the one who insisted upon eating dinner while dressing." And it had taken Clarissa's maid a good half hour to get her coiffeur, a confection of feathers and curls and ribbons, done properly.

"I'm an old woman," her mother said with a sniff. "I get peckish."

"You are *not* that old, Mama."

"No matter, Lady Margrave," Edwin said kindly and offered her his arm. "We're not late yet. Once I realized I'd have to change my plans for the evening, I came early enough to allow plenty of time for you two to dress, in case you wanted to attend *Olympic Revels* with me. I know how long such preparations take. Not for nothing do I have a sister Clarissa's age."

As she followed them down the steps to the carriage, Clarissa rolled her eyes at him. "You make it sound as if I'm miles younger than you. We're only eight years apart."

He handed Mama into the carriage, then turned to Clarissa, his gaze glittering in the glow of the gas lamps. "Eight years can be an enormous divide."

Unnerved by the coolness of his tone, she tipped up her chin. "Are you trying to convince yourself? Or me?"

He took her hand with a wary look. "Merely stating a fact."

"There's no need for the reminder," she said as he helped her in. "I already know we're utterly wrong for each other."

"Clarissa, for shame," Mama murmured as they

settled into their seats and he told the driver to go on. "His lordship is being very kind, squiring us about town like this. You should be grateful."

She sighed. Mama had a point. "Forgive me, Edwin." She was always willing to admit when she'd gone too far. "I've been in a foul mood all day, but I shouldn't inflict it upon you."

A cloud spread over his brow. "Nothing to do with Durand, I hope."

"No, of course not. I would have told you first thing." The truth was, Edwin's searing kisses two nights ago had left her all at sea. One moment he seemed to desire her, the next he was cold and remote as usual. She'd spent the entire two days trying to make him out, with no great success.

The worst was, she didn't want to care that he seemed to be withdrawing, but she did, and that alone was maddening.

"Per your instructions," she went on, "we didn't leave the house at all, not even to go shopping."

"Good."

As something occurred to her, she twisted the strap of her silk reticule. "You don't think he'll be there tonight, do you?"

"He may. But with such a crowd, he'll have a hard time finding us. Just stay close to me, and we should be fine."

She nodded, but her stomach knotted. She was being silly; Durand had probably lost interest once Edwin had stood up to him. She was worrying for nothing. Though she suddenly wished she hadn't worn *quite* so daring a gown.

Edwin seemed to sense her tension, for he softened his tone. "Don't let that arse keep you from enjoying yourself. If he's there, just leave him to me."

"Yes, my dear," Mama chimed in. "I'm sure his lordship is perfectly capable of routing that Frenchman. And you do like the opera, after all."

"It's not opera," she said mechanically. "From what I understand, they're doing burlesques."

"Oh, I love a good burlesque!" her mother cried. "Last year I saw one of *The Magic Flute*, and I nearly fell over laughing. That Mozart—what a droll fellow."

"Mozart didn't write the burlesque, Mama," Clarissa said. "He wrote the original opera from which they built the parody. And that burlesque could have used a dose of Madame Vestris. She has such a way of singing things that instantly makes one smile. Don't you agree, Edwin?"

"She does sing them very well," he said noncommittally.

"Come now, surely even you are susceptible to Madame Vestris's fine talent for comedic singing and dancing." She frowned at him. "Unless it's her famous 'breeches' roles that make you disapprove."

"A woman in breeches can be very funny," Mama put in. "You were quite comical when you dressed as Romeo for the masquerade last year, my dear."

Clarissa saw Edwin's shoulders stiffen and couldn't resist tweaking his nose. "Hard not to be comical in Papa's old breeches. They came down to my ankles and were so big in the waist, I had a difficult time keeping them up."

"I noticed," Edwin bit out.

"Did you?"

"Hard not to notice when you kept cinching up those braces until your . . . derriere was very prominently . . . well . . ." He muttered an oath under his breath. "Yes, I noticed you in breeches. The whole damned world noticed. The male half, at least. I can't believe Warren let you leave the house in that."

"*Let* me? My cousin doesn't dictate what I wear. Anyway, it was a masquerade. I wore a mask. No one knew who I was."

"The devil they didn't. And Warren considers it his duty to look after you. Which means making sure you don't attract unwanted attention."

"Warren didn't know what I was wearing until I arrived. I came down with my cloak already on." When his eyes narrowed as it apparently dawned on him that she'd done the same this evening, she added hastily, "This is why you and I would never suit, you know. You have no sense of fun."

That brought him up short. He crossed his arms over his chest. "That's not true. Didn't you hear Miss Trevor at the museum? She said I was surprisingly droll."

"That's one instance—hardly enough to form a pattern." She straightened her gloves. "Why, you can't even go ten minutes without chiding me for something."

"Nonsense. If I so chose, I could go an entire evening without chiding you."

"Could you? Prove it." The minute she said it, she questioned her sanity. Hadn't she ended up regretting her previous attempt to set a task for him?

Clearly, he hadn't forgotten that, for fire leapt in his eyes. "And if I do? What do I get as my reward?"

When his gaze drifted down to her arm, she swallowed hard, remembering the last reward he'd exacted. At least he wouldn't dare choose such an outrageous prize tonight, since Mama was listening to the exchange quite avidly.

Although Mama would probably approve whatever prize Edwin asked for. She wasn't exactly known for being a strict chaperone.

"Well?" he prodded.

"You get the satisfaction of knowing you are improving yourself."

"That's not much of an incentive." The sudden gleam in his eyes gave her pause. "How about this? If I succeed in going an entire night without making a single criticism of you—"

"Or my attire or my manners or—"

"Anything in your sphere," he said irritably.

"I'm just making sure we agree on the rules from the beginning." After last time, she wasn't letting him play fast and loose with her demands.

"Fine. If I behave to your specifications, then the next time I come to dine, you must wear breeches the entire evening." He paused, then amended, "Breeches that *fit*, mind you."

Oh, dear, he made that sound . . . rather wicked. It wasn't like him at all. In fact, it shocked her he would suggest such a thing, and he was rarely shocking.

Her mother, however, didn't seem to find it shocking at all, for she clapped her hands. "Oh, that would be such fun!"

"Mama! It's far too scandalous!"

"Pish," her mother said with a wave of her hand. "If it's just us at dinner, no one will care."

Clarissa would care. As usual, Mama was more than willing to skate past the proprieties if they stood in the way of her enjoyment—or her determination to get Clarissa married off. Sometimes Clarissa enjoyed the freedom. Sometimes, she wished her mother wasn't so . . . well . . . accommodating.

This was one of those times. While it might not be *too* risqué to dress in men's attire for a masquerade where everyone else was wearing outrageous costumes, doing it in a more private setting with Edwin, especially when Mama was so inattentive, was taking things too far. Why, the very idea of him watching her backside . . .

"The servants will gossip," she protested.

"Since when do you care about servant gossip?" Edwin said dryly.

Mama chimed in, "And they won't think a thing about it, anyway, if we all dress up. We can make a game of it. I do love games."

"Yes, by all means, let's make a game of it," Edwin said, his glittering gaze drifting down to fix on Clarissa's mouth.

The hint of a dare in his tone got her back up. "You're already assuming you will succeed, Edwin, but you might not. And if you don't—"

"I'll give *you* something," he said. "Why don't we make it a true wager? If I win, you wear breeches for dinner. If *you* win, I'll give you . . . what? You'll have to choose what you'd want from me. That is, *if* I fail, which I won't."

The arrogant statement pushed her over the edge. "Fine. I agree to a wager." She tapped her chin. "Just let me think what I might want of you."

She must choose carefully, since he almost certainly couldn't go an entire evening without instructing her on *some* aspect of her behavior. Her gown alone would send him over the edge. So she would win, which meant she wanted the prize to be something that made an impact, that truly made him regret not behaving more like an amiable gentleman.

"A jewel perhaps?" he prodded. "A new hat?"

"I can only imagine what sort of hat you would give me," she said.

Besides, he'd never been tightfisted, so throwing money about would hardly be a punishment for him. Indeed, the only things that did seem to matter to him, other than his family, his estates, and his good name, were his automatons, which he had never even allowed her to—

"I know!" she said triumphantly. "If you fail, you must give me one of your automatons."

He blinked. "You want an automaton?"

"Not just any automaton. One that you created." She sat up straighter. "I don't want you trying to fob off on me some broken thing that your father owned."

The glint of amusement in his eye surprised her. "I wouldn't dream of it. But are you sure you don't want an emerald bracelet or some such nonsense?"

"No. I want an automaton."

"Very well. I agree to your terms."

He held his gloved hand out across the space between them, and she took it, an odd shiver of anticipation coursing down her when he squeezed her hand. But he didn't release it right away. He held it, his gaze burning into hers, and for the merest moment, she wished she'd asked for some other sort of reward. Something more personal, more intimate even.

Another kiss.

No, that was absurd. Their last one had been un-nerving enough.

The moment passed. She tugged her hand free and flashed him a lofty smile. "All right, my lord. We are agreed."

He broke into a smile. "Good. Let the games begin."

Eight

The crowds outside the Olympic Theatre prevented the carriage from moving at greater than a snail's pace. It was one reason that, until two hours ago, Edwin had been dreading his evening. Though he'd promised to attend, he hadn't been looking forward to it. But now . . .

Now he could hardly wait. He would hold his tongue tonight if he had to bite it off, because he fully intended to win this wager.

He'd barely had a chance to see Clarissa in her costume at the masquerade last year; she'd been surrounded by fawning admirers the entire night. But in her own home, with her mother sanctioning the visit, he could feast his eyes as much as he liked on the vision of her sweet little bottom lovingly cupped by a pair of boy's breeches.

The only thing better would be cupping that bottom in his hands.

He groaned. Best to get such thoughts out of his head right now, before his body betrayed him. The carriage was finally drawing up in front, and the last thing he needed was to make a spectacle of himself before curious onlookers by thinking of Clarissa in anything more than the most brotherly fashion.

They'd scarcely disembarked when a servant came to their side and said he'd been sent by madam to accompany them to a private box held for their use. The servant took Lady Margrave's arm to help her walk, leaving Edwin to escort Clarissa.

As they followed the fellow into the theater and up a staircase, Clarissa murmured, "Clearly there are advantages to investing in a theater. You didn't even have to take a box of your own."

"It's opening night. I doubt this will continue."

"Oh, don't be a naysayer." Her eyes darted about, taking in everything. "You have a private box at the opening night of the most anticipated performance in London. Do you know how many people would kill for that? And Mama and I get to join you. How thrilling!"

"I'm glad it makes you happy," he said, and meant it.

As her mother hobbled along in front of them with her escort, Clarissa called a bright greeting to this friend or that acquaintance. The closer they moved down the passageway to the box, the more her smile broadened. It was breathtaking.

She was breathtaking.

Normally, he would only notice how many people were crowded into the place and how noisy it was. But tonight he couldn't help seeing all the glitter and glamour of it through her eyes. Her enthusiasm was infectious.

As soon as they entered the box where the servant was already settling Lady Margrave into a plush chair, Clarissa gave a little cry of delight. "Not only do you have a box, but it's perfectly situated! Oh, this is wonderful."

"Here, let me take your cloak," he said.

Mischief glinted in her eyes before she put her back to him and untied the satin wrap. He took it from her, then froze at the sight before him.

Her bodice barely clung to the edges of her shoulders. Though he knew that such necklines were the fashion, the fabric seemed to fall rather more deeply in the back than he was used to. He could see her shoulder blades, for God's sake. And if it was cut that low in back . . .

She turned, and he caught his breath. Her cross-draped bodice formed a low vee that served up the sweet swells of her creamy breasts for all to see.

"God help me," he rasped. He couldn't seem to look away.

"Is there something wrong?" she asked with a sly smile.

"I should say so. Your gown—" He caught himself as he realized why she was smiling. Their wager. Bloody hell.

"Yes?" Glee positively danced in her eyes. "What about my gown?"

He scrambled for an answer that she wouldn't consider "chiding." "The fichu appears to have fallen out of your bodice. Perhaps I should go look for it in the passageway."

"Don't be absurd," she said with a laugh. "There's no fichu. This is how the gown is supposed to look."

She thrust out her bosom—he would swear it was deliberate—and he had to swallow his groan. All that lush female flesh was close enough to kiss, to touch. Turning away to hang her cloak on a hook, he fought for composure.

"Don't you like it?" she persisted.

Like it? He could easily slip his hand inside that bodice. He could probably slip it inside her corset, too. The gown was cut too low to accommodate a more formidable corset, so it would be an easy matter to shove one shoulder off and fill his hand with her perfect—

"It's lovely." As he faced her once more, he had to resist the urge to act on his fantasy right here in the theater. "A very interesting gown."

She mocked him with a grin. "I thought you would enjoy it."

Sly minx.

The overture began, and he said, "Perhaps we should sit down."

"Oh, certainly. If you're done giving me compliments on my gown."

"It's not the gown I'm complimenting," he said dryly, "but what's in it. Or rather, half out of it."

"Is that a criticism?" she said sweetly.

"Merely an observation." He was skirting the edges of their wager, but he didn't care. The mere thought of the male half of the audience seeing her bosom so well displayed made something twist low in his gut. Clearly, he'd gone quite mad.

"Hmm," she murmured, but apparently chose to take him at his word. Probably she assumed she'd have plenty more chances to catch him.

He began to think she might. Clarissa would do everything in her power to make sure she won.

Meanwhile, he had to look away as he settled her
into the chair beside her mother's. Otherwise, he might
stand there frozen half the night, gaping down at her
delicious breasts and wondering how they might smell,
feel, taste.

God.

He took the seat next to Clarissa, and a faint scent
of lavender oil wafted to him. Every time he saw her,
she wore a different perfume. Was it just boredom
that made her change incessantly? Or a genuine pleasure in trying different things? The first showed her to
be flighty; the second showed her to be adventurous.

He wasn't sure he wanted either in a wife. Not
that it mattered. He wasn't marrying her, after all.
And why the devil did he keep having to remind
himself of that? The blasted woman was getting
under his skin.

The audience erupted into thunderous applause as
Lucia Bartolozzi Vestris herself came onto the stage
to present an introductory speech. The half-Italian
actress was widely acclaimed a beauty, although he'd
always thought her only marginally pretty, at least
compared to Clarissa. But despite being a year or two
younger than he, Lucia possessed the grace and manners of a woman much older, which was why she was
so beloved among the theater set.

She'd taken months to prepare the Olympic for
the opening, and it showed. There was none of the
usual red velvet and heavy gilding of other theaters,
just light and airy pastels with embossed flowers
and fleurs-de-lis on the panels of the boxes. The sets
were sparse but well done, and she'd fitted the the-

ater with the latest in gas lighting. With the place crammed full to bursting and people still trying to get in from off the street, it appeared she'd already succeeded in having a first night to remember.

It took some moments for the theatergoers to quiet down enough so she could speak. Then, in her carrying tones, she began her introductory speech:

> *Noble and gentle—matrons—patrons—friends!*
> *Before you here a venturous woman bends!*
> *A warrior woman—that in strife embarks,*
> *The first of all dramatic Joan of Arcs.*
> *Cheer on the enterprise thus dared by me!*
> *The first that ever led a company.*

Clarissa leaned up to whisper, "It's true, you know. I read in the paper that she's the first Englishwoman to ever manage a theater. And look what a great success it is!"

"For tonight, anyway. She still has a hard path ahead of her."

"But *you* believe in her, don't you? You invested in her concern."

He smiled. "I've known her a long time, actually. Her father, a dealer in art and other goods, supplied mine with most of his automatons. And me, as well, before he died. She and I have been friends since childhood."

"*Friends?*" She bumped her arm with his. "You neglected to tell me that you knew her personally! Heavens, what other secrets are you keeping?"

None that he would tell her. "I have a fondness

for women in breeches," he said lightly. "But you unearthed that secret already."

"Do be serious. How well do you know Madame Vestris? What is she like?" Her eyes narrowed. "Wait, she's famous for her breeches parts—is that why you want me to wear breeches? Because you have some sort of . . . infatuation with her?"

"Shhh!" Lady Margrave hissed. "I can't hear her speech! And everyone is sure to be talking about it tomorrow."

"We'll finish this discussion later," Clarissa said under her breath.

They certainly would. After Clarissa had cautioned him about Miss Trevor and questioned him about Lucia, he had to wonder—could she really be jealous? It seemed impossible, but the signs were growing too strong to ignore.

Not that he wanted her to be jealous. Truly, he did not. But at least it put in a better light his own unsettling reactions to seeing men court her.

Of course, the cause of his behavior was a protective instinct, nothing more. Not jealousy.

Liar.

While that annoying word rang in his thoughts, the first piece of the four-part program began, a burlesque that showed the gods Hercules, Jupiter, Neptune, and Plutus singing a comic song while playing whist.

Musical or operatic parody wasn't his favorite form of entertainment, but clearly it was hers. He soon found himself watching *her* half the time and not the production. Because Clarissa even threw herself into being a spectator. She laughed, she frowned, she made droll commentaries on everything.

He'd never seen anyone get so much pleasure from a simple theater performance. While her mother was busy waving to other patrons, whispering in her daughter's ear, and looking for the opera glasses she'd dropped, Clarissa sat rapt, an incandescent joy on her face as she watched what happened on the stage. He only wished he could capture that expression.

By the time the intermezzo came, he was almost loath to see the first piece end. But he had little chance to ask her opinion of the performance before the box door burst open, and they were swamped with visitors.

Unsurprisingly, none of them were there for him. A few of Lady Margrave's cronies wanted to compare notes with the dowager countess, but most of the visitors were young heirs of titled gentlemen who'd come to flirt with Clarissa. So Edwin stood back and observed the scene, hoping to learn which of their tactics garnered the best response from her.

He told himself he only wanted to see what he could use in courting *other* women. But the truth was more complicated. He wanted to figure Clarissa out. She was like one of those intricate clockwork beauties at Meeks's Mechanical Museum. He just had to know what made her tick.

Not that he could tell. She treated the young gentlemen like gamboling pups for her to tease and toy with, but never let too close.

Was that her game? To draw men in, then keep them away? Had she been playing that game with *him* the other night? Or was it something about all men that kept her on her guard?

Just as he felt he was circling some great discovery about her character, Major Wilkins showed up to join her group of fawning admirers.

Devil take it. After Clarissa had mentioned the man's "ogling" her breasts, Edwin had asked the members at St. George's some discreet questions about Wilkins. According to them, as the youngest son of a nearly penniless duke, he was the slyest form of fortune hunter, hiding his poverty behind his title. His father had sired a passel of sons, which meant there was little money left for the youngest. Which was probably why Wilkins had his eye on Clarissa and her fortune.

"That is a most fetching gown, Lady Clarissa." The arse's gaze dipped down, and Edwin felt an unreasonable urge to pummel the man.

Especially when Clarissa snapped open her fan and began to flutter it, effectively hiding her bosom from the major's gaze.

"As always, Lady Clarissa has very good taste," Edwin said coldly.

"She does indeed," Wilkins said with a bit of a leer.

That did it. Time to use what else he'd learned about the bastard. "So, sir," Edwin said bluntly, "is it true that you were recently asked to leave your regiment?"

"Oh, Lord," Clarissa muttered.

The major flushed. "It wasn't as simple as all that."

"It sounded simple to me. I heard you were caught in behavior unbecoming a gentleman. Something about your trying to elope with a general's daughter?"

As the pups sat there snickering, Wilkins drew himself up. "That is a scandalous lie!"

Edwin's gaze narrowed. "Are you calling me a liar, sir?"

Wilkins looked suddenly as if he'd rather be anywhere but there. "No. I'm merely saying you've been misinformed."

"Deuce take it, someone has been misinforming people again," one of the pups chimed in. "You'd best nip that in the bud, Wilkins. Your father might hear of it and cut you off."

"I heard he's already done that," one of his compatriots said. "But perhaps I was misinformed."

The pups erupted into laughter, which the major didn't apparently find the least amusing, for he glowered at them all.

Gathering his wounded dignity about him, he nodded to Clarissa. "I believe I shall return when you aren't so plagued with visitors, madam." Then he shot Edwin a daggered glance before leaving the box.

The pups continued their fun after he was gone. "He's headed off to find that dastardly misinformer."

"I thought he was a scandalous liar?"

"Clearly he's neither, since the 'lie' sent the major off with his tail between his legs. What is that saying about fire and smoke?"

"Where there's smoke, there's fire?"

"No, where there's smoking, there's fire, and the major was smoking, to be sure."

"You see what you started?" Clarissa complained to Edwin.

"Don't blame me if your friends are idiots," he shot back.

"Hey!" one of the pups said in mock outrage. "I am not an idiot. I am a fool."

"At least you're not a misinformer," another said, and they split their sides laughing.

"Oh, you gentlemen are too awful," Lady Margrave said, tittering along with them, as did her cronies. "The poor major. And he does have such a fondness for my daughter, too."

"A fondness for her fortune, you mean," Edwin said sharply, not in the mood to endure Lady Margrave's lack of perception.

Clarissa lifted an eyebrow. "I do hope you're not implying that my only attractions are my fortune, Edwin."

"If he is, he's blind," chirped a pup lounging against the wall. "You're the jewel in England's crown, Lady Clarissa, with eyes of emeralds and ruby lips and hair of spun gold."

"Jewels? Gold?" she said tartly. "Sounds as if you still have my wealth in mind, sir."

The young man blinked. "I only meant—"

"She knows what you meant." Edwin met her gaze, which he found more the quality of warm, rich jade than cold emeralds. "And she knows perfectly well what *I* meant, too. She's just toying with us both."

She smiled sweetly. "Am I, indeed? Do I detect a note of criticism?"

"You do not. I'm merely making an observation."

Her smile broadened as she moved up next to him. "Take care, sir. With each of your 'observations' about me, you slide closer to criticism."

Lowering his voice, he stared down into her lovely face. "You will not win this wager."

"Ah, but I will." She tapped his chest with her fan, provoking a slow, steady simmer in his blood. "You can no more stop taking me to task than you can stop breathing."

"It's better than turning you into a pile of jewels."

He and Clarissa were close enough to kiss, to embrace, to behave in the most wildly inappropriate manner. He could smell her cinnamon-scented breath, see the taunting tilt of her smile. The others disappeared for him, and all he could think was how badly he wanted to seize her and kiss that impudent mouth over and over until he'd broken through to the real Clarissa, whoever that might be.

Her smile faltered a little, and a dark awareness flickered in her eyes, as if she'd read his thoughts and guessed exactly all the ways he wanted to taste and caress and plunder her.

Then a feminine voice sounded from the doorway. "Are we interrupting anything?"

Clarissa started, then glanced over and renewed her smile. "Do come in, Lady Anne. How good to see you."

"I hope you don't mind," the young lady said, "but I brought a friend with me."

"Of course I don't . . ."

As her words died, Edwin saw a change come over Clarissa. When she began to flutter her fan in front of her bosom again and her posture stiffened until she looked like a deer poising for flight, the simmer in his blood cooled to ice.

Edwin turned to find Durand standing there with Lady Anne.

Bloody, bloody hell.

Nine

Clarissa's stomach churned as Count Durand raked her with a slow, wolfish glance. Edwin must have seen it, for she heard him mutter an oath and felt him start forward.

Catching his arm, she said under her breath, "Not now. Not here."

He stopped, thank heaven, though she could feel the barely leashed tension in his muscles even through his coat sleeve.

She forced herself to speak again. "I trust that you're enjoying the burlesque, Lady Anne?" She refused to address that blackguard Durand directly.

"It's very silly but I love it!" Tonight Lady Anne wore one of her more outrageous hats, which was sillier than anything Madame Vestris could have come up with for the stage. "The count's box is only a short way down from yours, so we thought we'd come see what *you* thought of it."

"I take it that you and the count are well-acquainted," Edwin said to Lady Anne, his hard voice as much a mockery of civility as Clarissa's smile.

"We were introduced only this afternoon," the count answered for her, "but of course I invited the lovely lady and her mother to join me in my box this evening." He patted her hand. "How could I resist?"

Lady Anne blushed a bright pink. "Oh, you are such a flatterer, sir."

He flashed that sly smile that Clarissa had grown to loathe. Unfortunately, when he did it, his eyes were fixed on *her*, not Lady Anne.

Then he approached Clarissa's mother, who rose with a rustle of taffeta skirts. "Lady Margrave, enchanted to see you again. You're looking very well."

Mama had been impressed with Durand in the beginning, until she'd started noticing how much he upset Clarissa. After that she'd always taken her cue on how to treat him from Clarissa.

But tonight she was behaving oddly, even for her, with an almost unnatural friendliness. "Why, thank you, Count Durand, that is very kind of you to say. I'm feeling particularly strong this evening. Haven't needed my salts once."

Then she cast a knowing look at Edwin, and Clarissa realized what she was about—she'd fixed her sights on the earl as a husband for Clarissa, and she meant to use Durand as a weapon in that endeavor.

"That's good to hear." The count swept the room with a look, then said, in a voice loud enough to carry at least to the boxes on either side, "I suppose you're excited about your daughter's recent betrothal to Lord Blakeborough."

Silence descended upon the box, and every eye turned to Clarissa and Edwin. As her mother's mouth dropped open, Clarissa froze. How dared he? She was going to kill him!

This time *she* was the one to start forward, and Edwin was the one to grip her hand where it clutched his arm. "Not now, not here," he murmured, echoing her own words.

It was clear from Durand's expression that he hadn't believed the lie Clarissa and Edwin had told him. So he meant to corner them, to force them to either confirm his suspicion or admit publicly to an engagement.

If they didn't admit it, he would be back to hounding her everywhere. But if they did, Edwin . . .

"Engaged?" her mother squeaked as she recovered her wits. She rounded on Clarissa and Edwin. "You're engaged, my dears? How fabulous! I knew it would come—I *knew* it!" She limped up to Clarissa. "What did Edwin say? What did *you* say? How did it come about? Oh, do tell me everything!"

"You didn't know about the betrothal, Lady Margrave?" Durand asked, with a veiled glance at Clarissa.

"Of course not." Mama tipped her head to one side. "It just happened, didn't it?"

As Clarissa stood there in a panic, Edwin stepped into the breach. "Not exactly. Forgive us, but we were waiting until Warren's return to ask for his blessing at the same time we asked for your permission." His voice sharpened. "Count Durand knew this, but apparently couldn't abide by our wish that he keep silent on the subject."

A small frown appeared on Mama's brow. "Exactly how long have you had an understanding? And why would you tell Count Durand, but not *me*?"

"We didn't tell him. He discovered it by accident." Edwin leveled Durand with a cold glance. "And now he means to embarrass us with it, presumably out of a fit of pique over Clarissa's rejection of his own proposal of marriage."

For once, Clarissa was glad of his bluntness. Even though an audible gasp came from their guests, who looked scandalized by the public exposure of Count Durand's motives, the angry flush rising up the Frenchman's neck made her want to kiss Edwin.

Take that, Count. Perhaps next time you'll think twice before confronting me and Edwin.

Although she did feel sorry for poor Lady Anne, who paled as she apparently realized that the count had merely used her to get admitted to Clarissa's box.

"Edwin, for shame," Mama said with a *tsk*ing noise. "I agree that the man shouldn't have spoken out of turn, but there's no need for you to lord it over him because you gained my daughter's hand and he did not."

If Clarissa weren't still furious at the Frenchman, she would have laughed at his scowl in response to Mama's words.

"They've been engaged for nearly a week," Count Durand bit out, clearly determined to keep stirring up trouble. "I can't imagine why your daughter wouldn't at least mention it to you, madam."

But it had finally sunk in with Mama that Clarissa would be marrying at last, and the man's insinuations

couldn't ruin that for her. "A week, you say? Well."
She patted Clarissa's shoulder. "I do wish you'd told
me sooner, my dear, for we could have started the
wedding preparations that much earlier. But no matter. Have you talked about when to marry? Where?"

"Mama," Clarissa said, "let us discuss this later, if
you please."

"Why? We've no time to waste. We must start
thinking about it all." She began to muse aloud. "You
could marry in St. Paul's Cathedral. But it would have
to be in summer, for the cathedral is very damp, even
in spring. Or perhaps St. James's's? No, too small." She
turned to her friends. "What do you think? She could
marry from home, but I would prefer a London wedding."

Mama's friends agreed with her, of course. A London wedding in a prominent church would be the
height of fashion.

In the meantime, the rest of their guests were
whispering about Clarissa and Edwin and their secret
engagement. Her stomach roiled. By the time she
and Edwin left the theater, everyone in the place
would have heard of it.

And all thanks to the meddling Count Durand.
The next time the man's back was turned, she was
liable to push him right off the balcony!

But she dared not let him see her true feelings.
Given how intently he watched her, he was waiting
for her to explode, waiting for her to give something
away. She would *not* give him the satisfaction.

"Oh, well," she said as if she hadn't a care in
the world. "It's probably a blessing in disguise that
the count revealed our secret." With a syrupy smile,

she stared adoringly up at Edwin. "It has been so hard to hide it from everyone, has it not?"

Edwin gazed down at her, his expression bland. "Yes, very hard."

"And now we don't have to." She forced a smile to her lips for the count's benefit. "Thank you for that, sir."

Count Durand's eyes narrowed on them both. Ha! If he thought she was going to fall into hysterics because of his machinations, he was daft.

Fortunately, the music started up just then. "The next piece is beginning," she said brightly. "You'd all better hurry back to your boxes, or you'll miss it." She couldn't *wait* to be rid of the count, so she could talk to Edwin alone.

Of course Mama was having none of that. "Nonsense, Edwin has plenty of room here. They can all remain. Why not? It's a celebration of your impending wedding."

Stifling a groan, Clarissa said meaningfully, "I'm sure Count Durand is eager to get Lady Anne back to her mother."

When Mama paled, it was obvious she hadn't meant to include the count in her invitation. But she could hardly take it back now.

Especially since Lady Anne had apparently decided that Clarissa's loss could be her gain. "No reason for that. I'll just pop down and tell Mama where the count and I are. I'm sure we'd love to stay here." She tucked her hand in the crook of the count's arm. "Wouldn't we, sir?"

"I wouldn't miss it for the world," the wretch drawled.

"No doubt," Edwin gritted out.

Lord, what a mess! As she and Edwin took their seats, she noticed Mama trying to remedy the situation by inviting Lady Anne and the count to sit beside her. But Count Durand was having none of that, and he and Lady Anne situated themselves right behind Edwin and Clarissa.

Clarissa could only sit there stewing. However would she get a chance to talk to Edwin about how to deal with their "engagement"?

Edwin must have realized her state of mind, for as the scene began, he gave her hand a quick, furtive squeeze.

Meeting his gaze, she mouthed the words, "I'm sorry."

"Don't be," he mouthed back. "It will be fine."

She wasn't so sure.

The next hour was an agony. Too upset over the count's meddling, she couldn't concentrate on the hodgepodge of songs and comical scenes that made up the second piece.

Was she just imagining it, or was Count Durand's gaze boring into her back? Having him behind her and not knowing for certain if his eyes were fixed on her made her skin crawl. There was something distinctly wrong with that man.

Either that or she did actually put off an inexplicable scent or air or *something* that made men want to possess her at any cost. She always seemed to be fending off gentlemen who bullied their way into her life.

Except for Edwin, of course. She didn't have to fend *him* off. Ever since their kiss, he'd gone back to keeping a discreet distance between them.

So when she slid a glance in his direction, she was surprised to find him watching her with that dark, brooding look he got sometimes, the one that roused a strange quivering low in her belly.

It made no sense. He didn't like her. He didn't approve of her. Why must he look at her that way, as if he were trying to understand her better? Edwin didn't want to understand anybody, especially her. Did he?

She tore her gaze from his and tried to concentrate on the performances. But it was impossible. Because of the extra people in the box, they'd had to bring in more chairs and pull them closer together, so Edwin's leg lay snug up against hers from thigh to calf.

Did he realize it? If it had been any other man, she would have assumed that he did, but with Edwin, it was impossible to know. The man was so impenetrable, he could out-riddle the Sphinx.

Whatever the reason, the sensation of having his leg pressed against hers felt much too intimate for the theater. Much too intimate for anywhere.

How ridiculous. It was only a leg—everyone had them. So why was her blood rustling through her veins like a tiger stirring in deep grasses? Why was her breath coming in hard hitches?

She drew her leg casually away from his. She was just overly aware of him tonight because of Count Durand. Thanks to the Frenchman, Edwin would once again have to be jilted, and she hated that.

The second hour of *Olympic Revels* ended after what seemed like an eternity. But even as Edwin rose and asked her, "Would you like to go downstairs to view the renovations to the lobby?" a knock came at the door.

When it was opened, the same servant entered who'd escorted them to the box earlier. He bowed to Edwin. "My lord, Madame Vestris sent me to ask if you and your two guests would wish to pay her a visit in her dressing room."

Clarissa drew in a sharp breath. That was a distinct honor.

Edwin seemed conscious of it, too, for he lifted an eyebrow at her. "Well?"

"Do you really need to ask? Of *course* I wish to go!" She could meet Madame Vestris *and* escape the count.

She turned to her mother, who was busily chatting with her friends about wedding plans. "Mama, do you want to join me and Edwin? Madame Vestris has invited us to her dressing room."

"That is *most* kind of her," Mama said. "Though you know I cannot go. All that tramping up and down stairs is too hard on my poor hip. But I realize that you admire the woman, so you should visit her." Mama's gaze lighted briefly on the count. "And now that you and Edwin are betrothed, well . . . I do believe it would be all right for me to remain here and entertain our guests."

Clarissa fought to hide her relief that Mama was staying behind. Perhaps she could keep the count from dogging their steps, and that would give Clarissa a chance to speak privately to Edwin. "Yes, I'm sure it would be considered quite respectable," Clarissa said, though she wasn't sure of any such thing.

And one glance at Durand showed he was none

too happy about her and Edwin going off together. That alone made her determined to do it.

Her mother smiled. "But do tell Madame Vestris how pleased I am that we could come and see her newly appointed theater."

"Yes, Mama."

As Clarissa and Edwin followed the servant to the door, her mother called out, "Oh, and tell her how much I'm enjoying the burlesque."

"Of course," Clarissa said.

They were nearly into the hall when her mother's voice wafted to her. "And ask her to sign a playbill for me!"

"I will! We're going now!" Clarissa called back.

As she shut the door firmly, the servant paused. "Are you sure her ladyship does not wish to join us?"

"We're sure," Edwin answered.

His rumble of a voice made her heart skip. Just a little, mind. Nothing unsettling.

No, the unsettling part was how easily he guided her through the crowded passageways. For a man who wasn't good with people, he certainly knew how to maneuver around them.

Twice, he laid his hand in the small of her back to steer her, and she felt the heat of it like a brand. Once, he even tugged her close to prevent her being run down by a rushing maid, and Clarissa stumbled against him, forcing him to steady her with both hands on her waist.

"All right?" he asked, his gaze playing over her as if checking for injuries.

She nodded.

But she wasn't all right. This night had thrown

her into turmoil. First Durand's deliberate meddling and now Edwin's disturbing effect on her. She truly didn't know what to think or how to act.

As the servant boy led them through a warren of passageways to the backstage area of the theater, she wished she could just pull Edwin into a nearby room and discuss their increasingly precarious situation. But Madame Vestris was waiting, and Clarissa didn't mean to lose her chance to meet the famous actress.

Besides, she was curious about Edwin's friendship with the woman. He hadn't yet explained why he'd been asked to invest in the theater in the first place. If they had only been friends in childhood . . .

What if it was more? What if he was hiding some secret affair with the actress? Madame Vestris was rumored to be quite pretty, after all, and men *were* men. Even Edwin.

Oh, she was being silly. Edwin having secret affairs—the very idea was ludicrous.

Still, it was a bit unnerving to find that in person, the actress was more than pretty—she was gorgeous. With her shiny dark curls, large brown eyes, olive skin, and perfectly oval face, she had the look of a seductress.

And when the woman greeted Edwin by his Christian name and kissed him on the cheek, a sudden unexpected pang seized Clarissa's chest.

He nodded coolly. "Good to see you again, Lucia."

Lucia? He called the actress by her Christian name? Well, of course he did. They'd known each other from childhood. Clarissa was really letting her imagination run away with her.

After all, the woman showed no sign of caring that Edwin was with another lady. And when Edwin introduced Clarissa, Madame Vestris was more than gracious, asking what they thought of the performances and whether the box was comfortable.

Then her servant stepped up to whisper in her ear, and Madame Vestris shot them a broad smile. "I'm told, Lord Blakeborough, that Lady Clarissa is your fiancée. Please accept my congratulations."

Clarissa sighed. The news was already starting to spread. She'd forgotten that the servant had heard Mama speak of their betrothal.

"Thank you." Edwin took Clarissa's hand. "We're very happy."

He didn't *sound* very happy.

Guilt stabbed her. When she'd agreed to the scheme, she hadn't expected Count Durand to wreak such havoc on their lives. *Edwin's* life, in particular.

Madame Vestris, too, must have heard the reserve in his voice, for she assessed Clarissa with a searching glance. "Any woman who has succeeded in capturing the heart of his lordship must be exceptional indeed."

That sent Clarissa's mind racing again. Was the woman showing jealousy? Warning Clarissa that she'd have to work hard to deserve Edwin? Clearly, the actress admired Edwin for more than his investing, but could it have gone so far as to be intimate? How could Clarissa find out without being vulgar?

"He speaks well of you, too," Clarissa said. "And I have long been an admirer of yours myself. There aren't many women who can conquer the theater world so thoroughly."

The actress dipped her head. "How kind of you to say."

Her servant murmured something in her ear again, and she said to him, "Go tell them I'll be along shortly."

As soon as the lad darted out, Clarissa said, "I understand that you and his lordship are very old, very dear friends."

It came out more coldly than she'd intended, and that seemed to give Madame Vestris pause. She stared at Clarissa. "Are you asking if I am his lordship's mistress?"

The blunt words brought Clarissa up short. But at least the woman wasn't beating about the bush. "Well, are you?"

When the actress didn't answer at once, Edwin snapped, "No, she is not."

Clarissa glanced at him. "I should like to hear it from the lady, if you please."

"Have you ever known me to lie?" Edwin asked, his hand tightening on hers.

But Madame Vestris laughed. "Forgive me, my lady, for toying with you. I am not, nor ever have been, his lordship's paramour." Humor gleamed in her eyes. "Though not for lack of trying. After all, Lord Blakeborough is that rarest of gentlemen— handsome, generous, *and* intelligent. An intelligent man always deserves an intelligent woman, don't you think?"

"Indeed he does." She thrust out her chin. "Fortunately, he has found one." While she knew it was foolish to tout their faux engagement, she felt oddly possessive of her pretend fiancé. She liked Madame

Vestris . . . but not well enough to see the woman romantically involved with Edwin.

The actress softened her tone. "You have nothing to fear from me, Lady Clarissa. His lordship is indeed an old friend, but it was never anything more. And these days our friendship centers around his investment in my concern, naught else."

Her servant appeared in the doorway, and she looked up. "Yes, yes, I'm coming." She took Clarissa's hand and pressed it warmly. "I hope to see more of you, my dear. You are always welcome in my theater. Now, forgive me, but I must get the players in their places." Then she swept out in a swish of silk skirts.

Her servant looked at Edwin. "Can you and the lady find your own way back, sir?"

"Yes," Edwin said. "Go on."

As the servant rushed off after his mistress, Edwin led Clarissa out into the passageway. They had to push their way past actors and actresses rushing the opposite direction to take their places onstage for the beginning of the final portion of the *Revels*.

Edwin stood aside to let a clown pass, and Clarissa said, "Do you really know where we're going?"

He smiled indulgently at her. "I always know where I'm going." Then he took her hand and drew her down another hall.

There were fewer people here, and as she and Edwin traversed it, those remaining players vanished into the other passageway. When she and Edwin passed an open door to an empty room, she stopped him. "We need to talk, and this is as good a place as any."

Glancing either way down the hall, he nodded and

drew her inside, then pulled the door mostly closed, to give them some privacy. Through the walls, they could hear muted voices and the sounds of music starting up, but here they were alone.

"So," she began. "Now that Durand has called our bluff, what do we do next?"

Ten

Edwin didn't know how to answer her. Between that damned Frenchman's baiting of them and Clarissa's surprising reaction to Lucia, he was at a loss. But Clarissa was looking at him expectantly, and he had to say something.

"We behave as if we're engaged."

She huffed out a breath. "I figured that out myself. But for how long? The whole world is sure to hear of it before the night is over, and we'll be bombarded with questions. I merely need to know what to answer. Have we set a date for the wedding, for example?"

"Of course not." He scrubbed his hand over his face and added acerbically, "Forgive me, but I haven't thought through the details of our pretend wedding, only the ones for our secret pretend engagement. I didn't expect Durand to press the issue. It doesn't make sense."

"Yes, I recall your saying that it wouldn't suit his plans." She halted to stare at him. "Perhaps you should have mentioned that to *him*. Because apparently he thinks it suits his plans quite well."

"Clearly his purpose was to catch us off guard and have us admit that the whole thing was a lie."

"I realize that. And while I'm glad that we didn't perform to his expectations, it doesn't change the fact that we are now publicly engaged." Her gaze grew shuttered. "Which neither of us wants."

"No." It was very nearly true. But part of him couldn't help imagining Clarissa naked in his bed, with her sensuous lips smiling coyly and her arms reaching up to pull him down beside her. Her breasts would be there for sucking, and her lovely thighs—

"Edwin?"

Blast. He'd missed whatever she'd said. "Sorry. Could you repeat that?"

"You're not even listening to me!"

"I'm thinking through the problem."

She eyed him askance. "You didn't *look* as if you were thinking through anything. You looked like you were thinking of something far more enticing. Or even *someone*. Your friend *Lucia*, perhaps?"

Now, *that* was jealousy. He might not previously have been on the receiving end of it, but he could tell it when he heard it. And it had the most peculiar effect on him, heating his blood until he felt on fire.

He wasn't the only one igniting. As he circled her, he noted the sudden flush in her cheeks. "You seem very interested in my association with Lucia."

"You seem very *comfortable* with her. And she is quite beautiful, after all."

"She is indeed," he said, just to see her reaction.

"Despite being nearly my age, she has a youthful quality about her that never seems to fade."

Her mouth formed a mutinous line. "You're not that old, you know."

"You're the one who said I wasn't getting any younger."

"Well, you're not. But that doesn't mean you're about to keel over." She stared ahead, not meeting his eyes. "And she's only a bit older than your former fiancée. No wonder she has a youthful quality." She tipped up her chin. "Whether she will keep it is another matter entirely."

Biting back a smile, he said, "I thought you admired her."

"I did. I do. It's just that . . . well, I don't think—"

"That she's right for me?" he said, echoing her remarks the other night about Miss Trevor.

"Don't be silly. Of course she's not right for you. She's an actress."

"And it would bother you if I married an actress."

"Married!" She snorted. "You would never do any such thing. You're too circumspect for that. But you might . . . well . . ."

"She already told you that she isn't, nor ever was, my mistress."

Clarissa walked over to stare into the mirror of a nearby dressing table. "But you've had mistresses?"

The question surprised him. Gently bred females didn't ask such things. Unless they were very interested in the answer. "I should think that's my private business," he said, trying to provoke her into admitting her jealousy.

She whirled on him, her expression stiff. "Which means you *have*. Otherwise, you would have denied it."

"Fine. I have. Why do you care?" He held his breath. It suddenly seemed very important to hear her reply.

"I just never thought of you as . . . well . . . that sort of man."

That sparked his temper. "What sort of man? The kind with physical needs?" He stepped closer. "The kind who can find beauty intoxicating and intelligence stimulating?" When her breath began to quicken, he lowered his voice. "The kind who can be tempted to do what he should not?"

She nodded, her gaze dropping to his cravat, as if she were afraid to stare into his face.

Wanting to see her eyes, he tipped up her chin. "I'm not perfect, minx, as you know quite well. And certain women are a very potent temptation to me."

Temper flared in her eyes. "Like Lucia."

"Like *you*, you silly fool."

He lowered his head slowly, giving her a chance to balk. When she merely gazed up at him like a startled fawn, he kissed her.

God, how could he have forgotten how lush her mouth was, how sweet the taste of her? When she willingly opened to him, he exulted and deepened the kiss. He wanted to sink into her like a warm bath, to explore every inch of her lips and tongue and teeth.

She came up on tiptoe, and he fisted his hands in her sleeves to hold her closer. She stilled, and he did, too, afraid of frightening her off as he had the other night.

But then she melted against him, and he was

well and truly lost. He couldn't summon an ounce of his usual control—he wanted to devour her. Her mouth was a revelation, showing him the difference between merely desiring a woman's body and desiring her mind and her soul. He plundered her lips over and over, drinking her soft gasps, growing more aroused by the moment.

She tore her mouth free of his to whisper, "Why are you doing this? You know you shouldn't."

He bent to nibble her ear. "Do you want me to stop?"

"I . . . I . . . No. But I do want to understand why . . . this is happening between us." She nuzzled his cheek. "You don't like me."

Choking back a laugh, he murmured, "You don't like *me*. Yet here we are."

As he kissed his way down her neck to her throat, she uttered a shuddering breath. "I do like you."

"And clearly I like you, or I wouldn't be standing here giving in to temptation." He tongued the hollow of her throat, reveling in her soft moan and the way she slid her hands up his coat lapels.

"But this is . . . more than liking."

"Yes." He took her mouth again.

Definitely more than liking. Desire had him in its grip and he didn't want to be free. So, as long as she didn't push him away, as long as she was tangling her tongue with his and twining her arms about his neck, he would take advantage.

Clarissa couldn't believe she was *letting* Edwin take advantage. But he kept coming to her defense with Durand even when it ruined his own plans, and it made him so . . . so endearing.

That was the only reason she clung to him and pressed herself against him, the only reason her blood was racing and her heart hammering and her body heating to boiling. Gratitude for what he'd done, that's all.

Even she wasn't fool enough to believe *that* assertion.

Breaking the kiss, she turned to face the mirror and tried to get hold of herself. "We must stop. Someone might see us."

"Nonsense. We're out of sight of the hallway." He slid his arm about her waist to draw her back against him. "They'd have to enter the room."

He wasn't lying, judging from what she saw in the mirror.

"Even if they did," he murmured against her hair, "they wouldn't say anything to anyone. They're theater people—they mind their own business."

When he kissed a path along her bare shoulder, alarm briefly skittered down her spine. But his arm held her lightly, so lightly, and his kisses were tender, coaxing. For once, what uncurled in her wasn't panic or fear.

"Besides," he added, "we're engaged."

"Not . . . really."

His gaze locked with hers in the mirror as he stroked one finger along the edge of her bodice. "We could be."

She was so intent on what he was doing with his finger that his words didn't quite register. "We could be what?"

"Really engaged. To each other." His finger dipped just beneath the edge to skim over the rise of her breasts in a slow caress. Watching him do it in the mirror made it so erotic that she had to plant one hand on the dressing table just to keep steady. "Why . . . Why would we . . . do that?" she choked out.

"I need a wife." He nuzzled her ear. "You need protection from Durand. It would make things simpler."

"Except that I don't want to marry anybody, even you." Though the words sounded hollow in her ears.

He slid his hand inside her bodice. "Only because you don't realize the advantages of it."

She was finding it hard to breathe. "For whom?"

A lazy smile played over his lips, and he pulled down the cup of her stays inside her bodice to bare her breast to his hand. "For us both."

As he covered it, she caught his wrist. "Edwin, what are you doing?" But she knew, and it felt awfully pleasurable. Then again, it always did at the beginning. It was later, when the man grew rough . . .

"I'm doing what I've craved for years—touching you," he whispered, his eyes searching hers in the mirror. "To show you what it could be like between us."

Her nipple was pebbling beneath his hand, belying her caution. "I don't think that's a good idea."

When she tightened her grip on his wrist, he stopped moving his hand. "I promise not to hurt you."

Still, his expression, full of heat and want, gave her pause. When the Vile Seducer had fondled her breasts years ago, it had started out pleasantly enough. But then she'd protested and he'd ignored her and the whole experience had rapidly twisted into . . .

That won't happen, she reminded herself. For one thing, Edwin was at her back and they were standing—she could fight him off much more easily. There were people on the other side of the wall, and hatpins on the dressing table that she could use to stab his arm. She was probably safer here with him than she'd ever been with any other man.

Besides, the way he waited patiently for her permission before he would continue reassured her that if she so much as tugged on his hand, he would stop this right now. But if she did that, she might never have another chance to explore these things with him.

Did she want to explore these things with him?

Yes. Oh, yes.

She released his wrist.

For half a second she feared she might regret it, because something dark and daring glittered in his eyes. But before she could react to that, he turned her head to the side with his free hand so he could kiss her mouth over her shoulder.

Then he was devouring her lips, and his hand was fondling her and it felt so astonishing that she soon found herself *pressing* her breast willingly into his palm. With a low groan, he kneaded it so deftly that it made her feel urges she'd denied herself for years. They were sweet and hot and rousing and all the things she'd never thought to feel again.

She turned into his arms and his hand fell away from her, but only so he could hoist her onto the dressing table. "Edwin!"

"Yes, minx?" He began kissing his way down into the valley between her breasts. "I want to taste you. Will you let me?"

"A-all right." Her blood howled through her veins, wanting things, needing things. She was living dangerously now, but she had to know, had to see if Edwin would push and prod his way past her walls.

Half of her wanted him to. The other half was terrified he would.

Yet she buried her hands in his hair as he maneuvered one breast free of its trappings and covered it with his mouth.

The Vile Seducer hadn't done such a thing—just mauled her through her bodice. But Edwin . . . oh, heavens. His silky, warm mouth explored her, sucking and soothing until she dug her fingers into his scalp. "Ohh . . . that is so . . . so . . ." She let out a shuddering sigh.

"You like that, do you?"

"Don't *you?*"

He uttered a choked laugh against her breast. "As if you need to ask." His tongue flicked her nipple. "Can't you see how I forget myself when I'm with you?"

His hair spilled over her hands like black satin as she clutched his head to her bosom. "But why?" she breathed. "You're always . . . chiding me."

"That's to keep everyone from realizing that I want you in my bed." He stared up at her, eyes gleaming. "I feared the whole damned world could tell."

"That isn't why you chide me," she said wryly. "You disapprove of me, admit it."

"You do make me insane." He teased her breast lightly with his teeth, making her arch up against him. "And if we were to marry—"

"You would shoot me inside a month. Or I would shoot you."

"Would you?" He straightened, dragging his open mouth up her neck in a series of hot kisses. "You're not shooting me now."

"No. But you're . . . doing naughty things to distract me," she gasped. "Later, I'll regret letting you."

"So I'll marry you." His hands caressed her other breast through her clothes. "Then you'll have no regrets."

"Edwin . . ."

He took her mouth again, to silence her.

But his hands were on her above and below, and she felt consumed by *those* feelings again, and this time panic swelled up from below like a mighty wave. It was too much. Too much!

She shoved him back, then slipped from between him and the table, grabbing a hairbrush as she went, which she brandished in front of her like a cudgel. Frantically, she struggled to pull her bodice up with the other hand.

His gaze dipped to the brush. "Clarissa?"

The shock in his voice brought her up short. Lord, he must think her mad.

She forced herself to lower the brush as she fought for calm. He must never guess her sordid past. She could only imagine what he would make of it. Bad enough that she had let him go as far as this.

With a steadying breath, she said firmly, "I will not let you ruin me." *I won't let you hurt me.*

"Ruin you?" He seemed disturbed by the words, for his eyes narrowed. "Surely you know I would *never* ruin you. I would never dishonor you so."

The very mention of honor made her despair.

He couldn't understand, and if he ever learned the truth . . . "Men dishonor women every day, without a thought."

"True." He stepped closer, and she barely stifled her panic. "But I am not that sort of man. I am not my brother."

The mention of Samuel reminded her whom she was dealing with. This was Edwin. She was being absurd. She set the brush down on the table.

He released a long breath. "Indeed, I am willing to marry you."

Willing. But not exactly eager. "To protect me from Durand," she said as she finished restoring her clothing.

With a nod, he said, "It makes sense. We're friends, are we not?"

She swallowed. Edwin was ever practical. They were friends, so they should marry. Because it would "make sense" and be convenient. "It hardly seems a good basis for a lifetime together."

He came near enough to cup her cheek. "All I ask is that you consider it. Just think about it, all right?"

Her breath stuttered out of her. She was a jumble of nerves, and given the heat in his eyes, she was horribly afraid he might try to kiss her again. She wanted it; she feared it. Most of all, she worried she might do something stupid in response . . . like shy from him and give herself away.

But just as he bent toward her, slowly, carefully, the door opened.

"Well, well," Count Durand said in a hard voice. "If it isn't the newly engaged couple."

The cold rage that leapt in Edwin's face gave her pause. Then he smoothed it from his expression and turned, taking her hand as he moved and pulling her next to him so that they formed a united front.

"What do you want, Durand?" he snapped.

The Frenchman ignored Edwin to address Clarissa. "I was sent by your mother to find you, Lady Clarissa."

"My mother would never entrust that task to you," Clarissa said, fighting the gorge rising in her throat.

"You think not? She likes me, you know."

Before Clarissa could call that the lie she knew it was, Edwin moved ever so slightly in front of her. "Lady Margrave is friendly to everyone. But she's not mad."

"We'll be coming along in a moment, sir," Clarissa added. "Do go on and tell Mama so. If indeed she sent you to look for me."

His lips formed a thin line. "I was charged with accompanying you. So I will wait until you're done with his lordship."

"The devil you will," Edwin said. "You've already caused enough trouble for tonight by spilling our news prematurely."

"Am I causing trouble, my lady?" the count asked Clarissa.

His studied drawl didn't fool her. He looked on edge and thoroughly dangerous. She wouldn't go off alone with him for all the world.

"You know that you are, sir. But as I said earlier, it hardly matters. You merely succeeded in moving up the announcement we would have made soon anyway."

The count tightened his jaw. "Knightford hasn't yet approved of the match."

"He will. Edwin is perfectly eligible, and is Warren's closest friend besides. In any case, I'm of age. Warren doesn't have to approve our engagement. We merely wanted his blessing."

With a cold glance at Edwin, the Frenchman scowled. "Does that mean you still intend to wait to wed until his return?"

"We haven't decided," Edwin said. "Not that it's any of your concern."

"I could make it my concern," Count Durand said.

Her stomach churned.

"I'd like to see you try," Edwin snarled, fury coming off him in waves.

Like a hound at a bear-baiting, the count was deliberately provoking Edwin. She half expected at any minute for Edwin to rip out Count Durand's throat.

"Enough," she said with a forced lightness in her tone, determined to calm both men. "This is silly—the two of you snapping at each other. Mama is waiting. We shall all three return to the box together, before we miss any more of the performance." She tugged Edwin's arm. "Come, my dear, let's go."

It was like trying to drag the baited bear from the arena, with his hackles raised and teeth bared, before he had the chance to devour his tormentor. For a moment she feared Edwin would do something rash, like fight the count then and there, fomenting gossip throughout society.

Then, to her vast relief, Edwin relaxed his stance. "Of course, sweetheart. Whatever you wish."

But as the three of them returned to the box through the passageways, she knew she had only forestalled a coming battle. Because she feared that Count Durand meant to draw blood until Edwin flat-out murdered him.

Eleven

Durand left the box as soon as they returned to it, thank God, or Edwin would have thrown the blasted fellow out of it. Fortunately, they saw no sign of the count when they left the theater.

Edwin hoped the reprieve lasted a while, but he no longer knew what to think of the Frenchman. He'd never seen a man so determined to bedevil a woman. There had to be something else behind it than a mere desire to have Clarissa as his wife.

Granted, any man would want her, but to continue once Edwin and Clarissa started going about in public together? Once they announced their engagement? It was beyond odd.

It was nearly midnight by the time they drew up in front of Warren's town house. Edwin glanced over at Clarissa, his gut twisting into a knot to see how still and silent she sat. This business with Durand could not go on.

And what if she's silent because of you *and your rash actions in that dressing room?*

God, he couldn't bear the thought.

When the door opened, Edwin climbed out to help the two ladies disembark and tried to gauge their moods. Normally he wasn't good at reading women, but even he could tell that Lady Margrave was worn-out. It had been a long night, after all.

Meanwhile, Clarissa's furrowed brow and faraway look made Edwin want to put his fist through the flimsy wall of the carriage. The intensity of the feeling alarmed him. He'd never had such urges in his life as he did when he was around her. That couldn't be good. A man should always be wary of strong emotions. It invariably drove him to behave badly.

Edwin helped Lady Margrave up the steps, all too aware of Clarissa climbing slowly up behind them. He wanted to halt her, drag her into his arms, and comfort her until she returned to her usual buoyant self. It was too late to do more than accompany them inside, yet he burned to finish his conversation with her about a possible marriage between them. He couldn't shake the uneasy feeling that she was in more danger from Durand than ever.

And his feeling was confirmed when, as soon as they entered, the butler took him aside. "You asked me to keep an eye out for that Frenchman, my lord, and I did. He's here."

Anger burned Edwin's throat. "In the *house?*"

"No, down the street, in his coach."

He scowled. Durand must have driven to the house another way to await their return. Otherwise, they would have seen him on their way here. "How long has he been there?"

"Half an hour or more."

Clarissa came over. "What's wrong?"

"Nothing." Edwin didn't want her to feel unsafe in her own home. He could take care of Durand without involving her.

She searched his face, then shrugged. "Mama wants to know if you'll join us for a celebratory glass of wine before you leave."

He glanced over to where Lady Margrave stood beaming at him. "Another time, perhaps. I have something to attend to."

"At this hour?" Clarissa said.

"I'm meeting someone later." It was true, though the "someone" didn't know it yet.

"Oh." Coloring deeply, she lifted an eyebrow. "I had no idea you were such a night owl, Edwin."

Her arch tone and clear assumption that it was a woman scraped his nerves, especially given her stubbornness about marrying him. "Once again, I must remind you that you don't know everything about me. Perhaps it's time you look beyond your own nose where I'm concerned."

"I'm sure Edwin is just going to his club, my dear," her mother hastened to put in. "Even your father enjoyed gambling into the wee hours of the morning from time to time."

Damn, now he had Lady Margrave making assumptions about him and his character, too. "I won't be gambling," he told Clarissa. "And it's a meeting with a man. I can see you're going to be quite the jealous wife."

"Not a bit," she said defensively.

"Edwin," her mother broke in again, "since we missed our dinner with you tonight, you simply must come to dine tomorrow night."

He tore his gaze from Clarissa to say, "Of course. I'd be delighted."

"And be sure to bring an automaton for me," Clarissa said blithely, "since I won our wager."

That arrested Edwin. "You did not."

"The agreement was that if you chided me—"

"Which I didn't do."

Her gaze narrowed on him. "Were you not just saying something about 'looking beyond my own nose' and being a 'jealous wife'? Sounds an awful lot like chiding to me."

"That's absurd," he said irritably, impatient to be away, "as you know perfectly well."

"Now you're chiding me for being absurd."

"I'm not saying *you're* absurd. I'm saying your remark is absurd."

"Same thing." She tapped his hand coyly with her fan. "Don't tell me you're trying to renege on our wager."

"Oh, for God's sake, I'm not—" he began, then halted as he noted the tension in her face.

In a flash, he realized that this was how Clarissa always handled a difficult situation. She made arch comments. She poked and prodded. She even flirted. And if that was what she had to do to take her mind off Durand, then he could at least give her that.

He gentled his voice. "All right. I concede defeat. I'll bring you an automaton tomorrow night."

She eyed him suspiciously, as if she couldn't quite believe he'd given in. "It had better be a *nice* automaton, if you please. Something I can put on the mantel. And one you created, not one of those old—"

"Yes, yes, I remember," he said, biting back a smile. "You want only the best. As usual."

"You say that as if it's a flaw in my character," she said with a sniff.

"No, indeed." Taking her hand and turning it over, he lifted it to his lips so he could slowly, carefully, kiss the inside of her wrist. When he felt her pulse quicken and heard her sigh softly, he murmured, "I've always preferred the highest of quality myself. In objects . . . and in people."

The sudden shadow in her eyes was sobering. "I know that only too well." She slipped her hand from his. "But I suspect that you and I differ in what we consider the highest of quality in people."

The strange statement gave him pause. "I doubt that. But we can discuss it further tomorrow night." Seeing her already withdrawing from him made him add, "Along with making plans for our future."

"Our future," she repeated dully. "That should prove an interesting discussion."

She'd said she would think about marrying him, but clearly she was starting to balk again.

Why? Damn it, she was attracted to him—he was sure of it. No woman made such sweet little sounds when being kissed and caressed if she didn't desire the person doing the kissing and caressing.

But no woman had ever brandished a hairbrush at him for it, either. The memory of that rubbed him as raw as a burr under a saddle. The fact that he could have been so carried away as to make her fear him . . .

It didn't matter. He would remedy that, somehow. He might not be good at understanding women, but if he put his mind to it, surely he could woo one. And wooing Clarissa began to make more sense in light of the problems with Durand. He would simply have to convince her of it.

He bowed to the ladies. "Good night to you both, and thank you for joining me at the theater. I'll see you tomorrow night for dinner."

Then he strode out the front door. Time to deal with that blasted count.

The moment he was outside, he noticed a carriage stopped directly behind his. As he descended the steps, the carriage door opened and Durand stepped out.

"You and I need to talk," the Frenchman said.

Edwin halted a few steps above the man. "Indeed we do. But not here." He glanced up at the windows and prayed that Clarissa wasn't looking out. "Somewhere more private."

"Yes. If you'll follow me to the French embassy, we can discuss this like civilized gentlemen."

"That would require your being a gentleman, which seems unlikely."

Durand flicked some nonexistent dirt off his sleeve. "It's either here or there. Or perhaps we should go inside to talk about it with Lady Clarissa."

Devil take the bastard. "Fine. I'll meet you at the embassy."

Despite the hour, it should be relatively safe there, with the usual guards present.

Still, when they pulled up in front of 50 Portland Place, he retrieved the small pistol he kept in his carriage for protection on late nights such as this. After checking to make sure it was loaded, he tucked it into the pocket of his dress cloak. He wasn't taking any chances with Durand.

It was nearly 1:00 A.M. when he and the Frenchman entered the embassy. Though the guards seemed surprised to see the charge d'affaires so late, they merely exchanged a few words with him before leaving Durand and his guest to their own devices.

Durand led Edwin into an office, probably the one he'd been using while the ambassador was in France. Opening a box, Durand offered him a cigar, which Edwin refused. He didn't want to smoke, eat, or drink with the man. He just wanted him out of Clarissa's life.

After lighting the cigar, Durand puffed on it a moment. "Have a seat."

"I'd rather stand. I won't be long."

"As you wish." The count leaned against the desk. "We need to discuss Lady Clarissa."

"We do, indeed. And I'll make this simple. She's my fiancée. I want you to stop plaguing her."

"I'm not plaguing her. I'm merely reminding her of our suitability for one another."

Edwin stared him down. "She isn't taking the hint very well. Nor am I. So I don't want to see you anywhere near her again."

"Or you'll do what?" Durand cocked up one eyebrow. "In my position, I'm immune to any attempt to curb my actions. As I'm sure you know."

"Nobody is entirely immune, even you."

The count smirked at him. "You'd be surprised. France is in tumult now. No one there will concern themselves with the frivolous accusations of a young woman who's being very respectably courted by a nobleman of my stature."

"Respectably? That's what you call dogging her steps, accosting her continually, spying on her home?"

"I should like to see you try to repeat those claims to anyone else. They would say that you are over-reacting. That I am a well-respected diplomat, who would have no cause to trouble a lady. That yours are merely the rants of a jealous British earl having trouble securing his place as her suitor."

Edwin gritted his teeth. "Let them say whatever they want. I have sufficient consequence to make my voice heeded."

"Not sufficient enough that I can't take it away at a moment's notice." Durand blew out some smoke. "All I need do is expose your father's secrets."

That sent unease curling through Edwin's insides. "My father had no secrets." None of any importance, anyway.

Yes, Father had been a member of a private opium den, which Edwin had discovered when he'd been forced to track down his father after Mother's death. But that had been fifteen years and several French ambassadors ago. Durand couldn't possibly know anything about it. And even if he did, Father had been dead quite some time. It would hardly matter to anyone that the man had occasionally indulged in opium-pipe smoking.

The count pushed away from the desk to walk over to a cabinet. "Don't tell me you didn't know about your father's actions during the war."

The *war*? "What actions?" Edwin said snidely. "His

sitting in Parliament? His occasional gambling? His attendance at the theater?"

"I'm speaking of your father's spying for France."

The accusation hit Edwin like a sledgehammer. What the devil? Durand was daft. Granted, Edwin's great-grandmother had been French and his family had distant relations in Paris, but Father had been thoroughly English. He would never have betrayed his country.

"That's a bald-faced lie," Edwin said coolly. "But a clever one, since you know there's no way to prove or disprove your claims."

The feral glitter in Durand's eyes sent a shaft of ice down Edwin's spine. "Ah, but there is." Durand unlocked and opened the topmost drawer, searched through it until he found a file, then handed it to Edwin and closed the drawer.

Edwin stood staring at the file for a moment, his heart pounding in his chest. God, how could it be? His father had never been much engaged with his family, but Edwin had always assumed it was because he was a cold fish, incapable of caring. Or because of the slow, awful disintegration of his marriage.

Not this. Edwin couldn't believe it. He wouldn't.

"Look inside," Durand said, lounging against the cabinet. "And in case you consider tossing the papers in the fire over there, you should know that they represent only part of your father's reports."

Reports. Oh, God. With a sinking feeling of dread, Edwin opened the file to find, in his father's own handwriting, pages and pages of notes. He choked down alarm and began to scan them systematically.

The further he read, the more his stomach roiled.

Every report began with a letter to a Frenchman named Aubert and contained a series of notes detailing information his father had gleaned at the opium den.

Apparently, certain British naval and army officers had enjoyed indulging from time to time in the odd Chinese practice of smoking opium. On those occasions, they'd inadvertently let slip bits about strategies of the war in France and the Peninsula. Father had then pieced them together into these reports.

There were crudely drawn maps, troop movement sketches, gossip about where Wellington intended to strike next. It was a damning set of documents, indeed.

No, how could this be? "Where did you get these?" Edwin demanded.

Durand shrugged. "They've been in our files for years. Our spy Aubert passed them on to the embassy after the war, and we kept them, in case we needed something else from your father."

"In other words, needed something with which to blackmail him," Edwin said tersely.

The acrid scent of cigar smoke swirled between them as Durand took another puff. "Or his son."

Edwin's blood chilled. "What the devil does that mean?"

Durand flicked some ash. "All I need do is send this to the press, and you'd be ruined in society."

"You wouldn't dare." Edwin fought to hide the tumult inside him. "With all the talk of another revolution to depose Charles X, your superiors have their hands full. They won't appreciate your stirring up a hornet's nest in England."

"What hornet's nest? I'd merely be guaranteeing that your position in society drops to somewhere below that of a charwoman. Especially after the scandal that your brother's criminal conviction engendered. Your sister's recent marriage might have restored the family name to a small degree, but this would destroy it for good."

Somehow Edwin managed a shrug. "That would merely mean I'd no longer have to deal with the likes of you."

"Ah, but you wouldn't be alone in your loss of consequence, would you?" With a grim smile, Durand pushed away from the cabinet. "How do you think Lady Clarissa would react if her association with you turned her into an outcast in society, too?"

God rot the bastard. Edwin *knew* how Clarissa would react. She might not care that his father had been a spy, but she would most assuredly hate leaving good society. Not being able to go to parties and routs and be the belle of the ball.

Durand pressed his point with ruthless efficiency. "Do you think she'd even consider marrying you if there was a chance it might mean suffering in solitude with you for the rest of your life? Does she care about you that much?"

Edwin feared he knew the answer to that, and it made an unmanageable anger roar up inside him. "My relationship with my betrothed is none of your concern. And yes, she'd stand by me. Because unlike you, Clarissa has a sound character."

"I wouldn't be too sure of that," Durand said.

The crafty remark only further fired Edwin's temper. With a growl, Edwin thrust his face into the other man's. "If you're insinuating anything insulting about my fiancée—"

"No." Durand's face clouded over. "Though she isn't the woman you think she is."

"Because she won't marry *you*, you mean? That only proves her intelligence and good sense."

Durand stiffened. After stubbing out his cigar in a salver, he slid the file from Edwin's clenched fingers. "Careful, Blakeborough. If you keep provoking me, I might just send this to the press for the fun of it."

"Go ahead. Then you and I can be churned under the gossip mill together. You're not the only one who can spread slander effectively."

Durand's cold stare would have frozen fire. "Have you considered that I could implicate *you* in your father's activities? You were, what? Eighteen or nineteen at the time this was going on? Not too young to be helping your father spy."

"There's not a shred of evidence I had anything to do with it," Edwin scoffed. "I was away at university."

"Not all the time. And you were certainly old enough to accompany him to that private opium den."

Edwin suddenly found it hard to breathe. In the last year of the war, he hadn't been at university. He'd been at Mother's side during her final hours. And he *had* visited the opium den once, too. If someone were to remember, were to misconstrue that . . . "Why are you doing this?"

"I want Lady Clarissa. I had a claim on her long before you started courting her. I know you don't love her, and I doubt she loves you, either. The two of you behave more like friends than like prospective spouses."

A pity that Durand hadn't discovered them in the midst of their unwise caresses earlier, although the wretch would probably have found a way to use that against them. "Tell yourself that our engagement doesn't mean anything if you wish, but it won't change the truth."

"The *truth* is that I could show the file to Lady Clarissa. I don't have to make it public. I daresay that would be enough to make her balk at being your wife."

Considering that Edwin hadn't even succeeded in getting her to agree to marry him, it probably would. "Is that what you meant by blackmail? You intend to expose my father's secrets to her unless I do what you wish."

"Exactly. I want you to set Lady Clarissa free."

Edwin gaped at him. "Half of society has already heard that we're engaged. If I were to end the betrothal, it would ruin her."

"Precisely." Durand's eyes shone the color of dark, treacherous waters. "She'd have nowhere to turn, no possibility of marrying anyone else but me. Admit it—you're merely involved with her because Knightford is your friend. But your heart isn't engaged. Mine is. Leave her to me, and I'll shower her with jewels and consequence and all the attention that a woman like her requires. Then I'll destroy your father's reports, burn them in front of you. You'll never have to worry about anyone learning the truth. But if you do not do as I ask . . ."

Durand left the words hanging with the dramatic flourish of some operatic villain. Edwin couldn't breathe. This made no sense. Why was the bastard so determined to have Clarissa as his wife? No doubt he was seeking some advantage by wedding her, but Edwin couldn't for the life of him figure out what it was. As a highly placed diplomat, Durand could have any woman he desired. This fascination with a lady who had no interest in him was unnatural.

No more than yours.

Not true. Edwin would never want to gain Clarissa by shaming her. And the fact that Durand would stoop so low chilled Edwin through and through. He had half a mind to shoot the arse right here and now.

But since the guards all knew of Edwin's presence, he wouldn't get away with it. He'd be tried and hanged, almost certainly. That, too, would affect Clarissa.

And not just her. It would expose his sister to yet another scandal, a worse one than anything their cursed younger brother had fomented. Yvette was finally happy; he refused to ruin that for her and her new husband.

Besides, there was another solution to this dilemma, one that would nip all of Durand's machinations in the bud. But it would take a bit of time to put his plan into place. So, as much as he wished to throw the count's threats back in his face, he must be cautious.

"I need a few days to think about it." Edwin practically choked on the lie. Though it was a necessary one, he loathed implying that he'd ever consider capitulating.

Durand narrowed his gaze on Edwin. "Why?"

Edwin shrugged. "That should be obvious. If I withdraw my offer to Clarissa, she could—and probably would—have me charged with breach of contract. So I must consult my lawyer about the likely outcome of such a charge and what it might cost me financially. I must also consider which scandal would damage my family more—the revelation of my father's secrets or the sudden refusal to marry a woman I've publicly proclaimed as my fiancée. Then there is also the matter—"

"Enough. I take your meaning." Durand scrutinized him closely. "You really are a cold man sometimes, Blakeborough. I threaten to take away Lady Clarissa, and all you can think about is how it will affect your purse."

If Durand thought so, then at least Edwin was managing to shield his true feelings. "I like to think I'm practical. As you say, Clarissa and I aren't in love—but that doesn't mean I'm unaware of what effect giving in to your demands could have on my life."

The count seemed to consider that. "Fine. You can have two days. But I expect your decision at the end of the day after tomorrow."

"Thank you." Edwin affected the bored tone typical of a lord of his rank. "Now, since this conversation has grown tiresome, I'll leave you to your cigars."

"You can show yourself out, I suppose," Durand said.

With the merest of nods, Edwin calmly left the room.

But inside he was seething. It was all he could do

to contain his fury until he was safely in his carriage and away. Father, a spy for the French. His gut twisted into a knot at the very thought.

Though it did explain so much. Why Father had always been so inattentive to his family. Why, when Mother was dying, he'd continued his jaunts to London. And why Edwin had never noticed any signs of opium intoxication on the few occasions Father *was* home. Had he ever even used opium? Or had he just gone to the opium den for his French masters?

The other thing he didn't understand was why. What could possibly have made Father wish to involve himself in such affairs? Some fondness for his French relations? It didn't seem plausible.

But the documents had clearly been written by Father. It wasn't just his handwriting—it was his manner of speech, his use of certain words. And Edwin didn't dare turn to anyone for advice, for fear the news would get out and the family's name be dragged through the mud.

There was only one way out of this. Clarissa wouldn't like it, but he must do his utmost to convince her to marry him by special license before he met with Durand again. Short of telling her exactly what Durand had found out about his father, of course. She was skittish enough about marrying him; if she knew there was a small chance she could be cut off from society, she would dig in her heels.

And this must be handled quickly. Even if Durand was bluffing about his threats to expose Father's spying, the very fact that he was so adamant about marrying Clarissa was cause for alarm. The Frenchman might even attempt abducting her. Plenty of men did that with heiresses.

But not on Edwin's watch. He would see Durand hang before he let the bastard harm one hair on her head.

Twelve

Shortly after sunset the next day, too early to dress for dinner and too late for a nap, Clarissa lounged about her room. Should she wear the lace pelerine or the net fichu with her dinner gown? Edwin was unlikely to care either way. As long as her attire was presentable, he probably wouldn't even notice.

No, *he* only noticed when her bosom was half-bare.

Her eyes narrowed. Very well, no pelerine or fichu at all. Because tonight she wanted to make him notice her—to make him see her for herself, with all her flaws. To make him understand that she really wasn't the sort of woman he wanted to marry.

Although that hadn't worked last night. It had only made him randy, something she would never have expected of the staid Edwin. And if she flaunted her bosom at him, he might look at her with that piercing stare that made her shiver all over, and then she would forget her purpose. Which was to very kindly but firmly refuse to marry him.

Yes—that was her plan and she must hold to it, no matter how much he growled in that oh-so-enticing rumble that half negated whatever he was saying. Even if he took her aside privately and gave her one of his luscious kisses that went on and on and on. Even if Mama, in her foolishness, left them alone again, and he tried to kiss his way down into—

Fichu. Definitely a fichu. And while she was at it, perhaps a nice suit of armor to keep him from being tempted and her from giving in.

A clatter sounded against the French doors that led out to her balcony. What on earth? Another rattle sounded. And another.

Hurrying out onto the balcony, she peered into the garden below, which was faintly lit by the gaslights from the mews in the back. And there, dressed far too informally for dinner, was Edwin.

She gaped down at him. "What do you think you're doing?"

"I need to talk to you privately. Now. It's urgent."

"Then come in the front door like a civilized person and ask for me."

"I can't. I don't want your mother involved. I don't even want the servants to know I've been here. Come down. We can talk in the garden."

Alone in the garden? Not likely. The very idea made a thrill course down her spine. "Don't be ridiculous. I'm in my dressing gown." She turned for the door. "Come back for dinner—that's soon enough to talk."

"Very well. I'll just have to come up."

What? She rushed back to the balcony in time to see him scaling the tall, spindly beech that rose too far away from her balcony to be of use to him.

"Edwin!" she hissed. "Stop that at once! It won't hold your weight."

He ignored her and kept climbing.

She watched with her heart in her throat. "What do you mean to do? Leap through the air? It's too far!"

If she raised an alarm, that would put an end to it . . . but something held her back. Curiosity? His expression of grim determination? Her worry that if anyone came out and distracted him, he might fall?

"Edwin," she whispered as he reached the level of her balcony. "Oh, do be careful. Don't even *think* about jumping."

Already, visions of his body broken on the garden paving stones below haunted her. But curiously, he kept climbing. The tree started to bow with his weight, and he shifted to the side nearest her balcony. When it bowed even more, she had to bite back a scream.

Then the tree bent just enough to set him down right before her.

When he released the beech, it sprang back into place. Then he dusted off his hands and trousers, as if he climbed onto balconies so deftly every day.

She wanted to throttle him. "Are you mad? You could have killed yourself!"

He blinked. "Nonsense. I knew precisely what I was doing. I calculated the circumference and height of the tree against my weight and the pull of gravity, and figured it would be fine."

"Figured!" She poked him in the chest. "If you had figured wrong, you would have broken your neck!"

He grabbed her hand, his eyes glittering in the faint candlelight from the room. "You were worried about me."

"Of course I was worried about you!"

"Then you should have come down," he said very matter-of-factly.

"I would have, if I'd known you'd turned into a reckless fool overnight."

He curled his fingers around her hand. "I was a boy once, you know. We learn to climb trees with our mother's milk." He tried to tug her close. "I was fine. Really."

She snatched her hand free, her heart still thundering in her chest, and walked back into the room. Edwin, climbing trees. Who would have thought it?

As he followed her inside, she snapped, "So tell me. What was so all-fired important that you had to risk your life to speak to me alone?"

"Durand was here last night."

That halted her in her tracks. With her throat tightening, she whirled to face him. "What do you mean?"

"Down the street. He was watching the house." The deadly seriousness in his tone confirmed the truth of his words. "I confronted him, and he gave me an ultimatum."

Her stomach began to churn. "What sort of ultimatum?"

A muscle worked in Edwin's jaw. "Either I call off our engagement by tomorrow evening, or he'll reveal some unsettling secrets about my family."

"What secrets?"

"I'd rather not say. But they would essentially destroy whatever credit Yvette and I have in society. We would be outcasts."

Yvette? It had something to do with Yvette? And

him, too. Oh no. "If that happened, you wouldn't be able to find a wife," she whispered.

"Precisely."

A hard lump stuck in her throat. She considered prodding him to reveal what secrets Count Durand was holding over him, but if they were enough to make him this alarmed, they had to be bad. Which meant he wouldn't talk about them with her. He never revealed such things to her. Why, she wouldn't even have known about how uncaring his father had been toward the family if Yvette hadn't told her.

Edwin wasn't the sort of man to open his past to anyone, even a woman he contemplated marrying.

And it probably wouldn't change anything if she knew. "Well, then, it appears you have no choice." She swallowed hard. "You must end our betrothal. Or better yet, I'll jilt you. Honestly, I never intended to marry any—"

"You're not listening, Clarissa." Stepping closer, he fixed her with a bleak glance. "He wants me to end things because he wants you to have no recourse but to marry him."

"That's absurd," she said, though a frisson of fear skittered down her spine. "I always have a recourse. I will simply jilt you. It will make things difficult for you, I know, and I'm very sorry for that, but at least—"

"That won't work, damn it. Don't you see? He doesn't mean to give you a choice! *He was lurking in your street just last night.* He's obsessed with having you as his wife. If you continue to refuse him, one day he will simply abduct you and carry you off to Gretna Green. Or worse, to France. He could get away with it, too. Diplomats are immune to all charges except murder."

Slowly the reason for his sense of urgency sank in, along with a hard knot of anger at Durand. "But *why* is he obsessed, drat it? Why does he want me? I don't understand him!"

"You're a beautiful woman, full of vibrancy and good humor. Who wouldn't want you?"

The delicious words startled her. They weren't at all like him, which made her suspicious. "This is not the time to be trying out your newfound skill at compliments. There are plenty of women like me."

"Not as many as you'd think." Glancing away, Edwin rubbed the back of his neck. "But I'll admit that his fixation with you goes beyond the pale. I can only assume that by wedding you, he hopes to gain access to something he wants."

"Like what?"

He huffed out a breath. "Bloody hell, I don't know. I wish I did. Perhaps Warren is wrong about his wealth. Perhaps he lost it at the gaming tables."

"If it's just about money, there are any number of heiresses who would happily marry a French count on his way to great success as a diplomat. Why insist on marrying a woman who clearly despises him?"

"He doesn't seem to believe you do."

"Then he's blind, deaf, and dumb," she said stoutly.

"Or he doesn't care how you feel. Right now, it hardly matters what his reasons are. It doesn't change the fact that he has both of us trapped."

"Not you." She sank onto her bed. She was tired of dealing with Durand, tired of the up-and-down, of being sure he was out of her hair only to have him show up again. "You must protect your family and take his bargain. I'll jilt you, and Mama and I will keep to the house until Warren is home. Then he can handle Durand."

"The way he's *been* handling him?" Edwin's face darkened. "You know damned well Warren might not be back for weeks. I am *not* leaving you alone to be abducted by that bastard."

"So what exactly are you proposing? That he drag you and your sister—and her new husband—through another scandal while you nobly hold down the fort until Warren returns?"

"No. I have another plan." He strode over to look out the balcony door. "You and I should marry right away. Tomorrow morning, first thing. I've already obtained a special license, so I'll come to take you riding in the morning and we'll go straight to the church. Your mother allowed us to go in the phaeton with only my tiger before, so that will work. We needn't even involve her in the wedding, since you're of age and don't need her permission. I've already spoken to my parish priest—"

"Wait, wait, stop it!" She jumped up from the bed. "Marry? How does that keep Durand from revealing your family secrets?"

He faced her, the shadows throwing the sharp planes of his face into harsh relief. "Once we marry and he loses any chance to gain you, he's lost his weapon. Divorce is nearly impossible to obtain, even for a man of my stature, so he can't make you his bride. That would leave no reason for him to spill my family secrets, other than a fit of pique, since it won't achieve his original aim. Even Durand isn't stupid enough to risk his own career in diplomacy to spread slander about an English earl just to vent his temper."

Lord. What a plan. "I'm not so sure about that. As long as we don't know why he's—"

"I'm not just rushing into this, if that's what you think."

"I think you're quite mad."

He reached into the pocket of his frock coat and pulled out a folded sheaf of papers. "I had my solicitor draw up a marriage settlement this morning." Setting it on the bed, he added, "I think you'll find it more than generous, but take some time to look it over tonight. If it doesn't meet with your approval, we can go to his office first thing so you can dictate any changes before we head to the church."

While she was flattered that he trusted her with legal documents—most men wouldn't believe a woman could even read them properly—this was all moving rather quickly. "Edwin—"

"If you *want* to involve your mother, I understand—but she's not very good at keeping secrets, and Durand absolutely cannot know of it until it's done."

"I don't care if Mama is involved, but—"

"Our marriage needn't be a typical one, you know." His throat moved convulsively. "If you prefer to live separately, we can do that once we're sure that Durand is no longer an issue."

"Which would make it a trifle hard for you to sire an heir, and I don't—"

"Obviously, I'd prefer that we bear children and raise them together as husband and wife, but if that doesn't suit you—"

"Curse it, Edwin, enough!" She seized his hands. "What doesn't suit me is your giving up your entire life to protect me."

His eyes widened. "I'm not. You know I've wanted a wife for a long time."

"But I'm sure you would prefer to choose one for yourself. Not be bullied into it by some madman."

"He didn't bully me into marrying you. He *attempted* to bully me into *not* marrying you. I'm the one who came up with the idea of marrying right away. I did it with my eyes open, so you needn't worry about that." Lifting her hands to his lips, he kissed each one with that slow care that never failed to make her blood run hot. Then he added, in a guttural murmur, "And you must admit that we're attracted to each other."

Given the furious beat of her heart just now, she could hardly deny that. But it made no difference. "That's not the point. There are things about me that you don't know, things that you wouldn't like, things that—"

"I am not leaving you to that *bastard*!" When she started, Edwin modulated his tone. "I will not stand by and do nothing while he tries to ruin your life. And if we're married, he won't act—I'm certain of it."

"You're calling his bluff. I see that. But what if it isn't a bluff?"

"Then you'll be forced to suffer the scandal along with us, but I honestly don't think it will come to that. And at least I'll still be protecting you from his attempt to have you. We can face him together as man and wife."

Man and wife. Her heart twisted in her chest.

When Edwin was being noble, she wanted to scoop him up and kiss him forever. But he wouldn't stay noble. Not once he learned about her past. "It's not fair to you," she said. "Making you risk scandal for your entire family to protect me. I can't ask you to do that."

"You're not asking. I'm offering. It isn't the same." He searched her face. "We can have a decent life together, you know. Muddle our way through things. And if we're unhappy, we can have separate homes. Margrave Manor is already next to my estate. You could go there, raise our children there. As long as I'm always part of their lives, I would be content."

"Content? You deserve better than that, Edwin."

He shook his head. "I'm not a romantic man, Clarissa. Love was never a consideration. As long as I can have a companion—preferably one who doesn't mind sharing my bed—"

"And what if I *do* mind?" she whispered. "I'm not like other women. I have a certain . . . aversion to such things."

Edwin did excite her body, but every time she thought about actually having him on top of her, her throat closed up and her hands grew clammy, and she wanted to die. He kept mentioning children, but having children required having marital relations, and she didn't know if she could endure that, even with Edwin. What if she could *never* do so?

"You're frightened of me," he said hollowly.

"No." The sharp, immediate response seemed to calm him. "Of any man being . . . with me in that way."

"Ah." He smiled. "Every woman has those virginal

fears, my sweet. But I promise I am capable of easing them, if you'll let me." He chucked her under the chin. "I see it like this. It's either an amiable marriage with a man who will treat you tenderly. Or risk abduction by a man who will almost certainly not."

She glanced away, indecision wracking her. She could end this all now, just by telling him the truth: that she wasn't chaste. He would withdraw his proposal, she would formally jilt him, and she could go back to living her life—

In fear. Of a man who would be far more terrifying if he ever *did* get her in his power. And there was no guarantee that Count Durand would not, especially if she and Mama were left with no male protector. There wasn't even a guarantee that he wouldn't ruin Edwin anyway. What was to keep him from holding to his word?

The truth was, the thought of dealing with Edwin once he discovered all her secrets paled in comparison to the thought of the count's abducting and forcing her into his bed. She couldn't endure such an assault again.

She met his gaze once more. "All right."

The relief flooding his face should have heartened her. It did not. He didn't know what he was getting into with her. And she really should tell him. But the thought of his withdrawal when he learned of it—

No, she would tell him once they were married. Eventually. But in the meantime . . . "I have one condition, however."

His eyes sharpened on her. "What is that?"

"You must . . . give me time to adapt to marriage before we share a bed. I still feel as if we're practically strangers. I never thought of you romantically before, and now—"

"You do?"

"I don't know. That's what worries me. I don't even know how to think of someone that way. But you must promise that I will be the one to choose when we share a bed, however long it takes."

"That sounds ominous," he said dryly.

"I know. But that's my condition. And I want it in the terms of the settlement."

His face clouded. "Ah."

"I know it's not the sort of thing that a man would ever—"

"I'll add it."

"If you can't—"

"It's fine. We'll stop at the solicitor's office in the morning to have it put in and the signatures witnessed. Be sure to look over the settlement tonight to make sure you want no other changes."

She swallowed. "You should probably not come to dinner. Just send a note saying you're busy or something. Because it will be too hard for you to keep lying through Mama's incessant chatter about our grand wedding that will never be."

He scowled. "I didn't think about that. You won't get that grand wedding, and your mother will never forgive me for that."

"Nonsense. You're marrying me. She was afraid I'd never marry, so she'll be fine. And we can have a grand party later to celebrate."

"What about you? Will you regret not having that grand wedding?"

A sudden sharp pang in her chest told her that

some part of her would, but she squelched it. "I never planned to marry, so I wouldn't have had it anyway."

Her tone must have been more wistful than she'd realized, for his eyes darkened. "It will be all right, Clarissa, I promise. I will make it all right."

Cupping her face in his hands, he kissed her. It was sweet and tender and utterly unthreatening. And it gave her hope that he might be telling the truth about their future. Because if he wasn't, she didn't know if she could bear it.

Thirteen

Edwin had no idea what to expect when he showed up at Warren's town house the next morning. After a night alone, Clarissa might have changed her mind about marrying him. And then what could he do?

He'd already done his best to convince her that Durand wouldn't call his bluff *after* they married. If that happened, she would never forgive him for obscuring the truth by deliberately playing down how devastating the scandal of his father's spying could be for *her*. If Durand went to the press with his evidence—and threw in a few hints that Edwin had been involved, too—it would ruin them both.

Guilt made him wince. He should have told her all that. But she wouldn't have married him if he had—he was sure of it. Clarissa liked being the belle of the ball.

What she didn't like, apparently, was being the belle of the bedchamber.

But you must promise that I will be the one to choose when we share a bed, however long it takes.

Edwin sighed. It was that last part that stymied him. She'd spoken of his siring an heir, so she couldn't mean to deny him her bed forever. And her plan was a sound one—to wait until they were more comfortable with each other to become intimate. So why did it gnaw at him that she'd even ask such a thing?

Because it made him wonder yet again what precisely was wrong with him. Despite accepting his kisses, despite her flirtations and her teasing, she didn't want to be close the way a man and wife should be. It oughtn't matter to him—he'd expected his marriage to be more of a business arrangement than a love match.

But he'd also expected to bed his bride. It was almost unbearable to think of being denied that.

Blast it, he was being ridiculous. Clarissa was just having a fit of nerves. She wouldn't go on like that for long. Even if she did, he certainly knew how to tempt a lady into his bed. How hard could it be with a woman like Clarissa, who'd responded to his kisses with enthusiasm?

Assuming she didn't rescind her agreement to marry him.

Fortunately, he arrived at the town house to find her waiting for him, dressed in a rather elaborate ensemble involving feathers and bows and an enormous hat with a transparent veil trimmed in lace. She looked rather like a gift box wrapped in net and oceans of silk, utterly inaccessible.

It didn't help that her mother awaited him, too. "How lovely of you to take Clarissa driving in Green Park as an apology for missing last night's dinner!" she exclaimed.

Thank God Clarissa had thought to provide a suitable lie for where they were going. "I was very sorry not to be here," he said, which was the truth. His brief kiss with Clarissa in her bedchamber hadn't been nearly enough.

"Well, a drive in the park should be quite invigorating at this hour. And she does enjoy early drives. As do I. Indeed, I thought I'd go along, but Clarissa says there's no room in the phaeton for me."

"Yes, I'm sorry," he said quickly. "My equipage is small, I'm afraid. But if you want to go, you could ride behind on my tiger's seat, and I'll leave him here."

As he'd expected, Lady Margrave was aghast. "Are you mad? Balance on the back of your phaeton? It sounds very uncomfortable. Why, I could easily fall right off! For shame, Edwin. I can't believe you'd even suggest such a thing to your future mother-in-law."

Clarissa's lips twitched. "Yes, Edwin, how dare you?" she said, a mischievous twinkle in her eye.

That little glimpse of Clarissa's usual teasing calmed all his fears. They would be fine. He would make it so. "I suppose I temporarily took leave of my wits." He held out his arm. "Why don't we go, then, before everyone descends on the park?"

"Of course," she said brightly.

They headed out the door at precisely 9:00 A.M. As they walked down the steps, he murmured, "Thank you for coming up with a suitable tale for your mother. You know how I hate lying."

"Because you're very bad at it. I wasn't about to risk your undoing everything by attempting to deceive Mama. You would never be convincing."

"True." It further heartened him that she seemed to know him so well sometimes. Although there were other times . . .

No, he would not think of that. They would have years to come to know each other better.

As they left in the phaeton, she sat stiffly in the seat, her hands gripping her reticule. Was she nervous? Worried?

Wishing she was not on her way to be married to *him*?

He ventured to set her at ease with a compliment. "Your gown is very . . . er . . ."

"Let me guess—'fussy, frilly, and overdone,'" she said with a certain belligerence.

"Pink."

Her rigid stance softened. "Oh. Yes. I suppose it is."

"You look fetching in pink. Not that you ever look less than fetching in anything else, but it just seems that pink brings out the jade of your eyes and the ruby of your lips and—" He broke off as he realized he was babbling like that pup at the theater the night before last. And he *never* babbled. "You look lovely."

She eyed him through the net that draped her face. "Thank you, but I know it's a fussy ensemble. It was my only one with a veiled hat. And I wanted to have at least the semblance of dressing as a bride at my wedding."

Regret stabbed him. "I'm sorry that's being denied you."

"Stop apologizing. Count Durand is the one to blame. You're just trying to make things better."

Well, at least she was aware of that. They rode some time in silence, until he realized that his solicitor's office wasn't much farther. "Did you read over the settlement?"

"Yes." She stared ahead at the road. "You weren't exaggerating when you said I would find it more than generous. But I do have one observation."

He shot her a wary glance. "What is it?"

"The jointure you list is about twenty percent of the fortune I bring to the marriage. That seems excessive, given that the typical jointure is ten percent of what the bride brings to the marriage."

Now *that* was a remark he'd never expected from Clarissa. But perhaps she didn't understand the terminology. "A woman's jointure provides for her once her husband dies, so it's only fair—"

"I know what a jointure is, Edwin," she said irritably. "I simply can't figure out why you're offering double the usual amount."

He smiled. "I see that I'm about to gain a rather clever wife."

"Were you in doubt of that?"

"Of course not," he said hastily, recognizing a trap when he saw one. "But I didn't expect you to have a knowledge of settlements or, for that matter, complicated mathematics."

"I took care of most of managing the household even before Papa died." She leaned close. "As you might imagine, Mama is not good with figures."

"I'm shocked to hear it," he said dryly.

She swatted him with her reticule. "*I* can criticize Mama. You cannot."

"I see," he said with a smile. "So there are rules for our marriage?"

"A number of them."

"Are you going to tell me what they are?"

"In due time. Now, stop beating about the bush, and answer my question about the terms of the jointure in the settlement."

When Clarissa got the bit between her teeth, she never let go. He wasn't sure what that meant for a marriage between them. That he'd never have any peace, probably. "How do you even know what the 'usual amount' is for a jointure?"

"I knew what Mama's was. And Yvette told me about hers."

He gaped at her. "My sister discussed her marriage settlement with you?"

"We women discuss all sorts of things, you know, and thank heaven that we do. Since Mama would rather eat snakes than read a legal document, and my brother—or my cousin—isn't here to negotiate my settlement, I was glad your sister had talked so much about hers when she was preparing for her wedding. It gave me something to go on when I looked it over."

Trying to imagine his sister poring over such a document made his head hurt. Reading contracts didn't seem like something she'd enjoy. "So you were able to . . . er . . . decipher the legal language?"

"With the help of a dictionary. And one of my cousin's books." She yawned, covering it rather ineffectively with one hand. "Which is why I got little sleep last night."

He chuckled. "I'm surprised the language alone didn't put you to sleep. It would have done me. I hate legal documents. But having overseen Yvette's, I at least knew what was supposed to be in one." After taking a corner a bit too fast, he slid her a side glance. "So you found your jointure acceptable? And the pin money?"

"Of course. I merely want to understand the reason for your generosity." She shot him an arch look. "Are you trying to soften me up before you assert your authority? Or are you simply more reckless with your money than I realized?"

"I am neither a spendthrift nor tyrannical. Or, for that matter, calculating enough to try to 'soften' you up with money. I am merely trying to make up for the unorthodox nature of our marriage."

"I see." Her smile warmed him. "In that case, I have no complaints." She stared down at her reticule. "Though I still want that extra clause put in."

The one that denied him his husbandly rights until she deigned to accept him in her bed. "Yes. That will be done." Even if he had to bludgeon his solicitor into it, which he might have to do. The man was doddering on the edge of the grave, and would find her demand outrageous and shocking.

Edwin gripped the reins. It couldn't be helped. He'd already made a promise, and he would keep it no matter what. Though he sincerely hoped she didn't deny him her bed for long. He found himself extraordinarily eager to consummate their marriage. *Whenever* it happened.

Moments later they reached the solicitor's office, which was rather empty so early in the morning. He was glad of that. They'd be able to take care of their business and be off to the church before it got too late. Even Lady Margrave, as negligent a chaperone as she was, would fret if they stayed gone too long. And the last thing they needed was her fluttering around in a panic, alerting Durand to what was going on.

As soon as they were seated before his solicitor, the man once more expressed concern that the young lady didn't have a male member of the family there to look after her interests. He didn't remain concerned for long. A few moments' conversation with an irate Clarissa quickly convinced him not to worry about that.

Now came the most difficult part for Edwin. "My fiancée has one clause she would like added. She'll have to be the one to explain it, since I'm not entirely sure how she wants it written out."

Even as Clarissa blushed tellingly, she removed a slip of paper from her reticule and placed it on the table. "I wrote the words down exactly as I want them put in."

The solicitor read the paper and blinked. "My lord, you agreed to this?"

"I did," Edwin said in the stern fashion that generally squelched all further questions.

Apparently it wasn't sufficient to quash his solicitor's. "So you've read it, then."

"No. But I know the gist of it."

The solicitor shot Clarissa a wary glance. "Forgive me, my lord, but I would feel more comfortable if you made sure that it's written in a way that is . . . acceptable to you as well. The clause is . . . well . . . most peculiar."

Edwin gritted his teeth. "I'm fully aware of that."

"All the same, if you could just look it over . . ." The man held out the slip.

Snatching it from him, Edwin read the words

printed there in her neat, feminine handwriting: *Edwin Barlow, Earl of Blakeborough, agrees to consummate his marriage to Lady Clarissa Lindsey only at a future date of her choosing. In exchange, Lady Clarissa agrees that the period of time between the wedding and the consummation of the marriage shall not proceed beyond one year.*

A year! Bloody hell. She would deny him her bed for a year? His gaze shot to her, and he was about to protest when he saw fear flash over her face. At having him demand that she share his bed sooner than she was ready.

Then her features smoothed, and she was staring at him with her usual expression of challenge.

Perhaps he'd imagined the fear. He didn't always read people correctly. Maidenly hesitation he could understand, but could she *truly* be terrified at the very idea of being bedded by him?

It seemed unlikely. Unless, of course, her mother had fed her the typical nonsense about the pain, humiliation, and unpleasantness of being deflowered. That would certainly put any woman on edge.

But that didn't seem in character for Lady Margrave. If ever there was a woman who lived for pleasure, it was the dowager countess. And until Clarissa had made her one demand of him, Edwin would have thought the same of her—that she had an appetite for pleasure equal to his own.

As he stared down at the slip of paper, another possibility entered his mind. Could Durand have pressed his attentions on her more vigorously than he should have? The man had pinned her against the wall that day in the library. Had he done the unthinkable to her during those weeks in Bath? Was that why she despised him?

But that made no sense. If Durand had taken her innocence, he would have mentioned it to Edwin right away in hopes that Edwin would turn his back on her for being ruined.

She isn't the woman you think she is.

Durand's words taunted him, quickly joined by her own warning last night: *There are things about me that you don't know, things that you wouldn't like.*

He should have made both of them explain themselves. He hated sly hints and secretive allusions. On the other hand, he couldn't believe anything Durand said, and Clarissa was just as likely to be talking about her propensity to snore as anything more serious.

Or she might just find him unappealing.

But he hadn't been the only one caught up in all those passionate kisses. So he'd have to cling to the evidence that she was attracted to him. Enjoyed kissing him. And would one day surely enjoy sharing his bed.

"My lord?" the solicitor said. "Do you want me to add the clause?"

Edwin looked up and forced a haughty expression to his face. "Of course." He threw the paper on the table. "Put it in exactly as she wrote it."

From the moment Clarissa and Edwin left his solicitor's, she felt numb. The look of wounded pride in his eyes, the anger in his voice when he'd told the solicitor to add her clause, still chilled her. She must be out of her mind to be marrying him.

Yet nothing had changed. She still couldn't let Edwin risk his family's future. She still dared not risk her own with the deranged Durand.

When they arrived at St. George's in Hanover Square, she was heartened to have a beautiful bouquet pressed into her hand by the vicar's wife, who would be serving as one of the witnesses to the ceremony.

"Thank you." She buried her face in the sweet lilies. "It's most kind of you."

The woman smiled. "Your fiancé picked them out, my lady."

Startled, Clarissa glanced at Edwin, who was watching her with an expression she couldn't decipher. Wariness? Anticipation? She could no more read him than she could the man in the moon. "Then thank you, too, Edwin."

He gave her a genuine smile devoid of mockery and cynicism, and it changed his whole face, made him look almost boyish. She liked those smiles best, because they were so rare.

And he looked sinfully handsome today, in his dark-blue coat, fawn trousers, and white figured silk waistcoat. He really had excellent taste in clothes. But then, the Vile Seducer had dressed nicely, too. She'd learned far too young that you couldn't judge a man's character by his choice of tailor.

Still, she thought they probably made an attractive couple as they headed to the altar. Edwin had arranged everything most precisely. He'd pressed his tiger into service as the second witness, and he'd even thought to purchase wedding rings sometime between yesterday afternoon and this morning.

Even though he'd bought hers without having a measurement, she was sure the ring would fit. Knowing Edwin, he'd gauged her size by doing some complicated mathematics in his head involving her height, the circumference of her hand, and the length of her fingers. And quite possibly the latitude and longitude of the church.

For some reason, the idea of him doing something so typically *Edwin* reassured her. As he stood solemnly beside her, she wondered if he might even be having the same vacillating thoughts as she, especially after that moment in the solicitor's office.

But when it came to the vows, he never wavered. He said, "I will," as readily as if he were marrying the love of his life.

Then it was her turn. The vicar asked, "Lady Clarissa, wilt thou have this man to be thy wedded husband? Wilt thou obey him, and serve him, love, honor, and keep him, in sickness and in health; and forsaking all others, keep thee only unto him, so long as ye both shall live?"

The old-fashioned words spoken in the vicar's somber tones echoed in the empty cathedral like a funeral dirge. Could she do this? Did she dare?

As she hesitated, she glanced at Edwin and saw the muscle in his jaw tighten. But he didn't look at her, didn't try to coax her to say the words, didn't even reach up to squeeze her hand where it gripped his arm.

It truly was her choice. Except it was no choice at all.

"I will," she said.

Only when Edwin let out a breath did she realize he'd been holding it, awaiting her answer. And somehow that made everything a tiny bit better.

Then came the kiss, which he didn't linger over, probably overly conscious of their audience. And that was it. They were done. It wasn't yet noon when they headed back to the town house.

They rode a while in silence before she ventured to speak. "Well, that was . . . quick."

"Yes, of necessity. But I'm sorry that the ceremony couldn't be more lavish."

She arched a brow at him. "You know perfectly well you preferred it that way—no fuss and no crowds." When he looked uncomfortable, she regretted the statement. "But it is a lovely church. I've always liked it. And it's conveniently named for the same saint as your club. Or did you name your club after your church?"

"Certainly not. They named the church in anticipation of my club."

When she blinked, he cast her a smug smile, and a laugh sputtered out of her. "You made a joke."

"I do sometimes, you know."

"Not very often. And hardly ever around me."

"Well, then, I shall have to remedy that," he said, nudging her knee with his.

It was such a companionable gesture that it made a lump form in her throat. He could be so charming when he tried. And now his knee was squarely up against hers and she was feeling rather . . . heated. That would not do.

Determinedly, she changed the subject. "Shall I

now reside at your town house?" she asked brightly. "Or will we take a honeymoon trip?"

Returning his gaze to the road, he said, "I don't think a trip is wise just now. If Durand *does* call my bluff and spread slander about my family, I don't want to be too far away, making it seem as if I ran off to avoid it. People will give his tales less credence if I act as if nothing happened."

She tried to hide her relief. A honeymoon trip would be so very intimate. It would be hard to share a room with him in an inn somewhere without . . . well . . . having relations. She needed to put that off as long as possible.

First, because she had to work herself up to enduring the pain. And second, because she wanted him to get to know her well enough so he wouldn't be too appalled when he realized she wasn't chaste. She was *not* looking forward to that discussion.

Perhaps she should just let him have his way with her tonight and get it over with. She didn't have to tell him the truth. He already assumed that her fears stemmed from her being a virgin.

And could a man even tell that a woman was not? She didn't know. But if so, she would feel awful to have Edwin discover it in their marital bed.

Best to be honest when the time came.

To distract herself from that sobering thought, she said, "So I suppose we will be living in your town house from now on, then."

"Actually, if you don't mind, I'd prefer to stay at Stoke Towers for the next couple of weeks. It's near enough to London that we can be here quickly if anything happens, but far enough that Durand won't be sniffing about day in and day out. Your mother can stay here if she wishes, or at Margrave Manor, but I imagine she'll be more comfortable in one of those two than at Stoke Towers."

Clarissa arched an eyebrow. "She'll also be out of your hair."

The corner of his lip quirked up. "That, too."

"Knowing Mama, she'd rather be in London lording it over all her friends who haven't yet married off their daughters." She sobered. "But do you think she would be safe alone at Warren's?"

"The servants have been keeping an eye out for Durand for some time. And what could he do, anyway? Kidnap her to force you into unmarrying me? She should be fine." He cast her a sidelong glance. "And if she stays in town, it will allow us more privacy."

Oh, Lord. Just what they needed. "We're not leaving until tomorrow, I assume, to give you time to inform the count of our wedding."

"I already had the announcement scheduled for this evening's papers. He'll learn of it quickly enough. And in case he doesn't, I'll pay him a visit before we go tonight to make sure he knows."

"I don't want you meeting him alone." Her heart constricted at the thought of how Durand might take his anger out on Edwin.

"I won't be. I'll go while his staff are still at the embassy. Besides, I'm not afraid of him."

"But I am! He could do anything to you!"

With an indulgent smile, he reached over to clasp

her hand. "I won't let him. And you mustn't be afraid of him, either. I swear I'll do everything in my power to prevent him from hurting you."

She did adore that about Edwin—he had a protective streak that ran wide and deep. Papa had been like that. He'd had to be, given Mama's tendency to wander heedlessly into trouble.

Edwin threaded his fingers with hers, starting a quivering low in her belly. They were married now. Joined forever. How long would it take for her to get used to that?

"So," she said nervously, "we're going to Stoke Towers this very evening?"

"We might as well." Releasing her hand, he tooled his rig toward Warren's town house at the other end of the street. "Otherwise, you'd have to move to my town house for the night and then again to Stoke Towers tomorrow. As long as you're packing up a few things anyway, you should go home with me to Hertfordshire."

Home. With him. Another thing to get used to. She'd spent many a happy hour at Stoke Towers with Yvette, but this was entirely different. It would be the two of them alone.

Until the children came along. She loved babies, and these would be hers. If she had some. Which depended on whether she could endure the act of creating them.

"But when will you pack?" she asked.

"I already did. The carriages set off for Hertfordshire this morning before I came here."

Lord, he'd certainly planned well. "Well, I haven't packed a thing. So I should think it would be better to start off tomorrow." She slipped her hand in his elbow. "We can stay at separate houses for one night, after all. That way I'll have plenty of time to figure out what I might need in the country."

"Anything that you need can be sent for once we're there. And your family *does* own the estate next door, so it's not as if you can't go over to Margrave Manor to find a few things in your closets. We'll leave tonight."

"Yes, Edwin," she said in her best coaxing voice, "but wouldn't it make much more sense to—"

"I do hope you're not trying to manage me already, Lady Blakeborough."

His sharp tone wasn't what arrested her. *Lady Blakeborough.* She hadn't counted on how lovely that would sound. A married woman had more conse-quence than a single lady. A married woman was freer to live her life as she pleased—as long as her husband allowed it.

She made a face at him. "I would never try to man-age *you*, Edwin. You're much too clever for that."

"Hmm." He looked skeptical.

"Besides," she said truthfully, "I need to conserve my energies for what's to come as soon as we reach the house."

"Oh? And what is that?"

She stared grimly ahead. "Telling Mama that we had our wedding without her."

Fourteen

Everyone in the street could probably hear Lady Margrave scream when they told her the news.

Edwin grimaced. He hadn't intended to cause a rift between Clarissa and her mother.

Lady Margrave stomped about the drawing room with her cane, pausing occasionally to brandish it at them. "What do you *mean*, you were wed this morning? How could you just . . . just *sneak* off to get married, without a word to *me*! No lace, no wedding breakfast . . . no orange blossoms . . . I can't believe it!"

"We didn't have a choice, Mama," Clarissa said. "Besides, you know I hate that scent. I wouldn't have worn orange blossoms anyway."

"Yes, but you would have worn a more impressive gown," she said, taking in Clarissa's dress with a look of contempt. "Why, just this morning I laid out the recent copies of *La Belle Assemblée* for us to go over in picking your design." Her mother pouted spectacularly. "And I saw the most perfect little wedding bonnet in a shopwindow a week ago that I wanted you to look at. And now . . . now . . . you're already married!"

The dowager countess burst into tears.

Edwin blinked. Blast, blast, and double blast. He sincerely hoped that becoming a watering pot was not one of Clarissa's attributes.

With a side glance at him, Clarissa put her arm around her mother and said, "There, there, Mama, I know it's a disappointment. But Count Durand was threatening awful things, and we saw no way around it."

Edwin felt he should say *something* to help. "I saw him right outside your house the other night, Lady Margrave. I was afraid he might abduct Clarissa if we didn't marry at once."

"And it wasn't as if Edwin could stay here all the time. It wouldn't be respectable."

His wife was handling the woman with surprising aplomb. Come to think of it, she always had. Perhaps she wouldn't be so unsuitable a wife after all. Assuming he could get her to share his bed eventually.

God, he must stop thinking about that.

"But why couldn't *I* attend the wedding, too? And perhaps a few of our friends? We could have kept it small." Her mother began to tick names off. "Just Lady Anne and the Lamonts and the Sweeney sisters, since they're my closest friends, and of course—"

"Mama! That's precisely why we didn't include you. You would have started making a big to-do, Count Durand would have got wind of our plan, and he would have spread scandal in hopes of preventing the wedding. It had to remain secret until it was over." She frowned at her mother. "Admit it, you do not know how to keep things secret."

"That's not true," Lady Margrave said with a sniff.

"Who told Cook that I disliked her veal sausages?"

The dowager countess lifted her chin. "That was only so she would make better ones."

"And who told Warren last year that Yvette thought his mustache made him look villainous?"

"Well, it did. She was right."

"Yes, but she didn't want to hurt his feelings. She wanted to broach it gently, and you just blurted it out."

"He . . . he caught me off guard. Asked me what I thought of it."

"So you offered *Yvette's* opinion instead of yours. That way he would be annoyed with her and not you."

Her mother began to wave her hands. "This is all beside the point. You got married in some havey-cavey manner, and now you mean to blame me for it. But not a soul saw it happen—"

"I told you," Edwin put in, "we had witnesses."

The dowager countess glared at him. "No one who *matters* saw it happen."

"I don't really give a damn," he muttered, which earned him a frown from both women.

Not to mention that Lady Margrave simply continued to complain. "And everyone will assume that we couldn't afford a proper wedding with a proper gown and a proper breakfast—"

"So have a proper breakfast," Edwin said irritably. "Some big affair to celebrate the ceremony. I'll pay for it." He owed it to the woman, since he'd

deprived her of the one experience every lady anticipated—planning her daughter's nuptials.

That stopped the dowager countess right in her
tracks. She eyed him uncertainly. "We can't have a
wedding breakfast days after the ceremony—it simply isn't done. Besides, it would take at least two
weeks to plan a proper one."

"Fine. Then don't have one. It's your choice."

"Yes, you're quite right, Edwin," Lady Margrave
said. "It shouldn't be a breakfast. It should be a grand
fete. A real celebration."

"Mama!" Clarissa said, with a furtive glance at
him. "That's *not* what he was saying. And I don't
think you should spend Edwin's money on some
grand fete."

Her concern for his finances amused him. "Tech-
nically, it's your money, minx, since your fortune just
increased my coffers by a substantial amount. Even
if it hadn't, I can afford to do whatever your mother
pleases."

Lady Margrave gazed at him as if he'd just opened
the doors to Versailles. "Could we have it at Vauxhall, do you think? I know they're not open at present, but they would probably hire it out to *you*. And
then we can hire one of those balloonists to come."

Good God. "If you wish."

"Can we hire the orchestra to play for our guests?"

He stifled a sigh. "Certainly."

"And bring in our own chefs so we have food
that's decent, instead of those ghastly chickens?"

"Of course," he said readily. "The fare at Vauxhall
is wretched."

"Edwin!" Clarissa exclaimed.

"What?"

"You don't even *like* Vauxhall!" his wife said.

"It would be a private affair," he countered. "It's not the same. Besides, this fete isn't for me or even you. It's for your mother. And she has put up with a great deal from us, so it's the least I . . . *we* . . . can do."

"It certainly is," the dowager countess said. "Now, come, Clarissa. We should do a bit of planning."

Clarissa raised her eyes heavenward. "I have to pack, Mama. Edwin and I are leaving for Stoke Towers tonight."

"What? Already? You can't! You have to help me plan the fete!" Lady Margrave rounded on him. "You can't be taking her off so soon, Edwin. You must stay in London until our fete."

Edwin stared her down. "I'm afraid that's impossible, madam. We think it best to retire to the country while Durand is still causing trouble. Besides, Clarissa and I mean to have a honeymoon trip, even if it's only to Hertfordshire."

The woman's eyes went wide. "Oh. Of course." Color stained her cheeks. "I hadn't thought . . . I assumed . . . Well, you must have a honeymoon trip, yes."

"I'm glad you understand," he said in a hard voice.

"Will you be all right here alone in town, Mama?" Clarissa asked anxiously. "Because you can always come and stay at home nearby."

"Don't be silly. I shall be fine. I have a fete to plan! It will be difficult without you here to help, of course, but while you pack you can tell me what you'd like, and I'll make some notes. Then I'll consult with the Sweeney sisters so we can do as much of the preparation as possible before I come out to Hertfordshire to go over the plans." She cast Edwin an apologetic look. "I will only come the once and steal her for an hour or so."

"That's fine," he said. "And as Clarissa said, if you wish to return to Hertfordshire today—"

"No, indeed." She smiled knowingly at him. "The two of you need time to yourselves." Taking her daughter's arm, she tugged her toward the door. "Indeed, before you leave, Clarissa, there are things I should tell you privately."

Edwin stifled an oath. Just what he needed—Lady Margrave putting her daughter even more on her guard concerning their wedding night. Which he would not get to have, anyway.

But it couldn't be helped. "I'll . . . er . . . wait here."

By 5:00 P.M., he was starting on his second glass of brandy when a servant knocked at the door. "My lord? That French count is here to call on Lady Clarissa."

Durand, damn him. "I'll take care of it."

Edwin marched out and down the stairs to find Durand pacing the foyer. "I'll make this short and sweet, Durand," he said as he descended. "Get out, now."

Durand visibly started. "What are *you* doing here?"

"Waiting for my wife to pack up. Hadn't you heard? Lady Clarissa and I were married this morning. And now we're headed off on our honeymoon."

The count's gaze sharpened on him. "I read the wedding announcement in the paper, but I figured it had to be a ruse. It's why I'm here."

"Well, you figured wrong. So you can go."

"I shan't take *your* word for it." Durand glanced up the stairs. "I want to speak to her ladyship myself."

"Not bloody likely. But if you must see proof, here's the special license." He waved it in front of the man. "And if this isn't good enough for you, then check the parish register at St. George's in Hanover Square, where we were married this morning."

The count's face darkened. "You couldn't be that foolish."

"I don't consider it foolish to marry a woman I've been courting."

"It is, when you know what I will do to you," Durand hissed.

"Go ahead." Edwin fought to sound nonchalant. "Then you'll force us to decamp to the Continent to avoid the scandal, and you'll never see her again. Meanwhile, your reputation as a diplomat will be tarnished, and all you'll have accomplished is the ruin of several lives, including your own." He thrust his face into Durand's. "But I'm game if you are. Do your worst."

Durand's eyes could have sliced slate, they were that hard. But he knew when he'd been backed into a corner. "You will come to regret this."

"I doubt that."

"I can cause a great deal of trouble for you. All I need do is have a few words with your wife about your father and the scandal she'll have to endure."

"Come near my wife again," Edwin growled, "and I will personally flay the flesh from your bones. Do you understand me?" He turned to the butler standing ready. "Please accompany the count to his carriage."

The servant stepped forward to lay his hand on

the man, but Durand shrugged it off. "No need—I'm leaving. But this isn't over."

As Durand clapped his hat upon his head and strode out the front door, Edwin said, "We'll see about that."

~≈~

Clarissa backed away from the stairs, shaking. Edwin had certainly not been lying about Durand. The man was clearly not right in his head. And Edwin hadn't exactly been his usual self, either.

Come near my wife again, and I will personally flay the flesh from your bones.

She didn't know whether to be thrilled or terrified by Edwin's words. She'd never guessed he could be that passionate about anything. He always seemed so calm and collected.

Well, except for that day in the library when he'd faced down Durand the first time. And at the theater, when his kisses had overwhelmed her.

She pressed her hands to her flaming cheeks. Who was Edwin? Did she even know? Was he only capable of such anger and force against the likes of Durand? Or might he unleash his temper on her, too, if she denied him her bed?

Hearing him stalk up the stairs, she hurried back into her bedchamber.

"Did you tell Edwin that you're ready for the footman to come get the trunks?" Mama asked.

Clarissa started. "No . . . I—I remembered one more thing you and I should discuss."

Coloring deeply, Mama gestured at the bed. "About the . . . well . . . you-know-what?"

"No, Mama, you covered that quite adequately," she said, fighting to keep the sarcasm from her voice.

It had taken all Clarissa's strength not to laugh bitterly at Mama's delicate explanation of what she should expect in the marital bed.

He will touch you all over your body, and you must let him because he's your husband. Try not to cry. Men hate that, and it quite withers them.

Clarissa would have to keep that in mind if she got desperate, though her sobs hadn't had any effect on the Vile Seducer. Somehow she suspected that it depended on the man, as to how he would react to tears in the bedchamber.

You will grow used to what he does. At that point, her mother had blushed furiously. *You will even grow to like it eventually. Though it will take a while to get past the embarrassment of it.*

Well, Clarissa could certainly attest to the truth of *that.* But it was the pain she most remembered, not the embarrassment. The pain and the grunting and the rough handling of her body.

Her stomach began churning. Surely Edwin would be different. Please, God, let him be different.

"Are you nearly ready?" came his deep voice from the doorway.

She jumped, then forced a smile for her new husband's benefit. "Yes. Quite ready. I was about to go tell you."

"Good. I'd like to be on our way before sunset, if we can manage it." He glanced at his pocket watch. "That gives you about an hour to—"

"Don't worry, Edwin," she quipped. "I know how you are about schedules. I shall attempt to be ready according to yours."

He winced. "Take your time."

"If I didn't know how it pained you to say such a thing, I might believe you," she said gaily.

Taking pity on him, she did her best to hurry. So the next half hour was a flurry of loading trunks and saying farewells. By the time they set off for Hertfordshire, it was still half an hour before dark. The two of them sat opposite each other, and now that they were alone together, she was nervous.

Especially since Edwin looked tired and distracted, undoubtedly unsettled by the count's visit. Should she mention it? Would Edwin deny it if she did?

She was afraid to press him just now. Her marriage didn't seem quite real. It still felt as if she and Edwin were just headed off to another social event.

Except that the event they were actually heading to was private, and he could do as he wished with her, marriage settlement or no. The part of the document about their consummation was hardly something that could be enforced, after all. Really just a request.

"I've something to tell you." Edwin looked out the window at the bustling streets. "You're probably wondering why I didn't go visit Durand before we left town, to inform him of our marriage."

She didn't want to lie, so she said nothing as she removed her hat, which was too large for comfort even in the spacious confines of Edwin's carriage.

"As it turns out," he went on, "there was no need. While you were packing, he came by to talk to you.

He couldn't believe we had wed. I made it clear that we had. And then I kicked him out of Warren's town house."

"I see." Thank heaven Edwin had told her about the incident. At least he wasn't trying to shield her from everything. This marriage might eventually prove manageable after all.

Should she continue to pretend not to have known about the count's visit? No, there were secrets enough between them already. "Actually, I wasn't sure if I should mention it, but I did overhear the end of your . . . discussion."

His gaze shot to her. "So you know that he made some idle threats."

"They didn't sound so idle to me."

The muscles of his jaw tautened. "I can handle Durand."

"You shouldn't have to." She concentrated on folding her veil about her hat. "It disturbs me that you are risking so much because of me."

"*That* is what you gleaned from my discussion with Durand?"

"Of course. He's clearly determined to make things difficult for you, and considering that all you did was step in to defend me, it hardly seems fair."

He shook his head ruefully. "You're remarkable, Clarissa."

That startled her. "Are you being sarcastic?"

"Certainly not. Here you are, being dogged by that arse Durand, yet you worry over what he'll do to *me*, a grown man who can take care of himself. By now most women would be weeping and wringing their hands, or worse yet, falling for his handsome appearance without seeing the unsettled mind behind it."

Edwin leaned forward. "But you saw him for what he was almost from the very beginning. And despite knowing that something wasn't quite right about the man, you stood up to him. You refused to let him cow you, even when he frightened you. You're a very brave woman."

Such effusive words of praise coming from Edwin made her a tiny bit wary. "Are you trying to manage *me* now, Lord Blakeborough?"

He smiled. "Is that even possible?"

"No," she said frankly. "But I suppose it would be intriguing to watch you try."

"Is it so hard to believe that I could genuinely admire you, on occasion?"

"Yes, it is. I've spent years hearing you lecture me. Why, you couldn't even refrain from chiding me for one whole night."

"Ah, yes, that reminds me. I owe you a prize for winning our wager." He drew a middling-size box from beneath the seat and held it out to her. "Open it."

The wager. She'd forgotten all about it until now. "Is it what I requested?" After removing her gloves, she took the box from him.

"Open it and see."

She did as he bade to find something encased in velvet inside. Once she parted the folds of fabric, she caught her breath.

The figurine lying there was about eight inches high and three inches wide. Blond curls peeped from beneath an enormous hat, and the lady—for it *was* a lady, very theatrically dressed in breeches and a waistcoat that failed to hide her womanly figure—was affixed to a box that had a windup key.

"An automaton!" she exclaimed.

He smiled. "I always pay my debts."

"But is it one you made yourself?"

"Just as you requested."

Delighted beyond words, Clarissa removed it from the box. "She looks like a performer. What exactly does she do?"

"Try it and find out."

After Clarissa wound it up, a lively tune played and the lady in breeches began to twirl and dip, to lift her arms and lower them in a most elaborate dance.

"Ohhh," she breathed. "She's *lovely.*"

"Yes," he said. "She is."

Clarissa glanced up to find him watching her face with that heated look that made her hands grow clammy and her cheeks hot. She jerked her gaze back to the automaton.

Suddenly the figure stopped. Was it broken? Had it already wound down? Then the lady stuck out her tongue.

Clarissa burst into laughter, even more enthralled. "Now, *that* is one cheeky dancer," she said as the figure repeated the dance again.

"Very much like the woman she's based upon," he said.

"Based upon?" Clarissa looked more closely at the dancing lady and noticed that her waistcoat had a particular design, as did the hat. Both were the same as in the costume Clarissa had worn to the masquerade last year.

She gasped. "You didn't!"

"I did."

"It's *me*? But when could you . . . how could you . . . I mean, surely you didn't have time to create it in the past day or so."

"I made it nearly a year ago, because Yvette wanted to give you something special last Christmas. She used a fashion doll and dictated every aspect of the attire. Then I altered the figure to suit. But I couldn't get it completed in time for Christmas, so Yvette had to choose you another present. Since then, it has sat in my study. I was going to ask my sister if she still wanted to give it to you, but then you wanted one and . . ."

"It's wonderful. And I suppose it does look a bit like me."

"But not as pretty. I can't work miracles, after all."

She cast him a coy look. "That's two compliments in less than an hour. You're turning into a veritable flatterer, Edwin."

"I shall have to chastise you for something right away," he drawled. "Wouldn't want you to grow complacent."

With a chuckle, she returned to examining the automaton. As the dancer wound down, she peered beneath the waistcoat, trying to glimpse the mechanism.

"She has a hidden secret," he said, after a moment.

"Does she? Where?"

"See if you can find it."

Clarissa looked all around the figure, but she was afraid to move too many parts for fear of breaking it. "At least give me a hint."

He crossed to Clarissa's side of the carriage and drew off his gloves. Taking Clarissa's finger and placing it beneath the back of the voluminous hat, he had her press up on the brim from beneath. A cascade of golden tresses fell out of the hat and down to the figure's waist.

"Oh!" she said. "That's marvelous!"

He twined one finger about the hair. "That night at the masquerade I kept hoping your hair would fall out of your hat, and I would finally get a glimpse of it unpinned."

With a catch in her throat, she looked up at him. He sat so close now, his eyes shimmering in the fading light of dusk and his breath wafting over her.

Then he added, in a husky voice, "I would give anything to see your hair down."

She swallowed convulsively. "I'm sure that can be arranged," she managed through a throat suddenly gone dry.

With his gaze boring into hers, he took the automaton from her and placed it on the seat behind him, then began to remove the pins from her coiffure.

"You mean to do it *now*?" she asked. "What will the servants think when I disembark from the carriage looking like a trollop from the streets?"

"They'll think we're newly married. Which we are."

When he tugged at a pin that stubbornly resisted his efforts, she said, "Stop that. Let me."

As she took out her pins, he caught the locks that fell, twining them loosely about his hands, rubbing them between his fingers. "Your hair is like gilded silk thread."

She gave a shaky laugh. "When did you become so poetic?"

"When my wife told me I had to learn how to pay a woman compliments." He kissed one of her curls. "I'm not very good at it yet."

"You're good enough," she said softly.

His gaze played over her face, searching, drinking in. Then he clasped her head in his hands and brought his mouth down on hers.

Oh, heavens. This kiss was decidedly different from the one they'd shared in the church—sweeter, hotter . . . more intimate. She parted her lips for him, and with a groan, he plunged his tongue deep.

That's when everything got more interesting. He kissed like a marauder of old, plundering and taking and turning her into mush with every long, hot thrust of his tongue. She caught him by the neck; he caught her by the waist. He swept his hand up to thumb her nipple through her gown; she swept hers up to fondle his beautiful raven hair that cascaded luxuriously over her fingers.

His free hand skimmed her as if looking for chinks in her armor. And there were many; right now her armor might as well be made of paper.

Burying his mouth in her neck, he gave a sort of sucking kiss to the delicate skin that sent a thrill down to her toes. When she gripped his head, he said, "Do you like that?"

"I'm not sure. It's different."

"I want to touch you beneath your skirts." He nuzzled her jaw with his whisker-rough face. "Will you let me?"

Beneath her skirts. Oh no. That was how things started to go awry. "I . . . I don't know."

He must have sensed her alarm, for he stilled. "What if I just kiss you, then?"

"Yes, oh yes." Relief coursed through her. "Kissing is good. I like kissing."

"So do I." To her surprise, instead of seizing her mouth again, he slid off the seat and onto the floor of the carriage.

When he started pushing her skirts up, she grabbed his hands. "Wait, I thought you were going to kiss me!"

"I am." His eyes gleamed up at her in the thin light of dusk. "But here." Parting the long slit in one pantalets leg, he pressed a kiss to the inside of her bare knee. "And here." He kissed the thigh above it. "And definitely here." He kissed the other thigh higher up.

An errant shiver swept down her. "I see," she managed, though she didn't see at all. It hadn't occurred to her that kissing could be done . . . down there. Or that it could feel so intoxicating. The Vile Seducer had certainly never bestowed any kisses on that part of her.

Edwin's head was practically in her lap now, and for some reason it felt less alarming than when he was sitting on the seat beside her. His privates were nowhere near hers, only his mouth. He couldn't really hurt her with his mouth, could he?

Unless . . . "You're not going to bite me, are you?"

He chuckled. "No, I swear." Rubbing her linen-clad thighs with his hands, he said, "Open your legs for me, my sweet, and I'll do things to you that make you feel good. Things that you'll like. And naught else, I swear."

Only the fact that he was kneeling and she was seated made her willing to let him try. She opened her legs a little and was rewarded with a series of soft, delicate kisses to her inner thighs inside the long openings in her drawers.

To her shock, that excited her quite a lot. It frightened her a bit, too, but beneath the fright simmered a hot thrill that made her heart race.

Then he placed his mouth right upon her privates.

"Edwin!" she squeaked. "Are you . . . sure about this?"

Ignoring her question, he began to kiss and lick her down there. Inside her pantalets. Between her legs. His mouth covered her soft flesh, teasing and stroking her tenderly. It felt *shockingly* good.

"That is . . . more than kissing . . ." She let out a little moan when he flicked with his tongue right at the top of her cleft. Her body arched high, craving more. "Heavens, Edwin!"

She was still marveling at how amazing it felt when suddenly, his tongue darted inside her. She tensed a little, but his thrusts were silken and sweet, devoid of pain. Full of the purest pleasure. Oh, *Lord*.

The fear still lay in a knot at the center of her, but the longer he caressed her with his mouth, the more she was able to push it down. Soon she was clutching his head to her, urging him to greater boldness. "You are very good at . . . whatever this is."

He paused to glance up at her. "I've had enough opportunities to study seduction to know what I'm doing."

She could well guess why, but she didn't care what women he'd been with before. All right, she cared a little. Just not right now. Not if they'd taught him *this*.

Her body tingled, felt alive and full to bursting. She shimmied beneath him, trying to get more.

"You taste delicious," he growled against her.

"Do I?" What he was doing to her was certainly delicious. "You are . . . oh . . . that is . . . *incredible*."

Who'd have guessed such a thing would make her want to press herself against his mouth like a shameless tart? The urge to squirm grew almost unbearable, and her lower body seemed to move of its own accord, seeking more of the amazing sensations, more of the heat and intoxication. A wildly drumming thrill built inside her, pounding and thrumming and making her strain to feel every caress of the sweet, hard lashes of his tongue until . . . until . . .

"Edwin! Lord, yes, *Edwin*!" She clasped his head against her privates as lights exploded behind her eyes.

Then she tumbled over into a most delicious oblivion.

Fifteen

When Edwin felt Clarissa convulse beneath his mouth, he exulted. He *could* make her feel pleasure. And since that was possible, then all of it was possible. He'd just have to take special care with her.

Perhaps he'd have his wedding night after all.

Smiling against her luscious skin, he nuzzled her thigh, drunk on the smell of her, the taste of her. His wife. She might run him a merry dance, but they would have this, at least.

Her fingers loosened their grip on his head, and she uttered a drawn-out sigh. "Oh my. My, my, my."

Chuckling, he wiped his mouth on her drawers. "Yes."

"Mama most certainly did not tell me about that."

He gazed up at her. "What *did* she tell you?"

"Not much; she was blushing too hard. But I already knew . . . some of it, anyway. Just not this."

"Who told you?"

It was too dark now to see her face, but he could feel her muscles tense beneath his hands, which were still resting on her thighs. "Oh, girls talk about these things, you know."

"Really? And what do they say?"

"Oh, this and that and the other. You wouldn't want to know."

She pushed on his shoulders and he drew back, only to have her pull her legs together and jerk her skirts down to cover them.

"Ah, but I would like to know." With his erection still thick in his trousers, he rose to sit beside her and put his hand on her waist. "Why don't you tell me?" He brushed a kiss to her cheek. "Then I can show you which things they were wrong about. And which things they didn't even know."

She shifted away from him to look out the window. "Oh, b-but surely we're getting near to home. It's been ever so long since we left London."

Her withdrawal was too obvious to mistake, and he bit down on the impulse to push her, to demand answers. That wasn't the way to handle a skittish female.

But now that he thought about it, wasn't her reaction odd? Clarissa was never skittish about anything. She threw herself into every adventure, embraced every experience, was often too reckless for his taste.

So why be afraid of this? Unless . . .

"Durand didn't do anything to you in Bath, did he?" he asked hoarsely.

Her head swung around. "Like what?" There seemed to be genuine surprise in her voice.

"Like overstep his bounds."

"Oh. No, of course not. I mean, he stole a kiss once or twice, but no, nothing like that."

"That surprises me. He hasn't seemed to be good about staying within any boundaries heretofore, and he tried to push a kiss on you that day in the library."

Crossing her arms over her chest, she slid back into the corner, into the shadows. "That was the first time he was rough with me. Before then, he was persistent in his attentions, but a gentleman. I think my unprecedented absence from London must have provoked him."

Hmm. "So he never forced himself on you."

"No. Certainly not."

He digested that in silence a moment. She sounded perfectly truthful. And he was usually good at detecting lies, especially after years of dealing with his untrustworthy younger brother.

"Then why do you shy away from me?" He hadn't meant to ask the question, but now that he had, he refused to take it back.

"I—I don't." She settled her shoulders. "For pity's sake, you were just under my skirts."

"And now I'm not."

He could hear her breathing come harder in the dark of the carriage. She seemed to shrink into herself. "You agreed to my terms. To get to know each other better, to be amiable before we become too intimate."

"Yes, but we have already become more intimate than most." He moved closer. "Why do you seem to enjoy my attentions one minute, and then panic at them the next?"

"You're imagining that," she said, but her voice rang hollow.

"I'm not imagining the clause you made me add to the settlement. I'm not imagining the hairbrush you brandished at me at the theater." He bent toward her, deliberately crowding her with his body, just to see how she'd react. "I know that you feel desire for me sometimes, Clarissa, and I can't understand—"

"Get off of me!" She shoved at him. "Get off, get off, *get off!*"

The violence of her words startled him so much that he threw himself across into the other seat. When he could speak again, he said, "I'm certainly not imagining that."

For a moment silence filled the carriage, punctuated by her shuddering gasps for air. Then, it was as if she'd brought a veil down over her face. Her breathing evened out, and she straightened in her seat, smoothing her skirts as he'd seen her do a hundred times.

"I told you," she said, her voice calmer, though still threaded with tension. "I'm not . . . the affectionate sort. It's nothing to do with you. I simply don't like people being too close to me. I find it overwhelming."

But not when you kiss me.

He didn't speak the words. He'd learned long ago with his sister that if you boxed a woman in with logical arguments and she didn't want to hear it, she struck out. Or retreated into silence, which would gain him nothing. So he just waited for her to speak again, hoping she would feel free to go on. Because there was more to the story. He was sure of it.

Unfortunately, when she spoke again, it was to withdraw from him even further. "I will grow used to it in time."

Grow *used to it*? He didn't want a wife who had to brace herself to be bedded. It reminded him painfully of his mother, how she had reacted to his father for a long time after that horrible day in the drawing room. How she'd jumped when her children came up behind her, cringed at Father's touch.

How the gulf between his mother and his father had grown deeper and wider by the day. Damn it, that was not what he'd wanted for his marriage—all that roiling, suppressed anger and unmet needs.

But if Clarissa wouldn't talk to him about her fears, then he didn't know what to do.

"Do the servants know that we got married?" she asked.

The abrupt change of subject made him want to grab her and shake her, to demand to know why she could only let him touch her so far and no more, why she got panicky when he crowded her in. Why she only liked his touch when he was kissing her, and for anything more, he must be behind her or under her skirts . . .

He choked down bile. What if *that* was what it was? As long as she didn't really have to look at him, she could close her eyes and pretend he was someone else when he grew more intimate. What if she simply disliked *him*?

God, he was being ridiculous. She responded to his kisses with passion; she grew aroused when he touched her. He wasn't so terrible a judge of women that he couldn't tell *that*.

And this was precisely why he'd wanted to marry some dull chit in the first place! This was why he'd wanted a mere companion for a wife. Because this seething mass of emotion was too much. He didn't like it.

"Well?" she asked. "Do the servants know?"

He gritted his teeth. "Yes. I sent them a letter at the same time I put the notice in the papers."

Fine. He'd do things her way for a while. Spend time with her. Deal with incorporating a new wife into his estate. Try to control his runaway desire to bed her.

Court her.

He started. He *hadn't* really courted her, had he? He'd just rushed her into a marriage. And every time in the past that he *had* done something vaguely courtship-like, it had ended in a most pleasurable interlude. The night at the theater. Just now with the automaton. Each time, he was able to get a little further with her.

Interesting. Apparently women liked thoughtful gifts and compliments. *She* liked thoughtful gifts and compliments.

Very well, then that was what he would do. Court her properly. Take the lessons she'd given him for courting other women and apply them to her.

"I do hope your staff don't mind having me as a mistress," Clarissa said.

The hesitation in her voice firmed his resolve. He could do this. Make her comfortable with him. And perhaps not too long from now, she would be ready to reveal what made her so frightened of sharing his bed.

"I'm sure they will be delighted to have someone

as accomplished as you running the household," he said smoothly.

At least now he had a strategy to pursue.

The first thing Clarissa noticed when she entered the dining room two hours later was the rose lying across her plate. The second thing was Edwin, looking breathtaking in his black superfine and snowy cravat, standing at the other end of the table and watching her with the intensity that always made her shiver deliciously.

Guilt stabbed her anew. She hadn't had a moment alone with him since their arrival. The staff had bombarded her with enthusiastic welcomes and then had ushered her up to dress for dinner in the suite of rooms meant to be hers. Amidst the chaos of unpacking and dressing, there'd been little time to dwell on her appalling behavior in the carriage.

But now, alone with him at dinner, she could no longer ignore it. Struggling for what to say, she took her seat and picked up the rose to sniff it. "How lovely." She strove for a light tone. "Should I expect one of these *every* evening at dinner?"

"That can be arranged."

His unconscious echo of her words earlier that had sparked their intimate interlude renewed her guilt. She had overreacted. Badly. She had to stop acting like a frightened ninny with him. She already had him asking questions she wasn't ready to answer.

She *would* tell him everything eventually. Just as soon as she got her bearings in their marriage.

Coward.

"That's a fetching gown," he said conversationally.

The polite nicety startled her, especially coming from Edwin. But at least she knew how to play that game. "Thank you. It's one of my favorites." She settled her napkin in her lap. "You look rather splendid yourself this evening."

She rather wished he didn't. Because whenever he looked good enough to tempt her, it always seemed to end in disaster.

Well, not *always*. The part in the carriage where he'd pleasured her had been incredible. It was her own stupid fault that things had deteriorated from there. And she *hated* that. She hated being weak and afraid.

The footman placed a bowl of soup in front of her. "This looks delicious," she said, fearing that she sounded utterly inane.

"If there are any particular foods you would prefer, just tell Cook." Edwin sipped some soup from his spoon. "I believe you're already familiar with her abilities."

"I should say so." She picked up her spoon. "Your mother chose her well."

"Mother was always very good at hiring servants." He glanced at her. "And I'm sure you'll be equally adept at it."

His oddly soothing tone made her halt her spoon in midair. "I shall certainly try to be."

"That's all I ask. And with that in mind, I was thinking that tomorrow we might tour our dairy and then the orchards."

"I've been in your dairy and your orchards more

times than I can count." Why was he behaving as if she hadn't visited Stoke Towers nearly every day in her youth? "I'm not sure what more I could learn from a tour."

A small frown knit his brow. "Very well, then we can call on the tenants so I may introduce you to them as my wife."

"That's an excellent idea. We should start with the Gronows. No, wait, perhaps the Leslies up near the river—Mrs. Leslie has probably had her baby by now, and I would so love to see it."

He sat back to stare at her. "How is it that you know almost as much about my tenants as Yvette?"

She shrugged. "I spent nearly every day of my childhood with her here."

"I knew you and Yvette were close, but I had no idea you were at Stoke Towers so much."

"How could you know? You were away at school; then I was away at school. And when I *was* home, you were too busy to pay much mind to a couple of girls romping about and going shopping in Preston."

"Ah, yes. I forgot about all the shopping."

"I can't imagine how. You were forever lecturing Yvette about the bills."

He stiffened. "You two thought me insufferable, I suppose."

"What? No. We knew you were preoccupied by your father's neglect of the estate, and by Samuel and his troubles. You had no time to spare for two chattering girls preparing for their debuts. Besides, you were always very serious and studious and we were always . . . well . . . not."

He eyed her askance. "Yvette was studious. *You* were 'not.'"

She couldn't help laughing. "Now, *that* is the blunt and honest Edwin I know and like so well."

To her surprise, he flushed. "Blast it, I was trying *not* to be so blunt."

"Why? We've always been honest with each other, haven't we? That shouldn't change simply because we're married. How does Shakespeare put it? 'Thou and I are too wise to woo peaceably.'"

"God, I hope that's not true."

The words fell between them like a gauntlet. Too late, she remembered the requirements he'd listed for a wife when she'd been helping him decide on one.

"Right," she said past the tightness in her throat. "You wanted a quiet, responsible, and calming wife. Instead, you got me."

He grimaced. "That isn't what I meant. I was only saying . . . *trying* to say, that I hope you and I . . ." Rubbing the back of his neck, he muttered, "God rot it. Pay me no mind. I'm a bit out of sorts."

She took pity on him. This was as hard for him as for her—perhaps even harder. He was doing a very noble thing and, in the process, giving up his own plans for the future.

"So," she said, determined to change the subject, "a visit to the tenants tomorrow. That sounds fun. What shall I wear?"

He met her gaze, seemingly startled by her amiable tone, then smoothed his expression. "Well, it's probably best if we go on horseback, so a riding habit would be appropriate. And if you happen to have . . ."

To her vast relief, there was no more talk of anything serious after that.

But later, once her giggling maid had left her dressed for bed and she sat propped up against the pillow attempting to read the latest *La Belle Assemblée*, she wondered if he would try to seduce her tonight. If he did, would she let him?

Part of her wanted to. The other part hated that she couldn't predict how she would react, once he came over on top of her and tried to enter her. She didn't think she could bear to witness again the shock on his face if she got panicky and said or did something untoward.

So when the door adjoining his room opened and she instinctively clutched her magazine to her breasts, she could have kicked herself to see frustration flash in his eyes.

Though it was swiftly gone, it left her chilled.

"I wanted to make sure you were comfortable before I retired," he said with infinite politeness, as if they were mere friends who happened to share a bedroom suite, rather than a newly wedded couple who ought to be consummating their marriage.

"Quite comfortable." She deliberately let the periodical drop onto her lap, not wanting him to think she was frightened of him. She wasn't . . . not entirely. "I shan't be up much longer. I'm quite tired."

"I would imagine so."

He continued to stand there a moment, as if unsure what to do. And Lord, he looked so much more approachable in a dressing gown than in his usual oh-so-correct attire. It dawned on her that she hadn't yet seen even a portion of him undressed.

No glimpse of what seemed to be a rather broad chest. No glance at what were probably quite fine arms. And just the thought of what he might look like without his clothes on sparked her curiosity.

Until she remembered what else she hadn't seen yet. The part she dreaded to look upon, much less feel pushing and tearing its way inside her.

"Clarissa, earlier, when I said—"

"It's fine. I knew what you meant."

He halted, his jaw going rigid. "Of course you did."

"Good night, Edwin," she said firmly. "I'll see you in the morning."

"Yes." He swept his gaze over her with a thoroughness that did nothing to soothe her. "Sleep well."

Then he was gone, shutting the door behind him.

She ignored her swift pang of disappointment. If she encouraged his desire—and her own—tonight, only to end up cutting him off again . . .

No, better to wait until she knew she was ready. She blew out the candle.

Still, it took her a long time to go to sleep, and when she did, she slid seamlessly into a dream.

A forest rose before her, dark and gloomy. She didn't want to go inside, but she had to. It was crucial that she enter, though she couldn't figure out why. The deeper she wandered into the forest the colder she got, until she reached a black lake that glistened in the light of the moon overhead.

She dipped her toe into the water. It was surprisingly warm, so much warmer than the forest. It would be lovely to go in and get warm. Slowly, she walked into the lake, sinking into the warmth.

Then something grabbed her leg beneath the surface and began pulling her toward the center, which had become a whirlpool, swirling faster and harder by the moment. She struggled to swim back to shore but she couldn't fight the current, which was pulling her down, down into the whirling void, down into the black, into the depths where she would surely drown . . .

She awoke on a scream. It took her a moment to catch her bearings, and by the time she did, the door swung open and Edwin appeared in the doorway, disheveled and wild-eyed and holding a lit candle.

"Bloody hell, Clarissa, are you all right?" He lifted the candle to scan the room as if searching for intruders.

"It was just a nightmare," she said hastily, starting to feel like a fool. "I . . . I get nervous in new places," she lied. "That's all."

"It sounded far worse than that." He stepped farther into the room.

The firelight now caught him fully, and she swallowed. He wore nothing but his drawers—no nightshirt, no nightcap, nothing but a thin layer of linen that covered him from low on his hips to his knees. And he was as well made as any woman could want—muscular chest, flat stomach, and very impressive calves. Not to mention arms that looked as if they could lift anything.

Or hold down anyone.

She shuddered. He wouldn't hurt her. She couldn't believe that he would. "I'm fine," she whispered. "Truly I am."

"You're shaking."

"I'm a bit chilly, is all. I dreamed of drowning."

The sympathy on his face sliced right through her fear. "Do you want me to stay?" When she hesitated, afraid to say yes, but not wanting to be alone, he added, "I'll sit right over there in that chair until you go back to sleep. If you'd like."

"It hardly seems fair to you—"

"Don't worry about that. I know how upsetting nightmares can be. I had a great many as a boy. And my mother would sit with me and rub my back until I could go to sleep." He approached the bed slowly. "I'll do the same for you, if you like."

"Edwin—"

"*Just* rub your back. I promise. Nothing more."

She let out a long breath. "That sounds lovely."

His smile of pure relief tugged at her somewhere down deep, where she rarely let anyone in. So when he came to sit beside her on the bed, and urged her to turn onto her stomach, she willingly gave herself up to his hands.

As he began to knead her shoulders through her nightdress, she moaned. "Ohhh. That is *wonderful*."

He rubbed her muscles expertly. "So, tell me about this nightmare. You were drowning?"

"Mmm," she said, her fear of the dream already fading, "I'd rather put it from my mind. Tell me about *your* nightmares. Somehow I always imagined you as a stalwart little boy afraid of nothing. What did you dream about that frightened you?"

"Skeletons."

She shifted her head to look up at him. "Skeletons? Truly?"

"Well, they started out as people when they came

after me. But then the flesh would melt from their bones until they were nothing more than skeletons lumbering toward me with their bones creaking." He shuddered.

"Good Lord, that's a rather macabre dream for a little boy."

"I suspect it started when I saw a puppet show at a fair, which featured a skeleton puppet dancing about the stage and scaring the audience. I dreamed of them for a few years after."

"You poor thing!"

"Actually, it's why I became interested in Father's automatons. They scared me because they vaguely reminded me of my nightmares, so I deliberately started examining them, determined to get past my fear. Before long I became genuinely interested in figuring out how they worked. The more I knew, the more fascinated I got, and before long, the dreams stopped."

"I do hope you're not going to suggest that I try swimming in a dark lake in the middle of a forest to learn to get past my nightmare."

He chuckled. "No. That doesn't sound wise *or* safe."

She relaxed against the pillow. "Good. Because I can't swim."

"Perhaps I'll teach you sometime. Just not at a dark lake in the middle of the forest."

"No," she murmured, then yawned.

His motions grew slower, more soothing. "Better now?"

"Mmm. Much better." Her eyes slid closed. "Tell me more about when you were a boy."

He started into a story about his first time on a horse, normally a tale that she might find entertaining, but soon his words began to melt together into one long droning, and before long she fell asleep.

That night there were no more dreams of any kind. And when she woke the next morning, he was gone.

Sixteen

Days later, Edwin sat at the breakfast table early in the morning, scouring the *Times* for any evidence that Durand might have made good on his threats. So far there had been no whiff of that, thank God.

He drank some of his tea. Hard to believe that he and Clarissa had been married almost a week. After the night of the blood-curdling scream, after seeing the terror that leapt in her eyes when she first saw him enter her room, he thought it prudent to retreat from any overt physical advances until she was willing to reveal what made her so frightened.

At least he was making progress. Though she hadn't had any more nightmares, she let him sit with her at night, rub her back, and talk to her about their day. It was an exquisite agony to be so close to her without being the least bit intimate, but he'd done his best not to think about that. He'd taken to going for long, hard rides through the countryside to release his pent-up desire. And when that didn't work, he pleasured himself.

It was ridiculous, really. He'd gone months before without bedding a woman, and now all he could think about was making love to his wife. Undoubtedly because he knew he couldn't. It had nothing to do with how fetching she looked in her night rail. Or how her merry laugh could instantly brighten his day. Or how her every motion seemed designed to seduce—

"Good morning!" said a cheery voice from the doorway.

Speak of the devil. She was of course wearing some treat of a gown that made him think of strawberries gilded with cream. That he wanted to devour.

He shifted uncomfortably in his seat. "You're up early." He frowned. "Not another bad dream, I hope."

"No. I just . . . couldn't sleep."

Picking up the orange he hadn't eaten, he asked, "Want me to peel this for you?"

She made a face. "I despise oranges and anything to do with them. The smell of them alone makes me sick."

"Then I'd best dispose of this one." He aimed at the open window and lobbed the orange right through it.

"It never ceases to amaze me how good you are at judging distances and trajectories." She cocked her head. "Are you trying to impress me again, sir?"

"If lobbing oranges through windows impresses you," he said, "I have a bowl of fruit I can juggle."

She laughed. Coming over to sit next to him, instead of at the far end of the table, she saw the newspaper and sobered. "Anything in the *Times* to worry about?"

"Not that I could find."

"Perhaps Durand has given up."

"I doubt that. He's probably plotting something—we just don't know what it is yet."

"Well, Mr. Doom and Gloom," she said teasingly, "I think it's time we got you out of the house."

He eyed her with suspicion. "Why?"

"Because you need more entertainment than throwing oranges. You need a dose of sun and warmth and leisurely exercise. We should do something fun in the outdoors."

How he hoped that her idea of fun and his were the same. But somehow he doubted it. "What did you have in mind? Swimming?" *Naked, preferably.* "Going for a drive?" *To somewhere they could be naked.* "Riding?" *Please let it be riding. But not on a horse. And definitely naked.*

"I thought perhaps we could have a picnic."

He blinked. "A picnic! Why would we do that when we have decent food right here in the dining room, served up on plates by well-paid servants?"

She rolled her eyes. "Where is your sense of adventure, Lord Blakeborough?"

"I don't have one."

"Nonsense. Everyone has a sense of adventure if the situation is right." She pushed the newspaper aside. "In this case, we'll start with something less challenging—a walk through the deer park, perhaps. I've already charged Cook with packing a picnic lunch for us, and after our stroll, we can have our luncheon by the stream between our estates."

"Along with the flies and the snails."

"I thought you liked the outdoors. You ride all the time."

"Yes. Going neck-or-nothing with the wind in my face. Not sitting on the damp ground, surrounded by spiderwebs and squawking crows while I eat cold ham from a basket."

"I had no idea you were so missish, Edwin."

He scowled. "I am not missish. I just prefer my comfortable house to the vagaries of a forest."

"Fine. Then I'll go by myself."

"You will not! Durand might be skulking about somewhere."

She eyed him askance.

"Very well." He sighed. "We'll go on your 'picnic.' Though it seems rather silly to me."

Nonetheless, a short time later, he was tramping through his land with a basket on one arm and his wife on the other. And surprisingly, he was enjoying himself. The sun brightened the barley fields, the sparrows were chirping, and every beech was in bud.

After a while, he found himself telling her about the various parts of the estate and the roe deer that lived in the park. She mustn't have found it too boring, for she listened and nodded and asked questions.

It wasn't long before three very enjoyable hours had passed. They headed to the stream to have their picnic, which he was still rather skeptical about. But when he saw her spread out a blanket, it cheered him. Blankets could double as beds, after all.

While she began to unpack the basket, he scanned their surroundings. To keep from dwelling on how lovely she looked beneath the dappled light of the trees, he said, "It seems that the flies and snails are absent just now."

"You know perfectly well that it's too early in the season for either." She shifted to look out at the water and grew pensive. "I've always loved this stream. At this time of day, it glistens like a fairy highway leading to a magical realm."

He snorted.

Planting her hands on her hips, she said, "So you have no sense of adventure *and* no sense of whimsy."

"Neither one, I'm afraid." He peered at the impressive number of chicken sandwiches, the wedge of Stilton, the jar of pickles, and what appeared to be apple tarts wrapped in paper. "What I have is a prodigious appetite. And it looks as if Cook has packed all my favorites. I suppose that was your doing?"

She laughed. "As if Cook doesn't know every single one of your preferences. That woman is a jewel."

"We certainly agree on that."

Some time later, after they'd both eaten their fill, he lay back on the blanket Clarissa had spread for them and crossed his arms beneath his head while she tidied up. It really was rather nice here. That was a surprise.

She glanced over at him, and mischief sparked in her eyes. "My, my, do I detect a smile?"

He tried to stifle it, but it was too late. "Perhaps."

"You're having fun, aren't you?"

"I suppose I am."

"I was sure you would." Beaming her triumph, she stretched out on the blanket beside him. "I know you better than you think."

"I doubt that. I daresay I know far more about you than you do about me."

She turned on her side to look at him. "Really? That sounds like a challenge to me. And as I recall, I won our last challenge."

He cocked an eyebrow at her. "Very well, a challenge, then. Same terms as before. If you win, you get another automaton. You can even dictate what type and watch me make it. But if *I* win, you have to wear breeches at dinner."

"Why do men love to see a woman in breeches?"

"I'll explain it to you when you do it."

She sniffed. "*If* I do it, which is by no means certain since I plan to win this challenge. Though it would help if we had some rules."

"How about this? We take turns asking each other questions about our own likes and dislikes, and the first one to answer wrong loses."

Her eyes narrowed on him. "All right. Since you laid down the challenge, I'll start. Which do I prefer—prawns or fish?"

"Prawns. Which do *I* prefer?"

"Neither. You don't like to eat anything that swims."

He scowled. "That shouldn't count. You've been consulting with Cook over dinner every night. I'd be surprised if you *didn't* know of my dislike of seafood."

"Hah! You simply can't stand losing." She tapped her chin. "Let me see, what else can I ask . . . What sort of jewelry do I like—gold or pearls?"

"Since I've never seen you wear a pearl in your life, I'll have to say gold." When she chuckled, he said flippantly, "What sort of jewelry do *I* like—gold or pearls?"

"If you start wearing pearls, I shall leave you," she said with a laugh. "And you like blue sapphires and gold. I've only ever seen you wear a sapphire stick-pin. With gold cuff links."

He smiled. "I ought to have realized you would notice such a thing, given your love of fashion. But here's a hard one. What political party do I support? Tell me that, if you can."

"You're an ardent supporter of the Tories." When he frowned, she said gleefully, "I'm right, aren't I? And I'll bet you don't know which party I support."

"Do *you* know which party you support?" He'd never once heard her mention politics.

"How many are there, again?" At his shocked look, she said, "I'm joking, you fool. Of course I know which party I support. Now tell me which it is."

He had to think about that. But Warren was a Tory, and given her propensity to be contrary . . . "You support the Whigs."

She poked him in the chest. "You just guessed, didn't you?"

"I told you," he said smugly. "I know you very well."

"We'll see about that." She knit her brow in deep concentration, then brightened. "Here's one you'll never guess. What's my favorite play?"

"That's far too general a question to be fair. There's hundreds to choose from. But just to show I'm a good sport, I'll take a stab at it." He pretended to be unsure. "*Much Ado about Nothing?*"

Her mouth fell open. "How could you possibly have known that?"

"You quoted it at dinner the first night of our marriage. And generally, if someone knows something well enough to quote it, it's a favorite." He leaned toward her gleefully. "What's *my* favorite play?"

She scowled, recognizing the trap. "As you said, there's hundreds."

"Yet I knew yours. Come now, give an answer."

She threw herself back on the blanket. "You're a wicked man, Edwin Barlow."

"Yes, I am. And I'm powerfully eager to see you wear breeches to dinner. What's my favorite play, minx?"

"It has to be something dry and dull. A history play, perhaps. *Richard III.* No, wait, *The Merchant of Venice.* It has those mechanical boxes in it."

He gave her a superior look. "Actually, it's not Shakespeare."

"What? Of course it's Shakespeare. Who else is there?"

"It's *She Stoops to Conquer.* Oliver Goldsmith."

She sat up to gape at him. "No!"

"Yes. It makes me laugh. And yes, occasionally I do like to laugh. So you see, Miss I-Know-Every-thing-about-You, you *don't* know everything about me." He grinned at her. "And I have won."

"That is the most . . . most . . ." she sputtered. "It's not . . ."

"To quote my wife, 'You simply can't stand losing.'"

She glared at him. He chuckled. She looked so adorably put out at the idea that he'd won.

"Fine," she said primly. "I shall wear breeches to dinner. But only if you tell me why it's so dratted important. Why *do* men like to see women in breeches?"

He leaned over to whisper, "Because what we

really like is to see women in their drawers. And it's the closest we can get to that without bedding them."

"Ohhh," she said. "That makes sense."

Though her cheeks pinkened, she didn't flinch from his gaze or look panicked by his nearness. And when he lowered his head toward her and her eyes turned sultry, his breath caught in his throat.

It had been a week since he'd kissed her, a week since he'd touched her. And she was acting as if she might welcome a kiss.

There was only one way to find out.

The minute his mouth touched hers, she opened to him, welcoming the duel of tongues, meeting him stroke for stroke. She did want him. Finally.

But perhaps he should do another test before he allowed himself to believe she was ready for this. So he covered her breast with his hand.

She didn't even shy away. If anything she pressed up into the caress, her hands sliding up to encircle his neck.

Thank God. She was his. *At last*. He'd been patient, and this was his reward. Aroused and inflamed, he wanted to throw caution to the winds, rip her clothes off her, and cover every inch of her with kisses and caresses.

Take care, man. You must be very gentle with her. Whatever you do, don't frighten her off.

That was going to be damned difficult. Because he'd never desired a woman more than he desired his wife at this very moment. And he feared that the mere fact of his desiring her too much might send her running.

Seventeen

Clarissa liked this part, having Edwin touch her and kiss her and heat her up. She could endure the painful part just for this. She *would*, drat it. She refused to spend her marriage afraid of the very activity that marriage was created for.

She refused to be denied children just because of her fears.

She'd planned their picnic so that she could seduce Edwin somewhere she'd feel comfortable. Somewhere safe, outdoors, with plenty of light and air around her, but private, too, here in the woods. Somewhere she wouldn't panic, because all she'd have to do was scream to bring someone running.

Somewhere utterly different from the place where she'd been deflowered.

As soon as the thought leapt into her mind, she thrust it out. The Vile Seducer was dead. He couldn't hurt her ever again. And Edwin *wouldn't* hurt her—not intentionally, anyway.

Edwin tugged her pelerine off, then took his time

unfastening her redingote gown, which had far too many ties in the front. By the time he had her bosom bared, she was desperate to have his hands on her there.

His *mouth* on her, which he was putting there now. Oh, *Lord*. She could lie here all day while he teased her breasts, especially since he wasn't on top of her, but propped up on his side next to her. "You do that . . . so well," she murmured, burying her fingers in his luscious hair. "It's heavenly."

"It certainly is," he said in a guttural voice.

He sucked and tongued her nipples in turn, then moved up to give her another hot, drugging kiss while his hand took over fondling her breast. When he tore free of her mouth, both of them were breathing hard, and she felt warm and melty inside.

With his eyes gleaming, he began to drag up her skirts. "I've imagined having you like this for ages."

She tried not to tense up as his hand moved higher, though fear lay deep inside her like a snake waiting to strike. "For a week . . . you mean."

"Years, I mean."

She gaped at him. "What?"

"I told you before—I always desired you." He gave her a rueful smile. "I just didn't think it terribly wise."

"It's not," she said. Though if he really had desired her all this time, it gave her hope for their future together.

"You let me be the judge of that." Then he kissed her again, and her heart flipped over.

Suddenly she felt his hand inside her drawers, but before she could even get alarmed, his fingers were toying with her down there so lightly and carefully that her fear abated. Especially when he found that secret little spot that begged to be touched, the one she hadn't even known existed until he came along.

As he'd done with his tongue in the carriage, he used his hand to excellent effect, arousing her deftly, thoroughly, until she was squirming and shimmying beneath his touch. She tore at his coat, wanting him to be as exposed as her, and he shrugged it off, then returned to caressing her. She unbuttoned his waistcoat and slid her hands inside his shirt to feel the broad, strong expanse of chest.

Heavens, he had a fine and manly chest. She found his nipples and teased them until he groaned and stroked her more firmly below. She didn't mind. Especially when what he was doing made her want to vault up into the trees, to sing and shake and behave like a wild wanton. With him.

How could she have known Edwin could do these things? Who would have thought that being with a man could feel this pleasurable?

"You're so hot and wet, minx," he rasped against her lips. "You *do* want me."

"Yes." She did, she truly did.

Taking her hand, he pressed it to his trousers. "This is how badly I want *you*."

He was thick and hard and bigger than she'd ever imagined. She swallowed the beginnings of alarm that rose in her throat. Determined to face her fears, she deliberately unbuttoned his trousers, then his drawers, and slid her hand inside to fondle him.

With a moan, he pushed into her hand. "God, yes, sweetheart. Touch me. Please."

Please. How deliciously thrilling that she could make him beg! She rubbed and stroked him, reveling in the choked sounds he made, the way his breath quickened and his eyes slid shut. His skin was so silky, the flesh beneath it so firm.

She was enjoying arousing him when he brushed her hand away. "No more, my sweet, or I'll embarrass myself. I can't bear it any longer. I need to be inside you."

"Yes." She reminded herself that this was what she'd wanted, that this would make things better between them. So she forced a smile as he pushed up her skirts and slid between her legs. She could do this. She *could.*

But her body refused to listen. It clenched of its own accord, and when he braced his hands on either side of her, trapping her in, the panic took over and her heart began to pound and her vision to narrow until all she could see was Edwin's taut jaw, vaguely like the Vile Seducer's, and she couldn't think, couldn't breathe, couldn't see . . .

"No . . . no . . . no . . ." she began, scarcely aware of what she was saying.

"Clarissa," he murmured soothingly, "sweetheart . . ."

Shoving against his chest, she bucked up against him, trying to throw him off her. "No . . . stop . . . stop . . . *Stop, damn you!*"

The last words were screamed into the forest.

He froze, his face ashen, and rolled off her to lie on the blanket panting as he stared up into the trees. That and the whimpers she couldn't seem to quell were the only sounds other than the warbling of the stream.

After a few moments, he gave a shuddering breath. "Clarissa," he said hoarsely. "You must tell me what's wrong."

She wanted to. But how could she say that she didn't know if she would ever be right with this? "N-nothing's wrong. I was just startled."

He swore under his breath. "You were not startled. Don't lie to me." When she said nothing to that, he added, "I can't do this anymore. Not like this. One minute you want me, and the next—"

When he choked off the words, she felt a different kind of panic. "Please don't say that. Just give me a moment, and I'll try . . . *we* can try—"

"God, no." He didn't look at her. "You were terrified. I could see it in your eyes."

"Not of you."

"There's no one else here." Dragging in a harsh breath, he seemed to struggle to speak. "My mother's eyes looked like yours once, when I burst in while my father's closest friend was trying to force himself on her. I still remember her crying, the fear on her face. I never want to see that on any woman's face again, but especially not on my own wife's. Not because of me, for certain."

That took Clarissa completely aback. "Y-your mother was . . . assaulted?"

She was still reeling from that revelation when a servant thundered out from the woods.

"I heard a scream—" The footman stopped short as he spotted them lying there next to each other, rather obviously undressed. "Oh." His cheeks turned crimson, and he swiftly turned his back to them. "Beg your pardon, my lord. I didn't mean to . . . that is, I—"

"What are you doing here?" Edwin snapped. "Are you spying on us?"

"No, certainly not, my lord," the man said hastily. "Your sister sent me to fetch you, so I was heading this way when I heard . . . Forgive me, I clearly misunderstood what you and her ladyship . . . that is . . ."

"It's all right." Edwin sat up and began to button his drawers and trousers. "Bloody, bloody hell. Yvette and Keane are back from America?"

"Yes, my lord," the footman said. "Apparently, they heard about your marriage as soon as they arrived in London, and they came straight here."

"Lord help us." Clarissa, too, was already frantically trying to set her clothing to rights.

Edwin stood. "Go and tell them we'll be right there."

"Yes, my lord." Without looking back, the servant left.

As soon as he was out of earshot, Edwin held out his hand to help her rise. She took it gratefully, but when she was standing and he tried to release it, she wouldn't let him. Squeezing his hand tight in hers, she said, "I'm so sorry."

"You have nothing to be sorry about." It was hard to believe him, when he looked so remote and controlled. "But I want you to know that I won't trouble you anymore by attempting to coax you into my bed."

"Edwin—"

"I mean it. I realize now why you had me add that clause to the settlement. Because you really do need time to . . . adjust to me." For a moment, his self-contained expression faltered. "Damn it, Clarissa, I wish you'd told me before . . . I wish I had understood . . ."

As if realizing how vulnerable he sounded, he stiffened. "It doesn't matter. When you're truly ready to consummate our marriage, however long that takes, you'll have to be the one to initiate it, just as you requested from the beginning."

"I *am* ready!"

"No, you're not. Being willing to *try* relations isn't the same as wanting them or being ready for them. And I won't have you shrinking from me in fear because you can't bear—" He broke off with a ragged breath as noises sounded beyond them in the woods. "Clearly we can't have this discussion now. But until you're prepared to talk about . . . why you shy away from me, I think you and I should not attempt this again."

"Don't say that," she whispered.

"Admit it. You're relieved that I said it."

Oh, Lord, perhaps she was. But only a little.

"Edwin, where are you?" came a lilting voice from not too far off.

Drat it all. Yvette had found them.

A murmuring sounded as if the servant were speaking to her, and she said, "Don't be silly—of course they want to see me."

Edwin barely had time to snatch up his waistcoat and coat before Yvette came out of the woods saying, "Cook claimed you two were on a picnic, but I couldn't believe it. I had to see for . . ."

She trailed off as she caught sight of them in their disordered state. Her cheeks reddened. "Oh. It's *that* sort of picnic."

Edwin's jaw looked hard enough to slice stone. "Don't be vulgar, Yvette. We were napping, that's all. And you woke us."

"Napping! You? In the outdoors? That's almost as unlikely as your having a picnic." Yvette swung her gaze from him to Clarissa. "Is he telling the truth?"

"Of course." Clarissa hoped she'd fixed her clothing enough not to give them away. "You know Edwin. He never lies." And being forced to do so now must be mortifying him.

"In that case," Yvette said, "I'm *so* glad to see you both!"

Edwin walked up to kiss his sister on the cheek. "As we are to see you. We didn't expect you in the country until next week at the very earliest."

"I got some news and made Jeremy come back sooner." Placing her hand on her visibly protruding belly, she said, "I suppose you can tell what my news is."

Only Clarissa noticed the quick flash of pain on Edwin's face before he forced a smile for his sister's benefit. "Congratulations. We're very happy for you." He turned to pull Clarissa forward to stand next to him. "Aren't we, my dear?"

His words were so obviously insincere that it cut her to the heart. She'd wounded him deeply. She hadn't even realized until now how much *he'd* been looking forward to having children.

Lord, she was making a complete mess of this marriage.

"Of course we're happy for you," Clarissa said, fighting back tears.

Yvette planted her hands on her hips. "I would

have been happy for you two, if I'd had any inkling you were getting married. How could you not tell me?" She arched an eyebrow at Clarissa. "Especially you. I never expect Edwin to tell me things, but *you* should have said something."

"It happened very quickly," Clarissa said. "I don't know if you remember what occurred when I took that trip to Bath last year, but—"

"We'll explain it all when we've got your husband with us, too," Edwin cut in. "No point in relating the whole tale twice. Shall we go?"

With a nod, Yvette started off, chattering about her and Jeremy's trip to America.

It was all Clarissa could do to make the usual responses. She was painfully aware of Edwin walking stiffly at her side, not touching her, not looking at her.

She hadn't intended to make him feel so awful. She had to fix this, to let him know it really had nothing to do with him. But that meant telling him the truth as soon as she could get him alone.

Did she dare? Or would it drive them farther apart? Given what he'd said about his mother, he might actually understand.

His mother—heavens. Clarissa had never guessed at any such tragedy in Lady Blakeborough's past. She had to know more. Assuming he would tell her.

It was rather a shock that he'd even mentioned it to Clarissa. It drove a stake of guilt through her heart to think that he'd been so devastated by her reaction to him that he had let slip something so highly personal about his family. It wasn't like him at all.

They emerged from the trees to see Jeremy striding toward them. "So there you are! I suppose Yvette has told you our news?"

"Of course," Clarissa said brightly. "You know your wife—she's deplorable at keeping secrets."

"Unlike her brother, who never says a thing. I should have known he was cooking up a plan to win you." Jeremy walked up to clap Edwin on the shoulder. "Not that I'm surprised, Blakeborough. The way you spoke of her a few months ago—"

"What?" Clarissa broke in. "How did he speak of me?"

Jeremy laughed. "As if you bedeviled him. And men are only ever bedeviled by women they fancy."

"I beg your pardon," Yvette retorted. "*I* bedevil him, and he certainly doesn't fancy me."

"You do not bedevil me," Edwin said lightly, obviously trying to get into the spirit of their banter. "You worry me. It's not the same."

"Hmph," Yvette said. "Does your wife not worry you, too?"

He slid a somber glance at Clarissa. "My wife worries me exceedingly. In truth, I don't know how I shall survive marriage to her."

"Nor do I." Clarissa tried to sound teasing, though inside she bled. "But you're stuck with me now, so you'll have to make the best of it."

"Well," Yvette said, taking Clarissa by the arm. "I want to hear all about it. When did he offer marriage? How did he do it?"

"God help us," Jeremy muttered. "Come, brother, I need something stiff to drink while those two reconstruct every moment of your courtship."

As the four of them headed for the house, with the two men going ahead of them toward the study, a sinking feeling of despair overtook Clarissa. It was going to be very hard to make things right with her husband while his family was at Stoke Towers.

She could only hope the Keanes wouldn't stay more than a day or two. Because the longer this rift stretched between her and Edwin, the harder it would be to mend it.

Eighteen

Edwin was glad of Keane's suggestion of having a drink; that way he could fill his brother-in-law in on *all* the details of the Durand situation, including the parts he didn't want his wife to hear.

But as they headed off to Edwin's study, where they could enjoy brandy and cigars in peace, it wasn't Durand that occupied Edwin's thoughts. It was Clarissa.

The wall between them seemed to grow more impassable by the day. She pushed him away as often as she let him close.

Had he made a huge mistake in marrying her? God, he hoped not. Because with every day that passed, he liked having her about him more and more as a companion.

But he couldn't bear the idea of a lifetime with a woman who couldn't endure his touch. Who had to buck herself up just to share his bed.

Never had he felt so alone.

He and Keane entered the study. As they settled

down to their cigars and brandy, he laid out the facts of the situation with Durand. The hardest part was telling Keane about the spying, but it wouldn't be fair to let his sister and brother-in-law be taken by surprise if Durand went through with his threats and told the world about Father's treasonous activities.

When he finished his explanations, Keane looked fit to be tied. "Blackmailed by a scoundrel like that? How dare he?"

"Durand has no shame. Or principles. Especially where gaining Clarissa is concerned."

"Damn."

"My sentiments exactly." Edwin drew in a long breath. "You'll have to decide if we should tell Yvette. I confess I have no idea what to do in that regard."

"It would devastate her. I mean, she's always felt unwanted by your father, but this . . ."

"It does explain why he was never around." It didn't *entirely* explain it, but Edwin wasn't about to go into the details of his mother's assault and the aftermath of it. He already regretted telling Clarissa so much. And not nearly enough.

"Perhaps knowing why your father was absent would make her feel better about it," Keane said. "Though I doubt it. She wasn't just hurt by that, but by the things he said, the way he treated your mother."

"Which is why I'm trusting you to tell Yvette as much or as little as you deem wise. You know her better than I."

"Only because you keep things from her." Keane searched his face. "You would keep this from her, too, wouldn't you, if you had the choice? Just to protect her from being hurt."

"Yes. It's my only way to make up for Father's and Samuel's lapses."

"The trouble is, she interprets your discretion as a lack of faith in her ability to weather trials and tribulations. You think you're protecting her, but you're really building a wall between you and her."

As he always did when Keane started talking about how he should treat his sister, Edwin withdrew into formality. "As I said, you can be the judge of whether to tell her or not. Since you seem to know better than I on the subject."

Apparently realizing how testy Edwin was getting, Keane said, "I didn't mean—"

"If Durand never reveals it, then she need never know that her father was a traitor. But I can't be sure he won't. That's why I'm telling *you*. So you won't find yourself suddenly immersed in a scandal out of the blue."

Keane nodded somberly. "Don't worry about me and Yvette. I don't give a damn about scandal, and she only worries about it for your sake. But if the two of you are in it together, she'll stand by you and thumb her nose at the world." He leaned back in his chair. "And you know me. I thumb my nose at the world as a matter of principle."

"You're an artist and an American. People expect that of you." Edwin stared out the window. "They don't expect it of me."

"And Clarissa? How does she feel about all this?"

He gritted his teeth. "I haven't told her."

"What?"

"I told her he's holding something over our heads, but I haven't said what. I had to reveal that much just to get her to marry me."

"I see." Keane sipped some brandy. "In other words, Durand's threats provided you with an excellent excuse for doing what you wanted in the first place."

Edwin's gaze shot to Keane. "What the devil does that mean? I did it for *her* benefit, not my own. I wasn't going to leave her to that arse's machinations."

"Right. It had nothing to do with your desiring her, I'm sure."

He glared at his friend. "Not everyone is as randy as you."

"You don't fool me." The man chuckled. "Even an idiot could tell how you feel about Clarissa. In any case, it's a good thing to desire one's wife, isn't it?"

"You have no idea," Edwin muttered. He could never reveal the mortifying truth to Keane—that his desire for his wife was something *she* didn't want. Not entirely. That he didn't even know why she rebuffed him.

He wanted to believe that it had nothing to do with him, but he couldn't. Because surely if someone else had hurt her, if all this was because of another man, she would tell him. And she had behaved very much like a virgin when he'd pleasured her with his mouth. It had startled her.

No, the fact that she wouldn't say why, the fact that she pulled back every time he got close to entering her, could only mean it was due to her dislike of *him*.

Just give me a moment, and I'll try . . . we can try—

God, the very idea of her having to drum up enthusiasm to share his bed sent chills down his spine.

He thrust that lowering thought from his mind. "In any case," he said coolly, "it's done now. Since our marriage, Durand has only made threats, but that doesn't mean he won't act on them down the road."

Thankfully Keane let him return to the subject of the count. "And you don't know what Durand's reasons for pursuing her are. Other than some odd obsession with her."

"No. As far as I know, he doesn't need money. Or so Fulkham and Rathmoor said."

Keane blinked. "You told them about the bastard?"

"Not exactly. I didn't want Clarissa's reputation tarnished, so I said I was asking on behalf of someone else in the club."

With a flick of ash from his cigar, Keane said, "I don't suppose you'd want to tell *them* about your father's spying."

"Right," Edwin said snidely. "I'll just run right out and tell Rathmoor, the man who stole my first fiancée, that my father sold his country to the French. Or better yet, I'll tell Fulkham, who practically runs the War Office." He shook his head. "Durand implied that he might implicate me in Father's activities. Imagine if *that* happened."

"He has no proof."

"He has solid proof of Father's activities. It wouldn't take much to connect those to me. Besides, the press doesn't need proof. All they need is a juicy story to foment scandal." Edwin downed some brandy. "No, it seems wiser to stay in the country for a while and hope that our marriage discourages Durand enough for him to turn his attentions elsewhere. It's not as if anyone could do anything to stop him, given his position and the delicacy of relations with the French right now."

"I see your point." Keane drew on his cigar. "But I do think you should tell Clarissa about it, at the very least."

"I can't." Not yet.

"Why not?"

"I have my reasons." He held her by the thinnest thread, if he held her at all. At least right now, she still saw him as her savior from Durand. But if she realized how awful the scandal might be if news of Father's treason got out, she would see him as the man who married her knowing he might be ruining her place in society. He wasn't ready for the recriminations that would follow.

"So, what if Durand does go to the press? What then?"

"Obviously, I'll have no choice. She and I will weather the scandal as best we can." And he would try to make it up to her somehow. If he could. "We'll go abroad, wait until the furor dies."

"You could always shoot the man," Keane said genially.

"Believe me, I've considered it, old boy." He sighed. "But since Clarissa has already lost her brother to exile because of a senseless duel, I hardly think she'd appreciate losing a husband to the gallows."

"True. I suppose we'll just have to hope Durand comes to his senses. Because if you and Clarissa leave

England for any reason, Yvette will get some fool notion about us taking over the care of Stoke Towers, the way Warren has with Margrave Manor—and I can barely manage the country house I just bought."

"I shudder to think what you would do if you ran this place," Edwin said. "You'd be having the dairymaids pose as gin-soaked washerwomen so you could paint them."

Keane paused with his cigar midair. "What a good idea. Or I could pose the footmen with them—add a bit of rowdy soldier flirtation to the scene. Of course, I'd have to acquire a number of military costumes—"

"Stay away from my servants, damn you," Edwin growled.

His brother-in-law burst into laughter. "You should see your face. That's what I ought to paint—you in high dudgeon. But trust me, I have no interest in having your servants model for me. I have enough trouble keeping up with the projects I'm engaged in already." Setting his brandy down, Keane turned serious. "So make sure you don't run afoul of Durand, do you hear?"

"I'll do my best. But the man is unpredictable." Edwin shook his head. "And I never know how to deal with unpredictable people."

Like his wife. He only hoped that in time *she* at least would become easier to read. Otherwise, he was in for a long, cold marriage.

As Clarissa finished her tale about Durand, Yvette let out a most unladylike oath. "The count did *what*? That *devil!* How could he? I mean, I know he was mad for you, but I didn't realize he was . . . well . . . *mad.*"

"I know. It's very strange. I cannot believe he keeps dogging me like this. Neither Edwin nor I can figure it out."

Unsure about the family secrets Durand was using to force Edwin's hand, Clarissa wasn't certain whether she should mention the blackmail. So far she'd only said that Edwin had feared Durand would try to abduct her and thus had married her to keep her safe. But prevaricating with her closest friend made her uncomfortable.

And that wasn't the only thing unnerving her. They were talking in Clarissa's new bedchamber, rather than in Yvette's old room, as they'd always done before. And it was Clarissa who'd summoned the servants to bring tea, Clarissa who'd given the orders about adding two for dinner. It felt rather odd to play lady of the house in front of the woman who'd always played that role previously.

Yvette now lay sprawled across the bed while Clarissa roamed the room, unable to sit still after her encounter with Edwin this afternoon. If she were married to anyone else, she could have begged her friend's advice about her marital troubles. But Yvette was liable to take her brother's side.

Not that there really *was* a side to this mess. Edwin had made a noble sacrifice and was now suffering for it. Meanwhile, Clarissa had stumbled into the very thing she'd been avoiding—marriage to a man who would want to bed her, who had every right to bed her. And whom she hurt with every refusal to let him do so.

"You're happy with Edwin, aren't you?" Yvette asked. "Even though you were forced into marrying him—"

"I wasn't forced," she said stiffly. "I *chose* to marry him. I could have refused, you know."

"And risked being abducted by Durand. Admit it, Edwin's a veritable angel compared to the Frenchman."

"I would never describe your brother as an angel," she said with a faint smile. "More like a knight-errant."

"Yes, he does tend to be overly protective of his womenfolk," Yvette said wryly. "I always found it annoying."

"I find it rather sweet. Except that knights come with armor that can be hard to pierce." Though *his* armor wasn't primarily the problem. It was hers.

"Give him time. He'll let you into his life bit by bit."

Clarissa raised an eyebrow at Yvette. "How many years did it take him to do so with you?"

Yvette shrugged. "That's different. Brothers routinely share secrets with their wives that they never tell their sisters, trust me. Amanda's hair would stand on end if she knew some of the things Jeremy has told me. There's an intimacy between husband and wife that can't exist between brother and sister, for obvious reasons."

Clarissa considered asking her friend about the assault upon the late Lady Blakeborough. But Edwin hadn't said when it happened, and there were eight years between brother and sister. Yvette might not even know about it. It certainly fell into the category of something Edwin would never reveal.

Probably for the same reason Clarissa had never told Yvette about the Vile Seducer. Certain things were so dark, so shameful, that one couldn't even tell one's best friend or sibling. After all, Niall had ended up in exile, trying to keep her ruin a secret. She wasn't going to dishonor his sacrifice by blurting it out to the world.

"You didn't answer my question about being happy with Edwin," Yvette said softly. "Are you?"

Lord, this was awkward. "We get along very well. He's . . . not what I expected. I knew he had a dry sense of humor, but I had no idea that he could actually be fun."

Yvette raised an eyebrow. "We're still talking about Edwin, right?"

"Yes." She felt an odd need to defend him. "He's not half the somber fellow I took him for." She walked over and picked up the automaton, which had held pride of place on her dressing table ever since her arrival. "He gave me this. He said that you had him make it for me last Christmas, but you never got the chance to give it to me."

Her friend's eyes gleamed with humor. "That's true. And did he tell you *why* I never gave it to you?"

"He said he didn't get it completed in time."

Yvette laughed. "Because he wouldn't stop altering it. Nothing was good enough, nothing was close enough, nothing seemed correct to him. 'The eyes aren't the right green,' he told me one time. 'Clarissa doesn't move like that,' he said another. I chalked it up to his usual attention to detail, but now I wonder . . ."

"Don't," Clarissa said, past the lump growing in

her throat. "You're attributing to him feelings for me that he doesn't have." His words floated through her mind: *I've imagined having you like this for ages.* "I mean, he *is* attracted to me, but—"

"But what?" Yvette sat up in bed to pounce on that admission. "Things are all right in *that* area, aren't they? I know that Edwin is stodgy, but surely—"

"It's not him," Clarissa blurted out.

Yvette's gaze narrowed on her, and Clarissa could have kicked herself for the admission. "What do you mean? If there's a problem in the bedchamber, it most assuredly *is* him. He knows more about doing *that* than you, I'm quite sure, so it's his responsibility to make it pleasant."

"Pleasant?" Clarissa said incredulously.

At her tone, Yvette paled. "Oh, Lord, he's not awful at it, is he? He hasn't hurt you or anything? I wouldn't have expected it of Edwin, but, well . . . one doesn't know such things about one's brother . . . I did always hear stories about Samuel, but Edwin—" She stopped as if realizing she was babbling. "You don't have to talk about it if you don't want to, but if it was as bad as all that—"

"We haven't yet done that," Clarissa said baldly.

She really must stop blurting things out. But if anyone could tell her how to get past the difficult part of marriage, it would be Yvette. For one thing, she had never minded discussing such things. For another, she obviously had a very talented husband in that respect, given how she doted on him.

"What do you mean, 'done that'?" Yvette asked. "Surely you're not saying that after a week of marriage, you still haven't made the beast with two backs."

"The beast with . . . What?"

Yvette waved her hand dismissively. "You know. You haven't *wapped* or *swived* or *joined giblets*."

A hysterical laugh bubbled up in Clarissa's throat. "Oh, Lord, I forgot that you collect street slang."

"And I taught *you* all the naughty words, too." Yvette crossed her arms over her chest. "So, have you done the deed or not?"

"Well . . . no. We haven't."

"Whyever not?" Yvette exclaimed.

Now came the tricky part. More than ever, she didn't want Yvette to know her past shame. Yvette would pity her, and Clarissa *hated* that. But there were certain things Clarissa wanted to learn, and Yvette seemed the only person likely to tell her.

"As I said, it's not him. I'm just . . . so afraid of the pain. You know how I am about pain. I am most sensitive to it."

"Nonsense." As always, Yvette saw right through her. "You've never been sensitive to pain a day in your life. And besides, it's only painful the first time. And even that isn't all that bad."

"Really?" Clarissa said skeptically. "That's not what I heard." *Or experienced.* It had seemed pretty awful to her.

"If the man knows what he's doing, and is careful with you—"

"What if he isn't?"

The bitter words seemed to give Yvette pause. "Has my brother ever hurt you? Has he ever given you reason to believe he would *not* be careful with you?"

"No. In truth, he's been very patient with me, willing to wait until I'm ready." She glanced away. "But once men are caught up in . . . their passion, they can be unpredictable." When she caught Yvette watching her with curiosity, she added hastily, "Or so I've heard."

Yvette eyed her suspiciously. "Well, I don't know who's been telling you these things—I assume it was your mother—but no matter what silliness we've always been taught, men are not bullies one has to endure in the bedroom. At least *my* husband is not."

"Perhaps your husband is different."

"I doubt it, or there wouldn't be so many wives taking lovers in our circles. They must get *some* pleasure out of the swiving. The first time is a bit difficult, but after that, it's wonderful. What did your mother tell you to expect, anyway?"

Clarissa could hardly admit the truth—that *her* first time had been agony. That she wasn't convinced it would be any better the second time. Or the third or the fourth. What if she wasn't . . . made right somehow? "It doesn't matter," she mumbled.

"It does matter." Yvette rose to put her arm around Clarissa. "Marriage requires trust. You either trust your husband to be careful with you, or you don't. I realize it's probably hard to trust a man you were forced into—" She caught herself. "*Coaxed* into marrying for reasons outside of love. But you trusted him enough to agree to his plan. You trusted him to keep you safe from Durand. Can't you trust him in this?"

Clarissa truly didn't know.

Yvette frowned. "Then again, I'm assuming that you desire him, too. Perhaps you don't."

"That is *not* the problem, believe me," Clarissa said

dryly. "Your brother has more of Samuel's talent for enticing a woman than I ever would have guessed."

"Does he, indeed?" Yvette said with a sly look. "How surprising."

Clarissa blushed. "Honestly, I cannot believe I'm having this conversation with his sister, of all people."

"Not just his sister. Your friend. I will always be your friend first, you know." Yvette squeezed her shoulder. "We women have to stick together, after all."

Impulsively, Clarissa embraced her. "I'm so happy you came to visit," she whispered. "You always did have the ability to cheer me up. And I'm very glad we'll be sisters now."

"Me, too."

They hugged fiercely, both of them teary-eyed.

Then Yvette held her at arm's length. "Answer me one question."

"What is it?" Clarissa asked, dabbing at her eyes with her handkerchief.

"Do you *want* my brother? Do you really want to be Lady Blakeborough in more than name only? To bear his children, be his companion, and have him be yours? Do you hope for the possibility of love down the road, once the two of you know each other better? Do you want a real future with Edwin?"

"Yes." The moment the words were out of her mouth she realized it was true. She had always wanted a life like that—the life she'd been bred for. But she'd assumed she couldn't have it.

Then Edwin had come along and made her rethink her assumptions, and now she was worried he would give up on her before she could beat down the terror deep inside her.

"In that case," Yvette went on stoutly, "you must fight for him. The Clarissa *I* know wouldn't let fear of pain govern her actions. The Clarissa *I* know wouldn't sit back and wait for things to change, but would go after what she wants, ignoring the opinions of propriety and society alike. The Clarissa *I* know would take the bull by the horns."

Clarissa straightened her spine. "She *would*, wouldn't she?"

"Bloody right she would," Yvette said with a shocking use of bad language. "So Jeremy and I will take ourselves back to London and leave you to it."

"Oh, that would be *wonderful*." Clarissa added hastily, "Not that I don't love having you here and everything, but—"

"I understand completely. And if there's anything else I can do to help, like loan you jewelry or a bottle of scent or clothes—"

Clarissa's eyes brightened as something occurred to her. "Actually, you *could* help me find something to wear. But it's not going to be what you think."

"Oh?"

"Edwin and I made a sort of challenge with each other this afternoon that I lost, so now . . . well . . . Did your mother happen to keep any of your brothers' clothes from when they were younger?"

Yvette broke into a grin, probably remembering how Edwin had reacted the last time Clarissa had worn male attire. "I don't know. But it shouldn't take us long to find out."

Nineteen

The ladies had been upstairs an inordinate amount of time. Edwin glanced at the clock in his study, where he and Jeremy were still sitting with their brandy and cigars. It had been over two hours, for God's sake. What were they doing up there?

He was about to comment on it when Yvette came hurrying in.

"Where's my wife?" Edwin asked, looking beyond her for the minx who drove him insane even when she wasn't nearby.

Yvette smiled. "She'll be down shortly. But Jeremy and I are leaving for London."

"What?" Jeremy said. "But we just got here!"

"Yes, and we interrupted their honeymoon. So now we're leaving again."

Edwin didn't know what to make of that. Had Clarissa said anything to his sister? Or was Yvette, as usual, simply better at reading people and situations than he was?

Jeremy scowled. "Just like that? Without any dinner? We haven't even had lunch yet!"

"It's fine if you wish to stay a bit longer," Edwin put in, taking pity on his brother-in-law. "We keep country hours, so you'd still have plenty of time to dine and return to the city before it got too late. I think Clarissa already told Cook to expect two more."

Yvette began putting on her gloves. "And *I* told Cook we wouldn't be here. So it's settled."

"But . . . but . . ." Jeremy sputtered.

"Cook has already made up a cold collation for us," she went on matter-of-factly, "including some of her special apple tarts."

That brought a change to Jeremy's face. "Freshly baked apple tarts, eh?" He rose. "You should have mentioned that in the beginning."

"Our cook does make exceptionally fine apple tarts," Edwin said as he, too, rose, his head spinning at the sudden change in plans.

Jeremy winked at him. "Sorry to leave you in the lurch. But I daresay you won't mind being sentenced to more time alone with your lovely wife."

"No," Edwin said. Though he honestly didn't know what to do with her. Especially now.

"Go on, darling," Yvette said to Jeremy. "I'll be along in a moment. I just need a few words with my brother."

That didn't sound good. Edwin braced himself for anything as she came around the desk. When she merely gave him a kiss on the cheek, he let out a relieved breath. "I'm glad you're back in England," he admitted.

"So am I. I missed you. And Clarissa." She seized his hand. "Be careful with her."

"Of course," he said tersely. "Why would I be anything else?"

"Because you can be a bull in a china shop sometimes, and despite all her boldness, Clarissa is the finest Wedgwood. So treat her with kid gloves, will you?"

He bristled. "How I handle my wife is none of your concern." When her eyes narrowed, he regretted speaking so sharply, but blast it, the idea of her and Clarissa talking over his . . . inadequacies made his blood boil. "What nonsense did she tell you about me, anyway?"

Her gaze grew shuttered. "Nothing of any consequence."

"I am not some monster, you know," he grumbled.

"Of course you aren't," she said soothingly. "And *she* certainly doesn't think you are." Her gaze grew steely. "All the same, if you ruin things with her by being your typical blunt self, I shall never forgive you."

As usual, Yvette thought everything was *his* fault. "Didn't you say something about returning to London?"

Perversely, that made his meddling sister laugh. "I'm going, I'm going." She headed for the door. "I understand that Lady Margrave is throwing a grand fete to celebrate your wedding, and Jeremy and I are invited. So I'll see you there in a week."

The thought of how extravagant an affair Clarissa's mother was probably planning made him shudder. "I can't wait," he said sarcastically.

Yvette paused in the doorway, her eyes gleaming

at him. "And here Clarissa was trying to tell me that you could be fun. I should have known better than to believe her."

By the time her words registered fully, his sister had already waltzed out into the hall.

"Wait!" he called out as he hurried after her. "Clarissa really said I was *fun*?"

Having reached the entrance door, Yvette paused to blow him a kiss. "See you next week!" Then she was gone.

By the time he got outside, the carriage was already pulling away, with her waving at him out the window.

After watching the equipage disappear onto the road, he walked slowly back into the house. Damn. What else had Clarissa told his sister? Had she spoken of their intimate relations . . . or lack thereof? Had she revealed what he'd blurted out about Mother?

God. There was no telling. Those two were as thick as thieves.

As he stood in the foyer, he glanced at the clock. A couple of hours until dinner. He had half a mind to tell a servant he was unwell, and retreat to his bedchamber to drink himself into oblivion for the rest of the day.

But he was no coward. Surely he could endure an evening of polite chitchat with his wife. He would simply put from his mind the memory of how soft she'd been earlier, how sweetly scented, how silky the skin along her thighs . . .

Damn it to hell. Now he wished Keane and Yvette had chosen to stay.

He returned to his study to deal with some correspondence. Perhaps that would take his mind off her until she came down to join him for a drink before dinner, as they'd begun the habit of doing.

Or would *she* play the coward and not come to dinner at all? He wasn't sure which he wanted.

Some time later, he was immersed in writing a letter to the board of the Preston Charity School when a voice sounded from the doorway.

"They've gone, I take it?"

Clarissa was here. "Yes, they've gone." He forced a polite smile to his face as he rose. "They were—"

He forgot whatever he was saying, just stood there slack-jawed. Because standing in the doorway was his wife in a pair of his old evening breeches from when he was a lad of twelve.

Over them, she wore his old white shirt without a cravat, unbuttoned almost to the vee in the placket; his old embroidered waistcoat, unbuttoned; and his old tailcoat. It was the most erotic thing he'd ever seen in his life.

God save his soul.

"Don't stand there with your mouth open, Edwin." She smiled hesitantly as she entered. "You'll attract flies."

He couldn't stop staring, couldn't stop imagining what lay behind the fall of those breeches. "What are you doing?" he barked.

"Paying my debt. You *did* win our challenge this afternoon. Or have you forgotten?"

"I . . . I . . . Yes." He swallowed hard. "I did."

Oh, God, what had he been thinking? He must have been out of his mind. Now he had an evening of torture ahead of him.

After their disastrous picnic, he hadn't expected her to "pay her debt," especially with things so uncertain between them.

He scowled. Unless she had done it on purpose, to arouse him. Which didn't make sense. He'd been very clear about why men liked women in breeches, and she'd been very clear about not wanting him to bed her.

As if she followed the train of his thoughts, her expression turned self-conscious. "I . . . um . . . would have buttoned the waistcoat, but it simply wouldn't close over my . . . er . . ."

"Fine attributes?" he said dryly.

She blushed. "Exactly. I could barely get the breeches on, either. You grew into such a tall, broad-chested fellow that this was all I could find that I wouldn't be swimming in, unfortunately."

"Yes, very unfortunately, indeed," he mumbled. Every inch of her attire was tight enough to show . . . several of her "fine attributes." "No cravat, I see."

"I gave up on figuring out how to tie one." A coy smile touched her lips. "Besides, I figured you would like the ensemble better without one."

"Can't imagine why you would think that," he said hoarsely as he fixed his gaze on her shirt. She didn't appear to have a corset on underneath. Or perhaps he merely imagined that he could see her nipples. "Where on earth did you find the clothes?"

"In an old trunk."

She strolled over to the wine decanter near the window, giving him a full view of her luscious backside. Those breeches were so tight, he could bounce a shilling off them. Had she even been able to get them on over her drawers? Or was she actually *naked* underneath?

Glancing back at him, she asked, "Shall we have our usual glass of Madeira?"

"Yes." *With a side of carnal relations, if you don't mind.* Damn. How would he ever make it through tonight?

She poured two glasses. "You don't mind that Yvette and Jeremy left so soon, do you?"

"No." He watched as she came toward him. "Why? Do *you?*"

"Certainly not. Though I did enjoy my chat with Yvette."

That arrested his attention. As she handed him his glass, he said, "And . . . er . . . what did you two discuss?"

Staring down into her glass, she said, "I told her all about Durand and why we had to marry. She thinks he's mad."

"He is. Though it's a crafty sort of mad."

She nodded. "Yvette agreed to write to me about whatever gossip she heard of him."

"That's good." Edwin downed his wine, then went to fetch himself another. It was the only way he was going to get through the next few hours with her looking like that.

Clarissa didn't seem to notice. "I didn't mention the blackmail aspect to her. I wasn't sure if you'd want her to know of it. Was that right?"

He forced himself to concentrate on the matter at hand. "Yes. I'd rather not worry her over it until it becomes necessary."

"It did occur to me, though, that . . . well . . ." She toyed with her glass. "I wondered if perhaps the blackmail had something to do with what you mentioned this afternoon. About your mother. And her assault."

He froze in the midst of pouring himself more wine. God, he hadn't even considered that she might think that. "No. Not at all. Something else entirely." Down went his second glass of Madeira.

When he said nothing more, she asked, "Will you tell me about it?"

Damn. The last thing he wanted to explain right now was his father's spying. "The blackmail, you mean?"

"No. Your mother's assault."

That threw him off guard. He faced her, eyes narrowing. "Why?"

She swallowed. "Because . . . well . . . it seems to have affected you profoundly, and I should like to know what happened."

It occurred to him that there might be deeper reasons for her request. What had Yvette said? *Treat her with kid gloves.*

Perhaps this was the way to do it. Show her his darkest secrets, so she might show him hers. He stepped nearer. "If I do, will you tell me why you shy from me?"

She blinked, then bobbed her head.

"Very well." He gestured to the chair in front of the desk. "But you'd better sit down. It's not a pretty story."

At those words, Clarissa felt a sudden queasiness in her stomach. But this was what she'd wanted, to know what had happened to his mother and how it might bear upon his feelings toward what had happened to her. Which she'd now promised to tell him, and wasn't at all sure she should.

But this couldn't go on. She might as well get it over with.

Edwin went to close the door to the study, probably so the servants wouldn't hear, and then to pour himself a third glass of Madeira. Clarissa frowned. She'd never seen him take more than one before, and it worried her. At least he only sipped this one, as if buying time.

When he spoke again, his voice was carefully measured. "It happened when I was eight and Samuel six. Father had just left to go to town one afternoon, so we were playing in the coat closet downstairs, having escaped our napping nurse. Father's oldest friend came to call, and we watched from our hiding place as Mother invited him to visit with her in the drawing room while he waited for Father to return."

His back stiffened. "We didn't know the man very well—he'd just returned from a long trip to America. But Mother knew him from before she and Father married, and they seemed cordial." He sipped some Madeira. "Anyway, Samuel and I got into a silly argument about something, and since we knew Mother was in the drawing room, we ran in there to have her settle it."

A shuddering breath escaped him. "It took a moment for us to register what we were seeing. At first, it looked like the man and Mother were playing some game on the settee, tussling like Samuel and I were wont to do." His voice grew choked. "But then I realized that the man's mouth was smothering Mother's, and he was holding her down while he dragged up her skirts. She beat on his back, but though she wasn't exactly a small woman, she couldn't get him off her."

Clarissa knew firsthand what that was like, having a man who was stronger and fiercer on top of her and not being able to get free. Just hearing Edwin's account made her hands clammy and her mouth dry.

He cleared his throat. "Samuel just stood there, unable to comprehend what was going on, but I wasn't about to let Father's 'friend' hurt her, so I cried out for him to stop."

Pivoting to face her, he stared blindly past her with a haunted expression. "The bastard clamped his hand over her mouth and told me they were playing a grown-up game, and I should go back to my nurse. But I saw the stark terror in her eyes, the tears running down her cheeks. So I launched myself at him, determined to get him off her."

His hand shook as he lifted his glass to his lips and drank deeply. "He had to abandon his assault of her to fight me, and then he had to fight both of us, and we made such a ruckus that our old butler came running. That ended it." Ice glittered in his eyes. "Or rather, that ended the *physical* assault. The assault on her character lasted the rest of my parents' marriage."

Her heart sank. "What do you mean? The man tried to rape her!"

"But he told our butler that Mother had encouraged his advances, and then had grown embarrassed when I came in upon them. That I'd misunderstood what was going on. And our damned butler, who'd never really approved of Mother, believed him and agreed to keep quiet about it. Then Father's friend took me and Mother aside and said that if we told anyone else about it, he would paint her to be a whore."

With an ugly oath, Edwin threw the wineglass into the fireplace, startling her with his anger. She watched with her heart in her throat as he paced before her, his jaw tight. "Mother, however, wasn't standing for that. As soon as the bastard left and Father returned home, she tearfully related what had happened. So Father went off to confront his friend, who apparently elaborated on his Banbury tale by claiming that Mother had tried several times previously to seduce him."

"That scoundrel!" The thought of poor Lady Blakeborough being falsely maligned made her stomach roil. "But . . . but surely your father didn't believe that awful man."

"I wish I could say he didn't." Edwin scrubbed his hands over his face. "But they'd been friends all their lives, and the man was clever enough to play on Father's jealousy, and the fact that Mother had always drawn men's gazes. So Father marched back home and questioned the butler, me, and Samuel."

He snorted. "Samuel was useless—he kept saying the two had been playing a game. I told Father that it hadn't been a game, but an assault. That didn't matter much when our butler said he'd come in upon my mother standing there in disordered clothing, looking flushed and agitated, while I screamed at Father's friend. All of it was true. But all of it could also corroborate her attacker's account."

"If one was predisposed to believe the wretch—which your father certainly should not have been."

"Unfortunately *he* did not agree with you." Edwin's voice went cold. "He believed the butler. Father said we were children and didn't understand that our mother had been playing the whore. Why else had she invited the man into the drawing room alone, after all?"

"Because she was being a courteous hostess?" Clarissa said, irate on his mother's behalf. "Because the man was supposedly your father's friend?"

"Father didn't see it that way. He saw it as her fault, and their marriage was never the same. Though he cut off his friend because the man had 'accepted his wife's advances,' he also withdrew from Mother and claimed that they'd both betrayed him. If she hadn't already been in the beginning stages of pregnancy with Yvette when it happened, I suspect my sister would never have been born."

"That's appalling! How dared he believe those wretches over your mother?" At least Niall had realized the truth about what had happened to *her*, had never doubted her word for one moment.

When he didn't say anything more, she eyed him warily. "You . . . you didn't come to agree with your father when you were older, did you? Blame your mother for . . . for . . ."

"Of course not," he bit out. "I might have been a child, but I could tell that she didn't want what that bastard was trying to do, even if Father was too stupid to realize it. My father broke her heart. I could see the pain in her eyes whenever he was cold to her, hear her crying at night when she thought no one knew. And as the years went by, I could see her grow hardened by it."

His expression was troubled. "She died without him at her side, because the man who'd claimed to marry her for love blamed her for that bastard's attack. It's why Father was never around, why his jaunts to London got longer and longer."

"Oh, Edwin, I'm so sorry. What a terrible thing to have to hold inside you. Is that why you've always been so strict with Yvette about what women should and shouldn't do—"

"Yes. Because I know that some men will use any excuse to justify hurting a woman." He locked his gaze with hers. "Better that women curtail their freedoms than end up broken and battered and betrayed."

"Better that men just stop hurting women," she countered fiercely. "Better that people stop allowing it, condoning it, excusing it."

That brought him up short. "Yes. You're right. That *would* be the best alternative. Sadly, we don't live in such a world." He approached her with a serious expression. "But I think you know that already."

Oh, Lord, the time had come. She had to tell him. Glancing away, she murmured, "Yes."

A shuddering breath escaped him. "Some man hurt you, scared you so badly that you've had trouble being touched intimately ever since."

He spoke the words so gently that it made tears clog her throat. "Yes."

Coming up next to her, he cupped her cheek. "He tried to do to you what that son-of-a-bitch tried to do to my mother."

Unable to bear his sympathy, which she didn't quite trust, she pulled away and turned her back to him. "He didn't *try*." Lord, but it was hard to say. Especially to Edwin. "He succeeded."

The long silence behind her made her wince. Then he let out his breath in a whoosh. "Are you saying that some man—"

"I'm saying I'm a ruined woman. That years ago, a suitor of mine got me off alone and . . . took my innocence." Now that the words were spilling out of her, she couldn't seem to stop them. "That's why I—as you put it—shy from you. It's why my nightmares, which I fought so hard to extinguish, erupted again recently."

She could feel his stare boring into her back. "That's why I . . . didn't want to marry you or anyone else." Bitterness crept into her voice despite her attempts to quash it. "Because I didn't want to spend my life like your mother—wed to a man who despised me because I 'let' some scoundrel assault me."

Twenty

"*Let?* No woman chooses that," Edwin said softly, determined to banish the bitterness from her voice. "And I do not despise you. I could never despise you."

Her shoulders shook violently, but when she spoke again, her tone was still harsh. "Perhaps you misunderstood me. I'm not chaste. I have lain with another man."

"I understood you. I simply don't give a damn."

It was true, oddly enough. Even as a boy, he hadn't understood the idea of being possessive of another person. Slavery was outlawed in England; people should belong to themselves and no one else. No matter what the law said, it had never made sense to him that women should be chattel.

And after his father's betrayal of his mother, he understood it even less. Love was supposed to mean accepting and trusting the object of one's affections over all others, wasn't it? Instead, it seemed a sort of license to mistreat someone.

So no, he didn't care that she was unchaste. But

that didn't mean he didn't care how it had occurred, and a thousand feelings were roaring through him. Frustration that she'd felt she couldn't tell him this before. Relief that it wasn't he in particular who frightened her. Fury that some bastard had hurt her.

Horror that she'd lived with this weight on her soul for years.

Years? How could that be?

"When did it happen?" he asked. He needed information so he could help her. Given the anger and belligerence in her tone, he could easily say the wrong thing, do the wrong thing. And any misstep, like a bell lightly struck, could reverberate down their future for a very long time. "How long ago?"

"Seven years, give or take a month," she clipped out. "During my debut."

His heart constricted in his chest. What a terrible thing for a young woman to endure during the period that was supposed to be her triumphant entrance into society. "Who was the man?"

She stiffened. "Why do you want to know?"

"So I can kill him for hurting you."

His hard words made her rigid shoulders relax a fraction. "You're too late. My brother already did that."

Bloody hell. "Niall?" Then he realized— "The duel. Oh, God, that's what the duel was about."

She nodded.

Suddenly a number of things fell into place. Why the circumstances of the duel had been kept so mysterious. Why Clarissa never spoke of it if she could avoid it. Why no one had seemed to know what woman the two parties had fought over.

But now Edwin knew who her attacker was. "The

Honorable Joseph Whiting. Damned bastard. No wonder Niall killed him."

The vehemence in his voice made her whirl on him with a look of surprise. "You knew Mr. Whiting?"

"I did. Not well, but he happened to attend school with Samuel. He thought he was God's gift to women. And as I recall, a number of women thought so, too, despite his reputation as a fortune hunter. He was a very handsome man with a glib tongue."

Her lips tightened into a line. "Yes, he was. And I was a stupid, foolish girl who fell for his . . . smooth advances."

The self-loathing in her voice pierced him. "You were barely eighteen, the kind of innocent whom men like Whiting prey on. He was older, more experienced, and a third son with a small allowance looking for a pretty heiress to marry." He reached up to cup her cheek, relieved when she let him. "I daresay his attack was part of his plan to force you into marriage. Am I right? Do you even know?"

Taking his hand from her cheek, she gripped it in hers as if holding on for dear life. "You're right. And ironically, that's probably why the gossips have never heard of my . . . ruin."

"How is that?"

She dropped her gaze to his chest. "The night that Mr. Whiting took my innocence, Niall came in upon us almost immediately after it happened. Mr. Whiting instantly offered to marry me, but Niall could see me lying there weeping and . . . bleeding and torn, so—"

"*Torn?*" Rage tore through him. "How badly? Where?"

She glanced up at him, clearly startled. "You know where. Down there. The way all women bleed and tear when they . . . do that."

All women? Oh, God. The situation might be more complex than he'd initially thought. What if she wasn't frightened of being bedded, but of being *hurt?*

The thought made him want to punch something.

But he controlled his anger, lest she think it directed at *her.* He must let her finish her tale. Once he had all the facts, he could pursue understanding how badly she'd been "torn."

"Go on, then," he said, sandwiching her hand between both of his. "What did your brother do when Whiting offered to marry you?"

"Niall wouldn't hear of it. In a fury, he challenged Mr. Whiting to a duel at dawn." She swallowed convulsively. "Mr. Whiting accepted the challenge, but said Niall would come to his senses in the morning and would realize that marriage was my only choice. That if he didn't, Mr. Whiting would happily shoot him and overcome any objection by the family."

"Bastard." It was getting harder by the minute to control his anger at her attacker. "That was a blackmail as bad as any Durand ever came up with."

She nodded. "I'd almost think the count had learned his tricks from Mr. Whiting, except that they couldn't have known each other. Count Durand had been in Paris with his family for years by then, and Mr. Whiting couldn't even afford to go to Brighton, much less France." She ducked her head. "I just . . . seem to attract men who won't take no for an answer."

"That's absurd. You attract men with a penchant

for beautiful women, like me and all those pups who were flirting with you at the theater, and half the fellows in the world. You've merely run afoul of a couple of bad eggs. *Very* bad eggs, unfortunately."

"At least Mr. Whiting's brand of blackmail didn't work," she said. "Niall was a better shot than the scoundrel realized. So after he killed Mr. Whiting, he fled England."

"That's one thing I don't understand. Public sympathy would have been on Niall's side during any trial. He probably would have been acquitted. Rarely do they convict a peer of murder in the case of a duel of honor, especially when it involves a family member."

With a squeeze of his hand, she pulled free to go over to the window. "I know. It wasn't fear of hanging that prompted his exile. He fled England for *me*."

The reason hit him like a hammer. "Because a trial would involve your telling the world what had happened."

She nodded. "Papa and Mr. Whiting's widowed mother agreed that neither family would be well served by having it come out that I was the reason for the duel. Apparently, Mr. Whiting had already told her that he was anticipating marrying me, so afterward, Papa had to convince her to say nothing about that in order to protect my identity. She agreed to comply, since she said she'd gone through this sort of . . . trouble with her son and young women before."

"Like my father with Samuel."

She nodded.

"But the seconds knew it involved you, surely."

"No. Mr. Whiting didn't tell them—he just said he and Niall were fighting over a woman."

"I'm surprised. You'd think he would have bragged about his conquest to his friends beforehand."

"Given what Mr. Whiting had told his mother, Papa assumed that at the time of the challenge, Mr. Whiting was still hoping to gain my hand and thus my fortune. Slandering his future wife wouldn't have fit into his plans for eventually cutting a fine figure in society with an earl's daughter on his arm. The morning of the duel, Mr. Whiting apparently just asked if Niall had changed his mind, and when Niall said no, they fought. And to everyone's surprise, Niall won."

"Thank God."

"*No!*" She whirled to face him, tears welling in her eyes. "I mean, yes, I was glad Niall wasn't killed, but I begged him not to fight in the first place. I told him to let Papa deal with it, but he wouldn't listen. And when it was over and he and Papa agreed that Niall should flee to protect me, I . . . I begged him not to do that, either."

"Why?"

"Because now he can never return! He won't risk putting me through a trial. He and Papa kept the whole thing utterly quiet—from Warren, from the rest of the family, from everyone. They didn't even tell Mama, for fear that she would let it slip. If she ever finds out that I was the cause of her son's exile—"

"You were *not* the cause of Niall's exile, blast it!" He strode up to seize her hands in his. "*Whiting* was. Your brother did a very noble thing by protecting you after the fact. And if I ever see him again, I will thank him for it."

"You don't understand."

"I do. You feel guilty over something that wasn't your fault."

"But it *was* my fault, don't you see?" Tears trickled down her cheeks. "If I hadn't gone into the orangery with the Vile Seducer—"

"The 'Vile Seducer'?"

"That's what I've always called him in my head. I can't think of him as a . . . as a person with a name."

"That I can well understand," he bit out. "Though you ought to call him the 'Vile Rapist.' Because that's clearly what he was."

"Was he?" Jerking her hands from his, she turned her back to him once more. "I went willingly with him. I let him kiss me—a lot. Like some tart, I let him put his hand on my breast."

"You did all that with me, and every time you balked at going further, I retreated. Because that's what a gentleman does—even with a woman who initially encouraged him. Even with his wife. A gentleman does not force a woman. *Ever.*"

As if she hadn't even heard him, she went on in a harsh rasp, "I should have fought him harder. I protested when he began to lift my skirts, but I didn't seriously struggle until he tore my clothes and held me down and . . . and pushed himself into me and—"

"Raped you," Edwin said fiercely. The very idea of that *bastard* tearing her clothes and holding her down made him wish he could march into hell and kill the man all over again. Bare-handed. "It's clearly a rape to me. And it clearly was to Niall, too. And your late father."

With a shake of her head, she wrapped her arms

about her waist. "I'm not so sure. A-after it happened, they could barely even look at me. Father never chided me, but I—I'm sure that he blamed me."

"If he did, then he was wrong. But I doubt that he did. The Lord Margrave *I* knew would never have blamed you. He was as different from my father as I am from Samuel. He was a man of character, and if he didn't look at you, it's because he couldn't stand to see you hurting. Couldn't stand the fact that he wasn't there to protect you."

Desperate to make her see, he came up behind her and pulled her back against him. "*I* can't stand the fact that I wasn't there to protect you, and I didn't even know any of this was going on."

She was crying now, though he could only tell because of the hitch in her breathing.

He held her as close as he dared, as close as she'd let him. "I've seen how you react to a man crowding you in, and being on top of you, sweetheart. I heard you scream after your nightmare. If that isn't the behavior of a woman who was raped, I don't know what is. I only wish I hadn't assumed that your balking was due to your dislike of me. Perhaps then I would have recognized it before."

"I *told* you it had nothing to do with you," she said in a small voice.

"Yes, you did. I just didn't believe you. Forgive me for that. Though if you'd told me in the first place—"

"I couldn't," she whispered. "I was afraid you would condemn me, would blame me for . . . for . . ."

"Being raped?" That wounded him to his soul. "I suppose your fear shouldn't surprise me, given that

Father condemned Mother, but I thought you knew my character better than that. I realize that you and Yvette think me cold and unfeeling—"

"*Not* cold and unfeeling." She twisted in his arms to face him. "I never thought you that, and she didn't, either. It's just that you were always so . . . rigid. So disapproving of my outrageous behavior."

"Because I worried about you." He brushed a lock of her hair from her eyes. "I knew what could happen to a woman with high spirits who was so damned appealing and intoxicating . . . and heedless of her own safety."

"Never that," she whispered. "Ever since the . . . attack, I always have an eye on who's behind me and where I am. I always know how many people are within screaming distance, because . . ." She shivered. "No one could hear me cry out in that orangery. It was too far away from the party, and there was too much noise in the house."

The very idea of her screaming and having no one come to her rescue until it was too late sent a shaft of ice through his heart. And reminded him of her screaming in the woods, and brandishing the hairbrush at the theater. The signs had all been there; if only he hadn't been dwelling on his own insecurity.

"Oh, sweetheart," he said through a throat tight with sorrow. "I hate that it happens to any woman, but to have it happen to *you*, to think of your being hurt so badly that you still have nightmares about it . . ." He clutched her close. "I can hardly bear the thought."

That's when she began to sob. She buried her face in his shoulder and cried, while he could only hold her, soothe her with nonsensical words of comfort, offer her his handkerchief.

It took her a while to cry it all out. She'd practically soaked his handkerchief through by the time she ventured to speak again. Dabbing at her eyes, she lifted her chin with a hint of the stalwart Clarissa he knew.

"I don't know why I'm . . . being such a watering pot," she said. "I've worked very hard to stop being afraid. I'd even managed to halt the nightmares. I've only had that one in some years—"

"The night we married," he said hoarsely. "The night I crowded you in the carriage."

She winced. "Yes, but . . . you were there after the nightmare to make it better." She flashed him a tremulous smile. "And I haven't had one since."

"Still, I wish I'd guessed at your pain years ago. I wouldn't have been so . . . so . . ."

"Snooty? Arrogant?" she said tartly.

"Disapproving. Without knowing what you were suffering."

"I'm *glad* you didn't know." She tipped up her chin. "It means I succeeded in hiding it from the world."

"You certainly did." But now that he knew, he could see her determined cheer and her impudence for what they really were—an attempt to put the past behind her and prove to herself she was no longer afraid, the way a boy whistles in the dark.

She'd been whistling in the dark for years. Until *he'd* come along and forced her to face the monster lurking there.

Her gaze dropped to his waistcoat. "No doubt you regret marrying me, now that you know everything."

"Not for one minute. Why would I?"

"Because men want chaste wives."

He chose his words carefully. "Some do, I suppose. Not all. As I said, I don't care one way or the other. Especially when my wife had no choice in the matter."

"Then you're the exception to the rule," she said acidly.

"Sweetheart, I am the exception to the rule in many things. I don't see why this should be any different." He tipped up her chin. "Except for your difficulties in the bedchamber, we've had a lovely time so far, have we not?"

Her ghost of a smile cheered him. "We have." Then her face darkened again, like the sun going behind a cloud. "But I don't know if I can ever . . . I mean, I had hoped that after all these years, the thought of marital relations wouldn't panic me so." She blushed. "I do want to be with you . . . I like all the beginning parts, the kissing and the touching. It's just later on—"

"It's all right," he said, seeing the anxiety come into her face again. "We will take it slow, get through it together." He refused to believe that his bold and sassy wife couldn't conquer this with a little help.

He caressed her cheek. "Tell me what to do to make it better."

Her breath hitched in her throat. "I don't know. Everything is fine until you get on top of me, and I remember the orangery and the Vile Seducer and I . . . go a little mad."

Thinking of how well she'd reacted when he'd been behind her, and below her, he said, "What if I don't get on top of you?"

She blinked. "What do you mean? How else can you . . . can we . . ."

A rueful smile escaped him. "I forget that you can still be as naïve and innocent as any virgin."

"That's not true," she said mutinously. "I know things."

Her taking umbrage amused him. He would never figure Clarissa out, and he wasn't sure he wanted to. "You know some things, yes. Clearly not others. Like the fact that a man doesn't *have* to be on top of a woman to bed her."

The hint of hope in her gaze struck him to the heart. "He doesn't?"

"No, minx, he doesn't. The woman can be on top, can make love to the man, just as easily as he can make love to her."

Her brow knitted as if she were trying to work it out. "I can't see . . . I don't understand—"

"Shall I show you?"

He regretted the words when she tensed up and glanced away. "I—I don't know . . ."

"Clarissa," he said, catching her head in his hands and drawing her gaze back to his. "We won't ever do anything you don't want to. We can stop in the middle as often as you want, as many times as you want—"

She raised an eyebrow at that.

"I'm not saying it won't frustrate me, because it will. But I imagine it's just as frustrating for a woman not to have a whole and fulfilling life with her husband because she's afraid of the past."

"Yes." She squared her shoulders. "I think you're right. And I do want children, after all."

She would do this to have children. Somehow that

made him sad. He wanted her to do it for herself. For him.

But no matter; he would work with what he had. "My point is, we have plenty of time to do this however we want. For tonight, all I ask is if you'll let me demonstrate how it works. Nothing more. We don't have to actually *do* what I show you. Or we can, and the minute you balk, we'll stop. The minute you're frightened, we'll stop."

Her gaze turned hard. "I once heard that a man can't stop. That it's almost impossible to stop."

He snorted. "That's a lie men tell women to get under their skirts. Have I not stopped more than once? Was I not fully aroused this afternoon?"

She sucked in a ragged breath. "Yes. But you said you couldn't keep going through that."

"I was wrong." He buried his fingers in her loosely pinned hair. "I can go through that as many times as it takes to make you comfortable. I only ask that you talk to me. To tell me what you're feeling, what you want, what you—"

"Kiss me, Edwin. Just stop talking and kiss me."

He didn't need another invitation. He took her mouth, feeling all at sea. While he was glad he now knew why she'd shied from him, it was hard to realize she both wanted and feared him. He hated having her fear him.

So when her lips parted to let him in, it touched him deeply. His determined wife was always willing to "try"—and now that he realized how difficult even *that* was for her, he couldn't be insulted by it.

They kissed, his heart thundering in his chest, her breath stuttering against his. She tugged at his coat, so he shrugged it off and let her unbutton his waist-coat while he spread openmouthed kisses down her cheek and jaw and throat. He pulled off *her* coat and waistcoat—odd to be doing that—and then tugged her shirt out of her breeches so he could slip his hands beneath the linen to fondle her breasts.

"Yes," she murmured. "I like that. It feels wonder-ful when *you* do it." She pulled *his* shirt out, and ran her hands beneath the fabric and all over his bare chest. "You're so hard, so strong. It thrills me. And scares me."

"Your softness does the same thing to me. I don't want to do anything to hurt you."

"You won't. In my head, I know that." She stretched up to brush a kiss to his lips. "It's only my body that doesn't know it."

"Perhaps you should show your body that there's nothing to fear." Taking her by the hand, he drew her over to the window seat that overlooked the garden. He shucked off his trousers and his drawers and sat down, letting his shirt cover his erection. "When *I'm* afraid of something, it always helps me to get a good look at it. So perhaps if you get a good look at my . . . er . . ."

"Cock?"

He blinked. "You know that word?"

"I learned it from Yvette's slang dictionaries. That's what men call their . . . their things, isn't it? Cocks?"

"Vulgarly, yes."

"Then I shall call it that, too." She edged close to pull his shirt up, and her throat worked convulsively as she saw him fully erect. But at least she wasn't turning away. "And now that I get a good look at it, I'm not surprised. It's rather impudent. And big. It's no wonder that dealing with that . . . that monstrous thing hurts. I don't know how other women stand it going in."

"You suffered more pain than you should have." His throat tightened. "It hurt because Whiting took you even though he knew you weren't ready."

"Ready?"

Reaching up to undo her breeches, he exulted when she didn't shy away as he pushed them down. She even stepped out of them.

As he'd suspected, she wore no drawers underneath, but her long shirt covered her privates from his sight. Perhaps being covered would ease her fears a bit.

Like a gamekeeper approaching a wild deer, he inched his hand beneath her shirt to the juncture of her thighs, where he stroked her with slow, careful caresses. "This wetness? It's to make it easier for you to let a man in." He dipped his finger inside, relishing her soft sigh. "I daresay Whiting frightened you so much that whatever might have been there in reaction to his kisses dried right up."

"I *was* very . . . upset."

What an understatement. It took all his will to keep his expression calm and even, instead of black with the rage he felt every time he thought of Whiting ravaging her. "But the bastard didn't care and entered you anyway. It's rather like when I try to fit two pieces of an automaton together. If they're not properly oiled, the friction of the movements can damage the metal. You weren't 'oiled.' That's why it hurt so much."

She blinked. "Oh. That makes sense. But women are always talking about the pain—"

"The first time can hurt for some, I'm told, but that's mostly because a virgin goes into the experience nervous and afraid. That doesn't help." Continuing to caress her, he glanced up into her wary face. "Nature created men and women to fit together, sweetheart. But we have to *want* to fit together. Whiting didn't wait for you to want him. *I* will."

"I know. I trust you."

The words were a balm to his aching heart. "Then may I lift your shirt?"

"I'll do you one better," she said, her voice a little shaky. Then she pulled it off over her head and dropped it to the floor.

He dragged in a hot breath. She was naked except for her stockings and garters. And he'd never seen anything lovelier in his life—skin smooth as alabaster, plump breasts with rosy little nipples, and a curly thatch a hand's width below her saucily crooked navel.

"Whiting was a fool," he said as he drank his fill. "To trample over all this glorious beauty without even taking his time to explore."

A faint smile curved up her lips. "Which means you'll be the first to explore. If you like."

His pulse tripled. "I like," he rasped. "I like very much."

"Then go to it," she whispered. "Because I like very much having your hands and mouth on me."

Twenty-One

When he reached for Clarissa, the look in his eyes heated her blood. How strange that it seemed natural to be naked before him, to be wrapped in his arms as his mouth kissed and laved and licked her breasts, her belly, her . . . tender parts. Which felt hot and aching for him. And wet. Very, very wet.

You weren't "oiled." That's why it hurt so much.

Oh, how she prayed he was right. But Edwin never lied. He was very matter-of-fact, even about her being unchaste.

I understood you. I simply don't give a damn.

He didn't, did he? He only cared about how she'd been hurt, and he showed it now by being so tender, it made tears well in her throat all over again. "Oh, Edwin . . . I wish I'd told you long ago . . ."

Pausing to gaze up her, he said, "You weren't ready to tell me. I understand that." He bent to lick her down there, sending her up on her toes with excitement. Eyes gleaming at her, he murmured, "Shall I do what I did in the carriage?"

"Later," she breathed. "I haven't yet had a chance to explore *you*."

He gave her a blank look.

"I want to see *you* naked, too. I want to caress all the parts of you." She reached forward to drag his shirt off over his head, then pulled away to look at him, but it was hard to see him properly when he was seated. "Lean back a bit."

With a lift of one imperious brow, he did, letting his legs fall open with a certain insolence that should have alarmed her.

It did not. Because he was down there, and she was up here.

And my oh my, how fascinating this was. She could look at him as much as she pleased without being afraid he might leap on her. Surprisingly excited, she swept her gaze over the muscular shoulders, chest, and lean waist she'd already seen but hadn't touched, for fear of sparking his lust.

Then once again she took in the sight of the thick cock thrusting up from his nest of black curls. She still didn't see how it could fit inside her, but she had to admit it had a strange beauty all its own.

And the way it bobbed under her gaze made her want to laugh. But she knew Edwin wouldn't find *that* amusing.

Her gaze continued down over the well-wrought thighs she hadn't yet seen to the handsome calves that always looked so fine in evening attire, and then roamed back up. "Can I . . . touch you?"

"God, yes," he growled. Then, as if worried he was being too fierce, he added, "Please."

With a little thrill of anticipation, she stepped

forward. All the male beauty she'd coveted was now hers to fondle without fear. He'd said they could stop whenever she wanted, and she believed him.

Amazing how freeing it was, to know she could balk if she wished. Perversely, it prompted her to be bolder, to smooth her hands over everything—his arms, his chest, his thighs—to relish the different textures of hair and smooth skin and rough calluses. To feel his muscles flex and tighten beneath her touch.

What delicious wickedness! And nothing at all like suffering the sordid gropings of the Vile Seducer.

She brushed the head of his cock, and he swore under his breath. Jerking her hand back, she said, "I didn't mean to hurt you."

"It doesn't hurt," he ground out. "It just . . . makes me want you all the more. Perhaps we should return to letting me explore you."

Suddenly nervous, but also intrigued, she gazed down at the hard male form before her. "Or you could show me what you were talking about. Show me how a woman makes love to a man."

He went still. "I could." He searched her face. "If you're sure."

"I am." She thought she was, anyway.

"Very well." Drawing his legs together, he leaned forward to catch her by the hips and tug her toward him. "We'll start with you sitting astride me, on my thighs."

How curious. "Like this?" she asked as she straddled him as far away from his cock as she could get.

"If I promise not to ravish you, will you come a *little* nearer? You're hurting my knees."

"Oh! Sorry." She scooted closer. Now his cock reared up between them, just brushing her damp curls. "I still don't see how it would work like this."

"It wouldn't," he said, his voice oddly strained. "But if you *were* to choose to make love to me, you'd plant your knees on the seat on either side of me. Rising up on them, you'd fit yourself onto my cock, however slowly or quickly you liked, rather like pulling a glove onto your hand. If it hurt too badly, you could rise up and get right off. If you found it pleasant, you could inch down more. *You* would choose how far up inside your glove my hand should go."

"Oh." So there would be no thrusting and shoving into her, no fighting a man's weight atop her. She eyed him with suspicion. "You really would accept it if I stopped in the middle and pulled myself off of you?"

"I swear on my mother's grave," he said solemnly. "You will have me utterly at your mercy."

"All right, then." She swallowed hard. "I want to try it."

His cock, which had been flagging through the discussion, shot straight up. "You do?"

"I—I can't promise to endure it for long, but I want to try."

"That's all I ask."

With a determined nod, she knelt above him on the seat, straddling his hips. Though she'd understood his directions, it proved trickier than she'd expected.

"I can help," he said. "Or you can take my cock with your hand and guide it in."

That hadn't occurred to her. And she did *that*. In

the meantime, he started rubbing her nipples with his hands, making her feel quite . . . heated, and before she'd even realized it, she was sliding down upon him. To her shock, though his cock felt intrusive inside her, there was no pain. No pain *at all*. Just some tightness.

Her gaze flew to him. "It . . . it doesn't hurt!"

"Good." He didn't say, "I told you so," or, "Ta-da!" or anything. Indeed, he looked as if he were having difficulty just breathing. His eyes were closed, his jaw taut enough to cut glass. "God help me, minx. You feel incredible."

The rough timbre of his voice sent a feminine thrill through her that made her relax and slide down a bit more. "Do I?"

"Like silk. Hot, enveloping silk." He gave an undulating move that sent him farther up inside her, then gritted his teeth. "Sorry. I wasn't supposed to do that, I know. It's just . . . you feel so damned wonderful."

"So do you. I think." Thank God Yvette had been right. How much it hurt definitely depended on the man's approach.

"You *think*?" he echoed, a thread of amusement in his voice.

She wriggled on him, and the groan that came from deep in his throat made her feel more alive, more of a woman than she'd allowed herself to feel for years. "I'll have to experiment some more to be sure." She settled herself on him, trying to find a more comfortable position.

"Stop that." His eyes flew open. "God, please stop."

She blinked at him. "That's what *I* usually say. But *you* can't possibly want me to stop this."

"Not 'this.' *That*. Moving around. It's just enough motion to . . . make me insane."

"Is it?" She wiggled some more. "How about that?"

"Don't torture me, my sweet. I can't bear it."

"I'm not trying to torture you. I just really don't know what to do."

"Right. Of course." He was breathing hard, his eyes heavy-lidded. "Try . . . moving up and down."

Up and down? Remembering how the Vile Seducer had driven into her, she realized that this would be that in reverse, with her controlling the motion. How intriguing.

"*Please*," he rasped. "Before I go out of my mind."

"All right," she said, and came up, then slid down.

His fingers dropped to grip her hips. "Yes, sweetheart, yes. Again."

"For a man at my mercy, you are very demanding," she said with a sniff, but did what he asked.

This time, he gave a low moan of pure pleasure. It was quite rewarding. And the up-and-down motion felt good to her, too. Rather enjoyable. So she did it again. And again.

It got easier each time. And when he began to finger her down where they were joined, she felt that quick leap of sensation she'd felt when he'd had his mouth on her in the carriage. "Oh, *Edwin* . . . oh my . . ."

He kissed her then, deeply, fiercely. He'd begun thrusting up inside her, too, but she rather liked that. It gave her an idea of the proper rhythm. And when he bumped her a certain way . . . it was glorious. Absolutely glorious.

Heavens. This wasn't what she'd expected *at all*.

No pain . . . no fear. Just Edwin beneath her, undulating into her, making her want to devour him, to engulf him, to show him she truly was his bride. *His* woman. His wife.

"You're mine . . . now . . . Edwin Barlow," she said as she clutched at his shoulders, riding him faster, harder. "My husband. For always."

"My wife," he choked out, his face alight. "Forever."

It had the sound of a vow. And now that rushing feeling was building down low in her belly, and her fingernails dug into his shoulders and she felt as if she were hurtling across the grounds on horseback, neck-or-nothing . . . heading for the biggest jump of them all. The one that would take her into the heavens . . . glittering there . . . just beyond her reach . . .

"Yes . . . more . . ." she cried as their motions reached a fever pitch. "Yes, my darling, *yes!*"

He drove up and spilled himself inside her. "Clarissa . . . *My* Clarissa!"

Mine.

With that exultant thought, she shot over the moon and into the stars.

～∞∽

It took some time for Edwin to come to his senses, especially with his lovely wife draped luxuriously over him.

That was amazing. *She* was amazing. And he couldn't believe he'd finally made her his. Thank God it hadn't taken a year; he never would have lasted that long. He'd have had to go live with monks for a while.

He nuzzled her hair, which had tumbled down

rather spectacularly in the midst of their frenzy. It smelled of lilacs and lavender. So very sweet.

"It's getting dark outside," Clarissa murmured.

She was in a position to see out the window behind him. Fortunately, none of the servants went into the garden at this time of the day. They were too busy preparing for dinner.

Still . . . "It won't be long before we can be seen easily from the garden. Unless one of us gets up to blow out the candle."

She drew back to flash him a sultry smile. "Is that a hint that I should move? Am I too heavy for you?"

"Hardly." He lifted her off of him. "Though you're heavier than I would have expected for such a small woman." When she laughed, he realized that he probably shouldn't have been quite that honest. "I mean . . ."

"Don't mince words with me," she said as he rose. "You're probably the only man I know who would have been as understanding of my . . . difficulties as you were. Besides, I'll take your bluntness any day over a lot of insincere compliments."

"Glad to hear it. Because clearly I am very bad at them."

She chuckled. Curling up into a ball on the window seat, she watched as he went over to the desk fully naked. "You're a very handsome man, Lord Blakeborough. And I am being utterly sincere."

He snuffed the candle. "Keep saying things like that, Lady Blakeborough, and I'll be wanting to ravish you again."

She fell quiet. As he realized what he'd said, he shot her a concerned glance, but she wore a dreamy look. "It's a pity it wasn't you seducing me in that orangery years ago."

It certainly was. How different their lives would have been. But . . . "It would never have been me." He tugged on his drawers. "Gentlemen do not seduce young ladies. They court them, they secure their affections, and then they propose."

A sudden gleam in her eye was all the warning he got before she rose to amble toward him with a most seductive walk. "So you don't think I could have tempted you to seduce me?"

His throat went dry at the sight of her so rumpled and lovely. "Tempted? Yes." He pulled her into his arms for a thorough kiss, then drew back to stare into her face. "But I would never have acted upon it."

Her smile faltered. "Are you quite sure it doesn't bother you that I . . . am not . . ."

"It doesn't." He kissed the tip of her nose. "I'm *very* happy with my choice of wife."

She eyed him askance. "Even though I'm reckless and impudent and always getting into trouble?"

"I'll take you any way I can get you, minx—reckless, impudent, and all." Even skittish and wary. As long as he could kiss the fear from her from time to time.

A sudden knock at the door made them both jump. "Milord, milady? Dinner is served."

"Thank you, John!" he called out. "We'll be there presently."

"We can't go to dinner yet," she hissed. "I'm naked!"

"And you do look very fetching that way, too."

With a roll of her eyes, she hurried to don her shirt. Or rather, *his* old shirt.

He followed her. "We have a choice, minx. We can

go to dinner late, with you dressed in breeches and me thinking the entire time how I want to get you out of them. Or we can ask for a tray upstairs and head up to my bedchamber or yours. Either way, we scandalize the servants, so—"

"We might as well go upstairs," she said in a throaty voice as she approached to place her hand on his bare chest. "I'd rather enjoy seeing how the woman-on-the-top thing works in a bed."

When she ran her finger down his chest and strolled away, he got dressed so fast, it was a miracle he didn't injure something. At last, they were having their wedding night. And he didn't intend to miss one minute.

Twenty-Two

A week later, Clarissa headed to London in the carriage with her husband and wondered where the time had gone. Days of easy camaraderie had bled into nights of passion. No nightmares. No fear. No horrible reminders of the past.

Well, she still couldn't lie beneath him without panicking, but he didn't seem to mind that she was always on top. At least she hoped he didn't mind. *She* had certainly come to enjoy their way of swiving. She liked arousing him. Making him lose control. Watching him fall apart beneath her. It was wonderful. They were together in every respect, and she'd never dreamed that could happen.

And if sometimes she wished she could try making love the other way, she shoved that from her mind. Because better that they do it the way they did, than not do it at all. It certainly did keep him in a far pleasanter mood than he'd been in during the first week of their marriage.

But not today. Staring over at him now, she could see how withdrawn he was from her, how pensive and subdued. Fortunately, she'd begun to understand that it was his way of dealing with things that worried him. He had to pull into himself to mull things over from every angle.

Still, they were going to their wedding celebration at Vauxhall, and she wasn't about to spend it with him looking dour and gloomy.

"I cannot wait for the party. It sounds like great fun, don't you think?"

"Indeed," he said, staring out the window.

She eyed him askance. He hadn't been so sanguine about Mama's plans when she'd come out to Hertfordshire three days ago for final approval. Annoyed that she couldn't find a balloonist, Mama had hired a female tightrope walker and an acrobat who did tricks with a hoop. After Clarissa had grown tired of fruitlessly trying to rein her mother in, she'd amused herself by cataloguing Edwin's many attempts to restrain his horror every time Mama mentioned some new excess.

So either he'd had a change of heart since then, or he wasn't paying attention to what she was saying now. She decided to test her theory. "Mama wrote me yesterday to say that she'd enlisted a snake charmer for the party, too."

"That's nice."

She stifled a laugh. "I told her that a lone snake charmer wouldn't be enough—we needed at least sixteen to do it properly. Preferably with enormous turbans in puce velvet."

"Uh-huh. Puce velvet. Right."

"I told her I was sure you would approve the three thousand pounds it will cost."

"Yes, that sounds—" His gaze shot to her. "What costs three thousand pounds?"

Of *course* he'd registered the part about the money. "Mama's sixteen snake charmers," she managed to say with a straight face. "For the wedding celebration."

"*What?* When did I agree to snake charmers, and why the devil would it cost three thousand—"

She began laughing, and as he realized she'd been bamming him, he threw himself back in his seat with a snort. "Very amusing," he drawled.

"You should have . . . seen your face . . ." she gasped between giggles, "when it d-dawned on . . . you that . . . Oh, my word!"

He crossed his arms over his chest. "Are you quite finished mocking me?"

With considerable effort, she made a stern face. "Yes, my lord. Of course, my lord. The situation is much too serious for humor, my lord."

"Now you're mocking me for complaining about your mocking me," he grumbled. "Though you must admit that your mother is turning our wedding celebration into a circus performance."

"I know," she said soothingly. "And I know you hate it, as do I. But let this be a lesson to you. Never let guilt persuade you to give my mother free rein in *anything.*"

"I'll definitely heed that advice in the future." He stared out the window. "But that's not what has me concerned. Aren't you the least bit worried about Durand?"

"I always find it easier to brazen out the things that frighten me than to cower in a corner. It doesn't always work, but I have to try. He isn't invited to our grand dinner, and even if he shows up somehow, I can always trust you to protect me."

His frown softened. "Yes. You can."

Except that it was *Edwin's* family secrets that needed protecting. She wished he'd say what they were, but she could hardly fault him for wanting to keep them close. He saw it as looking after his sister. One day, he'd trust his wife enough to tell her, and when he did, she would try to be as understanding as he'd been about her darkest secret.

"What good would it do Count Durand to cozy up to me now, anyway? I'm married." She smiled softly at him. "Happily, it seems."

That finally lightened his mood. "It does seem that way, doesn't it?"

"You see? I never thought that could happen, and now it has. So I have complete confidence that your bluff was successful and Count Durand has been routed at last."

He smiled. "You, sweetheart, are the eternal optimist. Even after all your troubles, you try to put a good face on things. It's one of many things I like about you."

Her good mood evaporated. *Like.* Not *love.*

She shouldn't care that he'd never professed to love her, since she'd never professed to love *him.* But she did care. Which she didn't want to examine too closely. "I like that my eternal optimism doesn't drive you mad," she said lightly.

"It does, but it's a pleasant sort of madness." He

glanced out the window. "We're nearly to Vauxhall, and I haven't yet given you your present."

"You got me another present?"

"Something very mundane." Reaching into his pocket, he pulled out a necklace with a silver leaf pendant with what looked like two jeweled raindrops on it. "For my whimsical wife."

"That isn't mundane at all. It's quite beautiful." Though she was rather surprised it wasn't another automaton.

When she reached for it, he stopped her. "It has a secret." He pressed one of the "raindrops" and the leaf pendant fell from the chain into his hands. He pressed the other and a wicked-looking blade shot out of the leaf sheath. "It's to keep you safe if I'm not around."

"Oh my." She took it from him and examined it. "Show me how it works again?"

It took only a few moments of demonstration for her to master opening it and also restoring it to the sheath and the chain.

Once she had it back in its original form, he closed her fingers around it. "Wear it or put it wherever you won't lose it. And I'll be much less worried about you."

A lump caught in her throat. "Thank you, I *shall* wear it." Staring into his eyes, she hung it about her neck. "Close to my heart."

He gazed into her face with such intensity that it started her pulse thundering. Then the carriage drew to a halt and the door swung open.

"It's about time you got here!" cried her mother, leaning heavily on her cane. "Everyone is waiting for you."

They stepped out to loud applause. Clarissa scanned the crowd, but saw no signs of Durand, thank God.

It was a good thing, because she needed all her strength for enduring the results of Mama's extravagance. The fete began with a rousing orchestral piece and got more dramatic from there—with acrobats, dancing, massive bowls of negus, and enormous platters of suckling pig and roast game cock.

It went on for hours, ending with a pyrotechnical display that nearly rivaled those done for the king's birthday.

Mama would either become a laughingstock in society because of it, or everyone would dismiss her eccentricities as they always did because she had such an amiable nature.

Through it all, Edwin miraculously maintained his composure. Clarissa wasn't sure if that was to please her, or because he spent the entire affair watching the crowd for Count Durand. So she was rather relieved when one of his club members engaged him in a discussion of how the pyrotechnics had been done, and she didn't have to worry about him so much.

Mama, however, was another matter. Leaning on a servant's arm, she came up to where Clarissa was standing. "There you are. We have a problem."

Those words had already been spoken half a dozen times this evening, and it always fell to Clarissa to solve those problems because Mama had such difficulty getting around.

"What is it this time?" She was tired and ready to leave.

"Those foreign pyrotechnical fellows are complaining about something in Italian. I *think* it has to do with what I paid them, but I'm not sure."

Mama gestured toward where the men were packing up their equipment behind the rows of boxes. Clarissa could just see them through the passage between the two closest sets of boxes overlooking the orchestra stage.

"My Italian isn't nearly as good as yours, so could you take care of it?" Mama laid the back of her hand dramatically on her forehead. "I swear, if I have to deal with one more matter or walk one more step, I shall collapse right here."

Clarissa stifled her irritation. "I'll handle it, Mama." Given how bad her mother's Italian really was, the men could be saying something as inconsequential as "We need a glass of water."

She strode off toward the Italians, but as she passed between the two sets of boxes, a man stepped into her path. "I need to talk to you."

Her heart sank. Count Durand! When she glanced over at the workmen, only to find that they'd melted into the night, she realized the count had planned this. He'd watched her deal with things for Mama all evening, and had been biding his time until he could create a reason for her to go off alone.

A quick glance behind her showed that in the passage, she was hidden from Edwin's sight. She was *not* going to let this happen. Turning swiftly on her heel, she started back, but the Frenchman called after her, "Do you *want* me to expose your husband's secrets to the world, simply because you won't allow me a moment of your time?"

She halted. Edwin's secrets. Drat it. She reached up

to release the leaf from the chain, then palmed it and turned to face him. "Very well. Say what you have to say."

"If you'll just come this way—"

"No. You say it here, or not at all."

That gave him pause. "Aren't you worried that someone might hear us talking about your precious husband's secrets?"

"No, because that will put an end to your blackmail."

"And your husband will land in gaol."

She dragged in a harsh breath. "There's no way on earth that my husband has *ever* done anything to land him in gaol. That is absurd."

When she started to turn away again, he said hastily, "No, but his father did. And I can easily make it seem as if your husband was part of it."

She froze. Drat Edwin and his secrets. She didn't even know how many of the count's claims were true. "What could his father possibly have done that would implicate Edwin?"

"He spied for the French during the war. And if you don't go with me now, I'll make sure the world sees the evidence."

"What evidence? I can't imagine you have any."

"I have his father's reports. And I can frame it so it looks as if Blakeborough helped him. But even if I don't succeed in proving *that*, there will be enough outrage to ensure that you, and he, and your respective families will never be able to raise your heads in good society again."

Edwin hurried up to Lady Margrave, who had just collapsed onto a bench. "Where's Clarissa? I can't find her." He'd turned away for only a moment, and his wife was gone. What the devil?

"She went to deal with those Italian pyrotechnic fellows," Lady Margrave said with a wave in the direction they'd been earlier. They weren't there.

His heart faltered when he saw them on the other end of the boxes, headed for the exit. There was no sign of Clarissa. Striding over to them, he asked in Italian where his wife was, but when they exchanged looks of alarm and started protesting that they knew nothing, he didn't waste his time with them. He broke into a run down the path behind the boxes where they'd just been working.

As he neared the end of the first row, he heard Clarissa's voice. With a relieved sigh, he slowed to a walk. Until her words registered.

"You're a liar, sir. There's no way on earth that my husband's father was a traitor. I don't care what evidence you claim to have, or what you think you can prove—"

Edwin vaulted around the corner of the box to find his wife facing down Durand. "Get away from my wife," Edwin growled, quickly putting himself between them.

"I *knew* you hadn't told her about the spying," Durand said with a sneer. "She would never stand for being married to a traitor's son. So if you'd said anything, the two of you wouldn't be here pretending that this wedding is a love match."

"It *is* a love match!" Clarissa spat from behind Edwin.

That momentarily threw Edwin off guard, even knowing she was just trying to get rid of Durand.

"Really?" Durand said coldly. "Blakeborough is in love with you? Does he know what a little whore you are?"

Fury inflaming him, Edwin caught Durand by the throat and squeezed. "I warned you not to bother my wife. I swear, I'll kill you right here and now, just for such a vile lie—"

"No, no, no, you can't!" Clarissa cried, dragging on Edwin's arm. "Or you will hang for it, and I cannot lose you, too!"

That last remark was the only thing that cut through the red haze in his head. He released Durand, who stumbled back choking and coughing.

After a moment, the bastard growled, "For that, Blakeborough, I challenge you to a duel at dawn. Over your wife's honor, which I maintain is scanty at best."

"Don't listen to him!" Clarissa cried as Edwin bristled again. "Can't you see he's goading you? He wants to kill you so he can get to me. You must not fight him!"

Durand gave a mocking laugh. "That's all right, Lady Clarissa, he's not going to accept. Everyone knows he despises dueling. Most cowards usually do."

"Ah, but this won't be a duel," Edwin said coldly. "It will be justice. For your tormenting my wife, trying to force her into marrying you. For frightening her and plaguing her, for nearly assaulting her, and daring to cast slurs upon her character."

"Edwin, *no*," Clarissa said.

Durand ignored her to stare Edwin down. "Does that mean you accept my challenge?"

"It does. Choose your seconds, and I shall see you
at dawn at Green Park. Pistols are my weapon of
choice." He turned to Clarissa. "Come, my dear, we're
leaving now."

By tomorrow, he meant to be rid of Durand once
and for all.

Twenty-Three

Clarissa managed to hold her tongue until their carriage pulled away. Only then did she face him, shoulders set. "You can't do this."

"I can and I will. It's the only way to stop him."

The hard edge to his voice made her despair. "I don't want to lose you."

"You won't. I happen to be very good with a pistol."

"I've no doubt of that. But if you kill him, you will end up accused of murder, forced to flee."

"Unlike your brother, I need only say that the bastard impugned your honor. No jury will convict an Englishman for defending his wife from a Frenchman."

"Not just a Frenchman. A French *diplomat*. With high connections in both governments."

He dragged in a heavy breath. "It will be difficult for us socially for a while, but . . ."

". . . not nearly as bad as if your father is revealed to be a traitor. Is that what you're thinking?"

Edwin released a coarse oath. "I never wanted you to know about that."

Her heart sank. "So it's true, then. Your father really was a traitor."

"It appears he was." Edwin rubbed the back of his neck. "Durand showed me the reports written in Father's hand, which were apparently made on Father's jaunts to a certain private opium-smoking club in London."

"Opium! Your father smoked opium?"

"I'm not sure. For years, I'd assumed so." His breathing grew labored. "When Mother died, I went looking for Father, so the servants were forced to send me to that club. That's how I learned of his association with it. He wouldn't speak of it at all, so I deduced he went there to indulge. But apparently he was going there to speak to soldiers and sailors and glean information for the French."

She sat back against the seat. "I can't believe it. I know your father had his weaknesses, but to be a *traitor* to his country . . ."

"It came as a shock to me, too."

"And you're sure these 'reports' aren't forged?"

"They certainly looked genuine. And clandestine activities would help to explain why Father was always running off to London and abandoning us."

Mulling that over a moment, she wondered what to say, what to do to help him. This duel clearly wasn't just about her. It was about saving his family—all of them—from scandal. It was about eliminating Durand as a threat.

She folded her arms over her waist. "How do you know that if you kill Durand, he won't have already instructed someone, in the event of his death, to expose your father's activities?"

"I don't. But it's better than waiting around for whenever he *does* choose to do it. And it will be a great deal more difficult for him to fan the flames of a scandal if he's dead."

"Not if *you're* the one who's dead."

He turned his head to the window, and the streetlamps caught the consternation on his face. "I won't let him kill me."

"You are not God, Edwin! You're fallible. And the thought of something happening to you—"

When she broke off with a choked cry, he shot her an alarmed glance, then moved to sit beside her. "Sweetheart, nothing will happen to me, I swear it."

"You don't know that!"

His hand clutched hers. "You're really worried about me."

"Of *course* I'm worried about you. You're my husband."

"And you're not angry with me for keeping the full extent of Durand's blackmail from you until now?" he said, sounding a little incredulous.

"Why should I be? Do you really think I care what your father did?"

"I'm sure you care that I married you knowing perfectly well that if Durand acted on his threats, you and I would be outcasts. Traitors aren't well regarded in this country, even long-dead ones." His voice roughened. "And if Durand succeeds in somehow connecting me . . ."

"How could he do that? I don't understand."

"I was nineteen when I was seen going into that

same opium den. It was only the one time, but all it takes is a single witness remembering my being there, and it will be enough to foment speculation and cause trouble for me."

Frustration twisted inside her. "That count is a blackguard!" she said stoutly. "I don't trust him. You can't play into his plans, whatever they are, by meeting him for a duel."

He stiffened. "I have no choice."

"That's not true! You have friends at your club— Lord Fulkham, for example. You should go to him for advice. I hear he's high up in government."

"All the more reason he won't want to be tainted by helping the son of a traitor."

She huffed out a breath. "So talk to one of the other gentlemen. There must be someone who can help you rout Durand. Those Duke's Men friends of Jeremy's, for example."

"Not a chance. I am not risking anyone else hearing of it. I will fight Durand at dawn, and that is that."

"But Edwin—"

"Enough! This is my decision, not yours."

The force of his declaration shattered her confidence. "You're upset because he called me a whore, aren't you?" Ever since Durand's words, she'd wondered if Edwin might have taken them to heart. *She* knew Durand had been goading him, but what if Edwin thought otherwise? "Are you afraid that he had a reason, that while he was courting me I allowed him to—"

"No, of course not. I asked you before if he forced himself on you, and you said he did not, and I believe you."

"B-but his words made you so angry . . . Are you sure that they didn't make you uncertain whether to trust me?"

"Don't be absurd. I trust you, I swear." He pulled her into his arms. "It's you who don't trust me . . . with your life, your future. Hell, you won't even let me make love to you in the usual way, because you're still afraid I might hurt you." When she groaned, he let out an oath. "I'm sorry, sweetheart, I shouldn't have mentioned that. It doesn't matter."

"Clearly, it *does*."

And she should have realized sooner that he saw her difficulties as a mark of her continuing distrust of him. Even the most understanding man in the world had his pride, and it wounded her husband's that she couldn't entirely trust him in bed.

"All of it matters," she went on. "Whether you ignore my advice and I ignore your desires *matters*. Because if we don't trust each other, what is left?" She clasped him about the neck. "And I *do* trust you. I trusted you from the moment you proposed marriage."

"Right," he said. "Except for demanding a clause in our settlement to ensure I didn't attack you."

She swallowed. "Looking back, I can see that perhaps that wasn't the *best* strategy, but it made sense at the time. And even with that clause, I never locked my bedchamber door to you—not once in our first week alone together. I could have, but I didn't."

That seemed to give him pause, for he dragged in an unsteady breath.

"Please, please, don't fight this duel, my darling," she went on. "I'm begging you."

He bent close enough for her to feel his warm breath against her lips. "What kind of husband would I be if I let him get away with all that he's done and is still trying to do to you?"

"What kind of wife would *I* be if I let you die defending me?"

Their gazes locked for a long moment. Then he kissed her.

Though it took her by surprise, she welcomed it, needing to be sure of him. His kiss was all-consuming, hard and sweet and urgent by turns, as if he couldn't bear to stop.

And she gave herself up to it with the same desperation. She had to make him see that what they had was too precious to throw away. That together they could get through anything.

"I want you, minx," he rasped in her ear. "Now. Here. It's mad, I know—"

"Not mad at all. I want you, too."

That was all the invitation he needed to start dragging up her skirts while kissing her as if it were their last time together. Which it very well might be.

No, she wouldn't let that happen. She couldn't. She would show him just how perfect it could be between them, tempt him not to be so foolish as to risk everything out of some noble pride or fear of scandal.

He unbuttoned his trousers, then tried to pull her astride him.

"No," she whispered, "not this time. I want you on top of me."

"Clarissa, I wasn't saying—"

"I know. I want to do it. I want you to take me

as you'd take any woman. As you'd take your wife if she were . . . any other woman."

She had to make him understand that she no longer saw him as a man who could ravage her, but as her husband, the only man she trusted with her body.

When he still hesitated, she said, "You're not remotely like the Vile Rapist, and I'm no longer the same Clarissa he raped, nor even the Clarissa of a few weeks ago. I'm finally ready to put that behind me. But I need to prove that to myself. And to you."

Even in the dim light, she could feel him searching her face. "Do you realize that's the first time you've ever called it a rape?"

That startled her. Was it? Her heart began to pound. Yes, it was. "He raped me," she said, trying out the sentence and feeling the truth of it.

"Yes." His voice was firm and sure, bolstering her confidence.

"It wasn't my fault."

"It was *never* your fault, my sweet. It's time you stop blaming yourself."

She clutched at his shoulders. "He had no right to rape me," she said fiercely. She'd partly acknowledged it in her head, but now she accepted it. Believed it. Was angry over it.

"No right whatsoever. As far as I'm concerned, he deserved to die. Who knows how many other women he would have assaulted if he hadn't?"

She'd never thought of it that way. It dampened the guilt she'd always felt over Niall's sacrifice, soothed the hurt of his exile a little.

But that didn't mean she would let her husband follow the same path. "If you're still determined to fight Durand, then I'm going to show you what you'll be missing if you're exiled or murdered." Scooting back into the corner, she tugged him toward her. "I'm going to show you how it could be between us if you'd only refuse to fight him."

He let her pull him against her until he was crowding her in the corner, as much of him between her legs and on top of her as they could manage in the confines of the carriage. "*This* is what I'm fighting for, my sweet," he growled. "You. Us. Our future."

"We'll *have* no future if you die."

"I won't." He seized her mouth once more, and for the first time, the weight of him on her was a reminder rather than a warning of how strong he was. That it made him fierce in her defense, determined and fine and noble.

Yes, the panic was lurking, but it had shrunk to a pea. So very small, she could ignore it. And one day, she would banish it, too.

She tore her lips from his to whisper, "Take me, Edwin. Fill me up."

With a growl, he entered her, more forcefully than usual but not enough to alarm her. And it was amazing. Not because he was on top of her and driving into her, but because she wasn't afraid. Because she knew she could stop him at any moment, that she could end things on a word.

This was what trust felt like.

He gave her no quarter, and to her shock, it thrilled her. He thundered into her, she rained on him, and it was like coming home. They were two parts of a whole, moving together in such intimate perfection it made her want to cry.

"Edwin," she whispered. "Yes, like that. Harder. More. Give me everything, my darling."

"Everything is already yours," he rasped as he fondled her breast through her gown. "That will never change."

For her, either. And as the truth blazed into her soul, she kissed him to keep from blurting it out.

She loved him. She wasn't sure how or when it had happened, but somewhere in the past few weeks, she'd fallen in love with Edwin. And now that she'd found him, was she to lose him?

No. *No!*

Slipping her hands down to his fine, taut buttocks, she cupped them to get him closer, deeper. She would drown him in pleasure, if that was what it took.

Instead, he drowned *her* in it, reaching between their bodies to finger her until she was fighting for breath and thought, fighting not to be the first one to succumb to her release. If she couldn't have his love, she wanted his surrender. *Needed* his surrender.

Shimmying and writhing beneath him, she ran her hands down the backs of his thighs, the tips of her fingers just brushing his ballocks between his legs.

He swore under his breath. "Come for me, sweetheart . . . please . . . I can't wait . . . much longer."

Neither could she. "Don't . . . wait." She kissed and caressed, touched and met each thrust eagerly, hungry for all of him . . . for the man who was her husband, the man whom she loved.

"I need you," he murmured against her ear. "God . . . stay with me . . . Clarissa. Never leave me."

"I wouldn't," she choked out. "I couldn't." Like

a rising tide, her release was rolling up in her, wave after wave, urge after urge, driving her up toward the surface, toward the sun . . .

"If I have to go into exile . . . promise you'll go . . . with me . . ."

"I will." She clenched on his cock as she felt herself exploding through the surface into sweet oblivion. "To the ends . . . of the earth . . . if I must."

With that, he, too, found his release. As they strained together, she milking him, he filling her, she held him close and thought the words she dared not say to the man who didn't believe in love.

I love you, Edwin.

Twenty-Four

By the time they turned onto his street, they'd made themselves presentable again. Or as presentable as two people could be who'd just been swiving wildly in a carriage.

Edwin didn't really care if anybody could tell. He meant to spend all night making love to his wife. Because this might be his last night with Clarissa for some time.

Or forever.

He scowled. No, he would not let Durand win. Surely Fate would not allow such a bastard to prevail.

It allowed Clarissa to be raped.

Which was precisely why it was long past time she got some reward for all her trials. She deserved it. He would give it to her.

You are not God, Edwin!

Great, now his conscience was quoting his wife. And no, he was not God. Because if he had been, Whiting would have been struck by lightning before he'd ever brought Clarissa into that orangery.

"Edwin, something's going on," Clarissa murmured.

He glanced out the window as their coach came to a halt. There was another carriage in front of his town house, which he recognized as one of Warren's. Had Clarissa's mother come here? No, why would she? They'd just left her.

So Edwin wasn't entirely shocked when the footman opened the door to the coach and greeted them with the words, "Lord Knightford is here to see you, milord."

"Warren is back?" Clarissa exclaimed as Edwin helped her out. Then her face turned ashen. "Oh no, something must have happened to Niall!"

Before Edwin could stop her, she raced up the steps, with him following. When they entered the house and were directed to the drawing room, they found a grim-faced Warren waiting for them with a glass of brandy in hand. Edwin tensed up.

"What's wrong?" Clarissa cried as she ran over to Warren. "Is Niall all right? Why are you back so soon?"

"Niall is well. But he told me something so alarming that I spent only a day with him before I rushed back."

Clarissa edged closer to Edwin, as if seeking support, and he looped his arm about her waist.

Warren's gaze narrowed on them. "And by the way, congratulations on your nuptials." He swallowed some brandy. "I go away for a few weeks, and you two get married behind my back."

"We had no choice," Edwin said. "Durand left us none."

"I can imagine. That's why I returned. Because after talking to Niall, I discovered that not only did he know of Durand, but he thinks he knows why the man has been plaguing Clarissa: Durand is Joseph Whiting's cousin on his mother's side. Apparently they were the closest of friends, and grew up together before Durand's family returned to France."

Edwin's gut knotted up. Bloody, bloody hell. This wasn't entirely about Clarissa. It was about Whiting. And Niall.

Warren stared at Edwin, and a bitterness entered his voice. "But I don't suppose you realize what that means. Niall had to explain it to me. Though I knew that Niall had killed Whiting in a duel, I didn't know why. Until now."

Edwin felt Clarissa sway against him, and anger welled up in him. "Actually, I know precisely what it means. Because she told me."

Warren stared at Clarissa with a wounded expression. "Yet you couldn't tell me, your own cousin? All these years of looking after you, not knowing that a bastard like Whiting had . . . had . . ."

"I couldn't tell anyone," she whispered. "They made me promise not to. Papa was determined that no one would ever learn of it. I'm surprised that Niall even revealed it to you, since he's kept it secret all these years."

"He didn't have much choice." Eyes hard, Warren swigged more brandy. "After he heard about Durand's pursuit of you, he got alarmed and told me the whole sordid story. He was terrified that the count would hurt you.

"But I was also worried that Durand would go after Niall, especially after Niall told me that his reason for decamping from Spain to Portugal—and calling on me for help—was his friends' warning him that someone had been asking around about him in Spain."

"Durand," Edwin bit out. "Or men he hired."

"Oh, God," Clarissa said. "And I talked to that devil about Niall, too! Nothing that would give away where he was, but still . . . Given that Count Durand claimed he wanted to marry me, it didn't occur to me to question his interest in my brother."

"So he's trying to find Niall and hoping to use Clarissa to do it," Edwin mused aloud. "I assume he wants revenge for his cousin's death. But why *now*? If it was so important to him, why not seek revenge seven years ago, right after the duel?"

Warren set down his empty glass. "I wondered that, too. Niall said Clarissa's father had made some deal with Whiting's mother that she wouldn't—"

"—speak of the matter," Edwin finished, impatiently. "Yes, we know that."

"So Niall assumes she broke her silence," Warren said. "He's just not sure why."

"Probably because she was dying," Clarissa said in a small voice. "She died of a lingering illness last year. I saw it in the papers. And if Durand had been anywhere around her at the time, if she were using laudanum or if she were even delirious—"

"She may have said something," Edwin put in. "And that sparked this whole thing. Having a relation die in an honorable duel over some anonymous soiled dove is one thing." His voice hardened. "But when the duel is with a respectable woman's brother, and the relation's offer to marry her was refused, the man might suspect something more nefarious was at work." He glanced at Warren. "When did Durand return to England as a member of the ambassador's staff?"

"Last summer."

Clarissa caught her breath. "Mrs. Whiting died last autumn." Her gaze flew to Edwin. "*That's* why Count Durand called me a whore tonight. It wasn't to goad you. It was because he knows everything, has always known everything. And he probably blames me for his cousin's death."

"That damned arse," Edwin growled. "If he'd had the tale from Whiting's ailing mother, she would never have admitted that his precious cousin was a rapist. There's no telling how she would have cast the tale in her final hours. Or if she might have demanded that he seek justice for the family."

"Wait a minute," Warren asked Clarissa, "Durand called you a *whore*? I will beat him within an inch of his life!"

"No need," Clarissa said dryly. "Your fool of a friend there challenged him to a duel for it."

Warren blinked. "Damn." He stared at Edwin. "Are you mad?"

"You were just talking about beating him yourself," Edwin shot back. "I'm defending my wife's honor!"

"Yes, but a duel . . ." Warren said. "You don't even believe in duels."

Edwin crossed his arms over his chest. "A man can alter his opinions."

"And a man can be stubborn to a fault," Clarissa replied.

"Nothing has changed," Edwin told her.

"*Everything* has changed! Since this isn't about Durand's wild obsession with me, he's not going to stop until he gets what he wants—the information about where to find my brother."

"And possibly," Warren put in, "the chance to humiliate Clarissa by telling the world what happened."

"He could have done that long ago if that's what he intended," Edwin pointed out.

"Yes, but then he would have lost his chance to find Niall," Warren said. "He wants them both—her ruined and Niall charged with murder."

"And if he's anything like Whiting," Clarissa said, "he will break every rule—even cheat at a duel—to get rid of his opposition, who happens to be you. And he'll get away with it because of his position! Then who will keep him from dragging *your* family through the mud? If he reveals your father's activities—"

"What activities?" Warren asked.

"All the more reason to kill him," Edwin said coldly, feeling beleaguered on all fronts. "Then he can't hurt anyone."

"Only if you win!" she cried.

When Edwin bristled at that, Warren said hastily, "Even if you don't, there would be repercussions, old boy. You can't kill a highly placed French diplomat, even in a duel over your wife's honor, without comment. You ought to go to his superiors."

"What superiors?" Edwin spat. "*He* is the most senior member at the French embassy right now! And there's no time to go through channels."

"Unless you refuse to fight him," Clarissa said stoutly. "You've bluffed him before and it worked. Just do it again. Tell him to go to the devil."

"And what happens to you when he has me dragged

before the courts on trumped-up charges of treason?" Edwin countered.

"Hold on, now," Warren said, "what's all this about *treason?*"

Clarissa ignored him. "You could consult with your friends at the club, talk to Warren's friends, gather some help and advice before you go waltzing off to die! But you simply won't."

"Because I refuse to embroil a bunch of friends and strangers in my private affairs. And certainly not in the private affairs of my wife!"

"Do *not* claim you're doing this for me, Edwin Blakeborough! I've argued myself hoarse begging you not to fight Count Durand, and you've ignored me. You're doing this for yourself. For your sense of justice and right, for your belief that a man should risk his own life to protect the reputation of a woman."

"Yes! He should!"

"Even if she doesn't want him to?" She planted her hands on her hips. "I've already lost my brother to exile because he was protecting my reputation. I don't want to lose you because of it, too. I would rather spend the rest of my life dealing with scandal than watch the man I love die trying to protect me, simply because he doesn't want 'a bunch of friends and strangers' to know his 'private affairs'!"

The man I love.

The words stunned him. She loved him? Truly?

As if she didn't even realize what she'd said, she added, "So I'm washing my hands of this whole thing." She tipped up her chin at Warren. "Perhaps you can talk some sense into him. I give up."

Then she stormed from the room.

Edwin could only stand there staring after her. The word *love* rang in his ears, shocking him with its power to beguile. If she *loved* him . . .

"All right," Warren broke into his thoughts. "Now that she's gone, you'd best tell me what the hell is going on. Why would you be accused of treason? What activity of your father's is Durand threatening to reveal? And how in God's name did you end up married to my cousin in only a few short weeks?"

"It's a long story."

"Then you'd better talk fast." He examined his watch. "Because unless we think of something, you'll be fighting a duel in four hours. And I'm not acting as your second for it unless I know what I'm getting into."

Edwin gritted his teeth. "Fine. And in case you're wondering, I never told you the spying and treason part because I didn't know about it myself until two weeks ago."

"*Spying?* God, this gets worse by the moment."

"You have no idea," he muttered.

Then he began to relate a highly truncated version of what had happened since Warren's departure. To Warren's credit, he didn't pepper Edwin with inconsequential questions. He just listened.

He did look rather speculative when Edwin got to the part about proposing marriage to Clarissa, but wisely didn't say anything.

When Edwin was finished, Warren headed for the door.

"Where are you going?" Edwin asked.

"You are in over your head, my friend. And no matter what you say, you need help. So we're going to talk to Fulkham and see what he can do."

"And what makes you think he won't just leap on the chance to make an example out of a traitor like my father?"

Warren stared hard at him. "*I'm* the one who convinced him to join St. George's. That means I vouch for his character. Do you question my judgment?"

Edwin gritted his teeth. "No."

"Good." Warren strode up to him. "Because if you did, I would have to remind you of the many ways I've championed you through the years. Of the times I helped you get Yvette and Clarissa out of youthful scrapes."

That brought Edwin up short. "And . . . I appreciate that."

"Do you? You're behaving like an ungrateful bastard at the moment. You *have* friends, Edwin, whether you accept it or not. There's me, there's Keane, there's the men at the club."

When Edwin just stared at him, Warren added, "They look up to you because they think you're sensible and rational. They know you'll always be in their corner. Can't you have the same faith in *them*? Accept that perhaps they will stand behind you because they're your *friends*?"

"You don't understand—"

"I understand that you have always operated as if you alone are responsible for your life, your fate. That you have no one to turn to. Well, that's not true. Your father may have pretty well abandoned you, but your family will not. Your friends will not. Your *wife* clearly will not."

"Leave my wife out of it," Edwin growled.

"Why? You said you were doing this for her. But

she's right: You're *not* doing this for her. You're doing this to prove that you're a better man than your father. That you can take care of your family. You're doing this in an attempt to protect Clarissa and Yvette, which is a noble idea on the face of it."

Warren leaned in. "But at the heart of it is pride. You don't want to ask for help. You don't trust anyone to give you help. You would rather risk your future with a woman who loves you than rely on the aid of your friends."

Glancing away, Edwin swallowed past the thickness in his throat. What if Warren was right? That he didn't trust *anyone*? That he would give up a future with Clarissa rather than take a chance on his friends and family?

The possibility made his stomach roil. Until now, he'd let his anger at Durand propel him forward. But Clarissa didn't want the risk he was ready to embrace. She didn't want a life without him.

The truth of that sang through his heart like a nightingale's trill.

She *loved* him.

And surely that was worth taking a chance on the men who believed in him.

"All right. Let's go find Fulkham. And I pray to God he has some idea for routing Durand. Because if he doesn't, you, my friend, will be going with me to fight that blasted Frenchman at dawn."

It took Edwin and Warren some time to rouse Fulkham's servants, and even more time to persuade them that he should be disturbed in the wee hours of the morning. They only relented when Edwin told them that there would be dire consequences if they turned away a marquess and an earl who were there on a matter of great import to the English people.

After being ushered into his lordship's study, they were forced to wait while Fulkham was roused from his bed. Unsurprisingly, when he entered in his dressing gown, he was none too happy.

"What in God's name is this about?" he asked as he crossed the room. "Couldn't it wait until morning?"

"Blakeborough here might be dead by morning," Warren said. "I'm hoping you can prevent that from happening."

Fulkham frowned. "You've caught my attention, that's for damned sure." He sat down behind his desk. "Why would Blakeborough be dead?"

"Because Count Durand challenged me to a duel at dawn, and I've accepted," Edwin said matter-of-factly.

"A duel?" Fulkham looked from Edwin to Warren. "Is this a joke?"

"Afraid not," Warren said. "The count is apparently trying to hunt down my cousin, the Earl of Margrave. In the process, he's been threatening the life and reputation of Blakeborough and Margrave's sister. Who just happens to be Blakeborough's new wife."

"Ah," Fulkham said, glancing at Edwin. "This has to do with that conversation we had a few weeks ago at the club. The one you claimed was about some other member."

Edwin nodded. "Forgive me for the subterfuge, but

my fiancée was involved, and I didn't want that information to be bandied about."

"Then can I assume this concerns the duel between Whiting and Margrave?"

Edwin and Warren exchanged surprised glances.

"You don't think I knew about Durand's connection to Whiting?" Fulkham fixed Edwin with a hard stare. "If you'd told me at the time that your concern over the charge d'affaires' activities was related to Lady Clarissa's family, I would have mentioned that Whiting and Durand were cousins. But you didn't offer that information."

"Offering information isn't my friend's strong suit, I'm afraid," Warren said dryly.

"Do you know what the duel was about?" Edwin asked.

"No. Do you?"

Edwin let out a breath. "Yes. Unfortunately, I can't say. But it doesn't matter anyway. The important thing is that Durand wants revenge on my brother-in-law for killing his cousin, so he's been trying to find Niall by cozying up to my wife. When she and I put an end to that with our betrothal, Durand threatened to reveal secrets about my father if I didn't break it off."

That arrested Fulkham's attention. "What sort of secrets?"

Edwin swallowed. Now came the difficult part. "That apparently Father was a spy for the French."

A cold anger suffused Fulkham's features with color. "That damned bastard."

"My father?" Edwin snapped.

The baron started. "No, no, not him. Durand. He's

mucking about in matters he should leave alone. I'll have to speak to his superiors and put an end to this before he creates more trouble. Relations between England and France are rocky enough as it is right now."

Edwin eyed him closely. "So you knew about my father's spying."

"Of course I knew. He was spying for us."

"That's not what Durand says. And he showed me—"

"Reports? Documents your father gave to the French? Damn them; they'd assured him that those records had been destroyed." As Edwin and Warren continued to gape at him, he sighed. "I need your word as gentlemen that what I'm about to tell you never leaves this room."

"Of course," Edwin said, with Warren nodding his assent.

"Because of your father's ties to France through his grandmother, and because of his occasional visits to that private opium club, the French approached your father in the final years of the war with a request to spy for them. They promised to pay him quite handsomely for such treachery."

Fulkham settled back in his chair. "As you can imagine, money wasn't much of an incentive for him, but he did see an opportunity to help England beat the French—so after agreeing to their proposal, he came to us. We engaged him to leak incorrect information about our troops to the French from time to time."

A wave of relief swamped Edwin, followed swiftly by a wave of shame. He should have realized his father could never commit treason. "How do you know all this? You're no older than I. You couldn't possibly have been in the War Office at the time."

"I wasn't. But your father continued to go to the opium dens, so when our focus shifted to India, he was able to give us information about that occasionally. I joined the War Office a couple of years before he died. I was the one who took over managing his information."

Edwin was still reeling. His father had spied for his country all that time. Without a word to his son. "You're telling me he was *not* a traitor."

"Never. He was a hero, as a matter of fact. Of course, he could never speak of his activities, and the French never knew him as anything but a spy for them. But they assured him that his reputation would never be impugned, because the documents connecting him to the activities were burned."

"Clearly, that was a lie."

"Yes," Fulkham said tersely. "Which is another reason to go to Durand's superiors. I don't need to reveal that your father helped us—just that Durand is trying to use what he did to blackmail you for his own purposes."

Warren leaned forward. "Going to his superiors won't solve the problem that he's dueling with Edwin in Green Park in a little over an hour."

Fulkham rose. "Then I'll have to go there with you, and tell him precisely what sort of trouble he'll be in if he persists in his madness. We won't allow an English citizen, no matter what his crime, to be assassinated by a Frenchman, even a diplomat."

The baron headed for the door to get dressed, then

paused. "It's curious, though. What does Durand think to accomplish with a duel?"

"By eliminating me," Edwin said, "he thinks to gain control over my wife and force her into telling him where Niall is."

"Then why hasn't he done that before? Why not abduct her off the street? Use brute force to convince her to do so?"

"He tried courting her, no doubt so he wouldn't tip his hand and give her a chance to warn Niall. When she persisted in refusing his advances, he started shadowing her, which is when I stepped in and married her."

"So she's been with you since then."

"At my estate, where it would have been hard for him to roam without comment. We only returned to town last evening for a celebration of our marriage. He tried to get her alone, and I stepped in. That was when he challenged me."

"Hmm." Fulkham stared at Edwin. "So where is your wife now?"

The question made him uneasy. "At home asleep, I hope."

"Or, if she's anything like my indomitable sister-in-law, preparing to go to Green Park and plead with you not to fight."

Edwin's blood chilled. "Damn it all to hell." He jumped to his feet. "She *would* do that, too. She doesn't know we're here. And if we don't return—"

"Go, go," Fulkham said. "I'll dress and head to the dueling field, while you two return home. You can probably catch her if you hurry."

Edwin rushed from the study, with Warren cursing behind him. They leapt into Warren's carriage, ordering his coachman to drive at top speed to Edwin's town house.

As the rig pulled away, Warren said, "Perhaps she won't go. She said she was washing her hands of the whole thing."

"She also said she loved me." Edwin's throat felt raw with fear. "And Clarissa is precisely the sort of woman who gives a man her whole self once she falls in love. She will fight for me with her last breath."

"The way you're fighting for her," Warren remarked. "You swallowed your pride for her, you gave up your plans for a peaceful life for her, and you clearly will do anything for her. I think she's not the only one in love, old chap."

As the truth hit him, Edwin sucked in a ragged breath. No, she wasn't the only one.

All these years, he'd avoided the tumult that love could bring, but it had slipped under his guard while he wasn't looking. The idea of something happening to her, of living without her, stole the breath from his soul. He couldn't stand to think of her suffering one second of Durand's cruelty. What was that but love?

Now that he knew what it felt like to crave her company and her teasing, to seek her touch in the middle of the night when the world seemed darkest, he couldn't imagine his father feeling any of that and still taking his friend's side over his wife's. Mother might have been in love, but Father couldn't have known the meaning of the word.

"She'll be all right," Warren said. "I'm sure she will."

"If she isn't, I swear I'll cut out Durand's heart and crush it under my heel. I'll draw and quarter him myself. I'll—"

"I get the gist," Warren said grimly. "But let's hope it doesn't come to that, my friend. Because I don't fancy watching you hang for the murder of a worthless arse like Durand."

Twenty-Five

It was no surprise that Clarissa hadn't been able to sleep after she saw Edwin and Warren leave the house. She tried, she really did, but she couldn't stop worrying. She kept waiting for them to return, not sure where they'd even gone, but by 4:00 A.M., she knew it was growing too late for them to get back before the duel began.

Which meant they were probably already on their way to Green Park. Curse them both.

She rose and got dressed, muttering at her cousin the whole time. Hadn't he been able to stop her husband, *his* friend? She'd blurted out that she loved Edwin in the vain hope that it would give him pause, but clearly even that couldn't have an impact on the dratted idiot.

After fretting a while longer, she decided enough was enough. She was *not* going to let her husband do this insane thing. If she had to, she'd stand between him and Count Durand. Because she didn't want to lose Edwin. She'd lost enough in her life.

No more.

She went downstairs and roused a servant, then called for her carriage. It came surprisingly quickly. It was only after she'd gone out the door that she realized it wasn't *her* carriage waiting for her at the bottom of the steps. She paused, but before she could react, someone stepped behind her and she felt a hard object shoved into her side.

"There you are, my dear," said the voice she'd grown to loathe. "I knew you couldn't resist going to the duel."

Count Durand. Oh, Lord. Her heart jumped into her throat. Damn him, damn him, *damn him*. "And I knew you would cheat," she said, fighting for calm. "So we apparently know each other well."

"Better than you can imagine." When she caught her breath, he added, "And I wouldn't scream, if I were you. I'll shoot you where you stand." He nudged her with the hard object to make his point.

"You always were a bully." As she fumbled to release her knife pendant from the chain, her mind raced. She needed to throw him off guard, buy some time until she could get the pistol away from her side long enough to stab him. "You're like your cousin—always running roughshod over women."

A long silence followed before he rasped, "Do not speak ill of a man you know nothing about."

"I know he raped me." She palmed her pendant. "He held me down and forced himself on me."

"That's a lie!" he hissed. "He was my closest friend in the world once. Then you incited your brother with your lies, and like that, he was murdered. I've seen you flirt, seen you entice men. I know what kind of woman you are. Why should he bother to rape a whore like you?"

Anger roiled up in her. "Would a whore keep you at arm's length the entire time you were courting me? No. He was evil and you are just as evil, and I don't deserve this."

"Shut up!" he growled. "You have a choice. Get in the carriage. Or die."

Her blood faltered. "You'll just kill me anyway."

"Not if you tell me where your brother is. We'll go see him together."

"And you'll kill us both. No, thank you." If he would move the pistol long enough for her to jab at him . . . "You know my husband won't stop until he destroys you."

Count Durand snorted. "There's little chance of that."

Another voice came from the shadows behind the carriage. "There's more chance than you realize."

Edwin. Thank heaven!

Catching her about the waist, Count Durand jerked her up close to him. "I'll kill her, Blakeborough. I swear I will."

"And then what? You'll lose your chance at her brother."

Edwin stepped out of the shadows, and she nearly had heart failure. "He has a gun, my love! Don't come any nearer!"

Ignoring her, Edwin moved more into the light. "You're not fool enough to murder a peer's wife in cold blood, Durand. You'd hang for it."

"You don't know a damned thing," Count Durand hissed. "I don't care if she dies. I'll find Margrave somehow. Even if I only wait for him to come after me to revenge his sister."

"You won't have to wait for him." Edwin lifted a hand and she saw a pistol in it. "Kill her and you die. It's as simple as that."

That seemed to give Count Durand pause, for she could feel his gun waver against her side. "Or you could let us both leave," he snarled, "and I'll allow her to live."

Clarissa suppressed her snort of disbelief even as she opened the leaf knife. Durand wouldn't get away with his perfidy if she had anything to say about it. She just needed the right moment.

Edwin's gaze swung to her and dropped ever so briefly to her hand. He knew what she meant to do. And was ready.

All of a sudden, Count Durand's coach started driving away.

"What are you doing?" the count shouted at the driver. "Damn you, man, come back!"

In that moment, while his attention was distracted and the gun had left her side, she jabbed up at his pistol arm and fell to the ground without even waiting to see his reaction.

Then Edwin shot him through the heart.

⟡

A short while later, Clarissa sat in her drawing room as the household erupted around her. Edwin and Warren, who'd been the one to unseat the driver of Count Durand's carriage and drive it off, were deep in discussion with Lord Fulkham, who'd just shown up. Footmen and servants were running about following orders occasionally barked at them by Edwin.

There *was* a dead body on the steps, after all. It had to be dealt with.

All she could do was sit there frozen as she listened to the discussion.

"I'll take care of this, Blakeborough," Lord Fulkham was saying. "The man was trying to abduct your wife. By the time I get through with the French ambassador for allowing Durand free rein to torment English citizens, they will be happy to keep the matter quiet. It may not even go to a trial."

"Even if it does," Warren said, "your servants are witnesses and we have Durand's coachman, who will testify to the truth of it if he knows what's good for him. Or Fulkham can have him charged as an accessory."

At that moment, Edwin glanced over and saw that she'd begun to tremble. His face paled. With a few words to the others, who instantly left the room, he came to sit beside her. He poured some brandy from the carafe on the table next to the settee and pressed the glass into her hand. "Drink it, sweetheart. It will stop the shaking."

"You—you're plying me with s-spirits again," she feebly tried to joke.

"We're married now. It's allowed."

She lifted the glass to drink and caught sight of her glove. Her red-stained glove. After setting down the glass, she tore her gloves off. "I have Count Durand's blood on me," she said, her stomach churning. "It's probably on my gown and in my hair and—"

"Yes," he said raggedly.

She looked over to see him crumbling before her

eyes, his shoulders shaking, his face contorted as if he fought tears.

"Edwin!"

"If I had lost you . . ." His breath came in fractured gasps as he lifted his tortured face to her. "I couldn't have borne it."

"You weren't going to let that happen." With her heart in her throat, she cupped his cheek. "As usual, you're my Saint George slaying the dragon."

"I love you," he said baldly.

He— Had she heard that right? "I thought you didn't believe in love."

"I didn't." His gaze bore into her. "But I was wrong."

Her breathing grew unsteady. Was this just his reaction to seeing her nearly killed? Fighting to keep the tremor from her voice, she said, "My goodness, that's the second time you've said you're wrong in a week. Actually, it's the second time you've said it in my lifetime." She laid her hand on his forehead. "Are you ill? Do you have a fever?"

"I mean it, minx." Covering her hand, he pulled it to his lips and kissed her palm. "I love you, body and soul. For so long, I've lived with a clockwork heart, refusing to feel, because I'd seen what love—or what I thought was love—had done to my parents, and I couldn't bear to go through that."

Scarcely daring to breathe, she clutched his hand in both of hers.

"But I was in trouble from the moment Warren talked me into looking out for you. I told myself, 'Beware, if you let her in, she may destroy you.' Because deep down, I knew that if anyone could make my clockwork heart bleed, it would be you."

She swallowed hard, not sure how she liked that.

"Instead," he said, breaking into a smile, "you made it beat. Hard. With life and joy and, yes, love. You, sweetheart, transformed my clockwork heart into a real one."

With tears filling her eyes, she said, "Good. Because you deserve better than life with a clockwork heart. And I could never stand for an automaton husband, even one of your exquisite craftsmanship. I much prefer the flesh-and-blood man I've fallen in love with."

He kissed her then with a sweetness that made her heart soar. When they finally pulled apart, dawn was breaking through the window.

"Looks like you were right, last night," he said as he slid his arm about her shoulders. "Ours *is* a love match after all."

She slid her arm about his waist, then leaned up to whisper in his ear, "That was my heart's desire, so you got it for me. What a clever husband you are."

And as they laughed together, the sun rose.

Epilogue

Edwin was bent over a table in his workroom, carving a bit of cork, when his wife entered.

"What are you making *now*? We still have nearly four months until the babe is born. At the rate you're going, she'll be able to open her own toy shop."

Ever since Edwin had heard that Clarissa was with child, he'd launched into creating every clockwork toy he could think of: a trilling nightingale, a dancing bear, a book with letters that sprang up when you opened it, and a mechanical dog that jumped through a hoop held by an acrobat. He had to be ready. This was his firstborn, after all.

He shifted in his chair to look at his lovely wife. God, but she was gorgeous when she was full with his child. Her face glowed and her breasts were even plumper. It was all he could do to remind himself that he must be careful with her. Careful of the babe she carried inside her.

"First of all," he said, "the 'she' will be a 'he.' I feel it in my bones."

She rolled her eyes. "Yes, and you are nothing if not famous for your ability at predicting the sex of a child."

Ignoring her, he settled back in the chair. "Secondly, I'm not making these for the baby, but for me." He held up the two carved pieces of cork, then stuffed them in his ears. "Lately, you've been snoring."

She cocked up one eyebrow and said something he couldn't hear.

Excellent, they were working. He cupped his hand behind his ear. "What's that?"

Marching over, she plucked the corks out of his ears and stuffed them into hers. "Thank you for these. Now I don't have to hear you go on and on about what we need to buy for the baby and make for the baby and arrange for the baby. You're worse than my mother, I swear."

She had a point. He and Lady Margrave had surprisingly grown more friendly while plotting the future of his child and her grandchild.

He drew Clarissa between his legs. Reaching up to take out the corks, he said, "I'll make you a pair, too. You can use them when your mother visits." He spread his hands over her belly, his blood leaping to feel the subtle movements. "He's really kicking today, isn't he?"

"*She* is dancing. She has to practice making her father laugh."

"Her mother already does plenty of that." He kissed Clarissa's clothed navel, then scattered more kisses up her stomach to her swollen breasts. "Among other things." He nuzzled her nipple. "We should make love in this room. I've imagined it so many times."

She looked scandalized. "In your *workroom*? Truly?"

"In every room in the house. Long before you married me, too."

"I don't believe you."

With a sly smile, he rose and took her hand. "Come with me."

He took her through the house to the conservatory, where he nodded to the dais by the window. "I've pictured you lying there naked, bathed in sunlight, while I take you."

Reveling in her blush, he led her through the halls into the music room. "The possibility of sitting on that pianoforte bench while you rode me has seen me through many a dull recital."

She gaped at him. "Not Yvette's, I hope."

"Good God, no. But yours, for certain."

"Are you saying that my playing bores you?"

"I'm saying that it always provided a fitting backdrop for my fantasy."

Raking her with a long, slow glance for emphasis, he laughed when she said, "Oh, Lord, now I'll never be able to look you in the eye when I'm playing for guests."

"Shall I go on?" he asked.

A look of challenge crossed her face. "I'll bet there's one room you haven't imagined making love to me in. The kitchen."

"Are you mad? Of *course* I've pictured you there, splayed on the table to provide me with a delicious feast." When she looked surprised, he said, "Mind you, we could never serve food from there again if I acted on it, but God knows I've imagined it."

She looped her arms about his neck. "When I

married you, Lord Blakeborough, I had no idea you were such a naughty man."

"Obviously, or you wouldn't have assumed I could wait a bloody *year* to bed you."

Remorse tinged her cheeks pink. "What if it really had been a year? Would you have complied with my terms?"

"Of course. But you wouldn't have lasted that long. You're too much of a naughty *woman* for that. And I was too bent on seducing you."

She got that melting look in her eyes that never failed to enrapture him, and he was on the verge of dragging her into his arms and ravishing her, when a voice came from the door. "I hope we're not interrupting."

Edwin cursed inwardly . . . and then realized that the voice was vaguely familiar. No—it couldn't be.

But it could. "Niall?" Clarissa said, turning for the door. "Niall!"

She broke away from Edwin and ran to hug her brother. The man Edwin had remembered as being tall and gangly had filled out into quite a stalwart fellow. His hair was darker than Clarissa's—more like sun-streaked bronze—but his expression was hard. Clearly his sojourn on the Continent had changed him.

Behind him stood Warren, who watched the siblings with a smile.

"What on earth are you doing here?" Clarissa asked. "Did you sneak into England?" She shook him. "You cannot be here—you're a fugitive. They could hang you!"

"Doubtful," Warren said as he glanced beyond Niall to Edwin. "After all the trouble Fulkham and I took to get him back legally, it wouldn't make sense for the government to turn around and hang him. And I would be most annoyed."

"So would I," Niall said dryly. "I don't fancy having a rope for a cravat."

She whirled on Edwin. "Did you know about this?"

"Are you mad?" Warren put in. "Edwin would have told you at once. Which is why we didn't tell *him*. We weren't sure if it would work out, and we didn't want you to get your hopes up."

Edwin stepped next to her to slide his arm about her waist, feeling oddly protective. "So exactly how did you get it to work out?" he asked the two others.

"As it happens," his brother-in-law said, "Durand was already becoming a problem for both the French and the English—making rash diplomatic decisions, squirreling away documents that were supposed to be destroyed, breaking agreements that had long been held. The attempt to blackmail you was the last straw. So Fulkham convinced his superiors that without my involvement, the man would never have been routed, and his attempts to 'unveil' a peer as a spy would have ended in disaster."

"In other words," Warren put in, "Niall got a royal pardon. And it didn't hurt that after Prinny's death, our new king was eager to issue a few royal pardons as part of his ascension to the throne. One of those went to Niall."

"Without having to reveal any of your past, dear girl," Niall added.

With a sniff, she patted her belly. "Clearly, I am *not* a 'girl.'"

Niall laughed. "No, clearly not." He sobered as his

gaze met Edwin's. "And if your new husband doesn't take care of you, I shall challenge *him* to a duel."

"Don't worry," Edwin said solemnly. "I would go to the ends of the earth for her."

The serious statement brought the other two men up short. Then Niall glanced at Warren. "I can't believe it, but you were right. He *is* in love."

Clarissa slid her arm about Edwin's waist. "Of course he is. I have that effect on men."

The flippantly spoken words lightened the mood, as his wife had no doubt intended.

With a genial smile, Niall said, "I do hope we got here in time for dinner. I'm famished."

"Yes, dinner will be served shortly." Clarissa turned to her cousin. "Warren, are you staying?"

He shook his head. "I must return to London. Something has come up. But you and Niall enjoy your reunion. I'll see you in a few weeks at the party at Keane's."

"All right." She kissed her cousin, then turned to Niall. "Go on to the dining room. I need a quick word with my husband."

Niall looked a bit taken aback by her bossiness, but then, he hadn't seen her in seven years. He didn't know the Clarissa whom Edwin knew and adored. The Clarissa who'd changed his life. Who'd made him whole.

Who'd proved that he did believe in love, after all.

Niall departed for the dining room, leaving the couple alone together.

Clarissa turned to Edwin with a sultry smile. "So, to return to our earlier conversation, would you like to know what room *I've* imagined making love in?"

That got his attention instantly. "Damned right I would."

"Perhaps we should make it a wager." She dragged one finger down his chest, making his blood heat. "If you guess the correct room, you get a reward."

He swallowed hard. Amazing how she could still rouse him with one word, one look. One sensual insinuation. "A reward, eh? What sort of reward?"

Her minxish smile increased the pounding of his heart. "Oh, I don't know. You can kiss my arm, I suppose." With a knowing glance, she touched the inside of her elbow. "Right here."

"I have a better idea. If I guess the room, then I get to make love to you in it. After your brother has returned home tonight."

"Hmm." Her eyes gleamed. "That sounds like an excellent reward. But what do I get if you *don't* guess correctly?"

"The same thing you get if I do—my heart, my body, my soul."

"In that case, I can't lose," she said, her love for him shining in her face.

"Neither can I." He drew her into his arms. "And that, my love, is the best kind of wager."

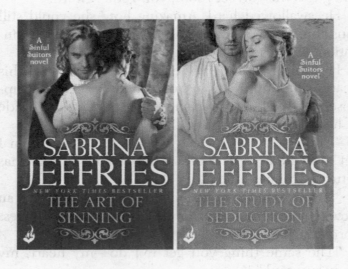